WEDDING DAY MURDER

When Libby glanced down at Leeza Sharp her first thought was: this is a practical joke. Her second thought was: I don't have time for this nonsense. Her third thought was: Amber and Bernie are dead meat.

"Not funny," she said, whirling around to face Bernie. Then she saw the horrified expression on Bernie's face and Libby's stomach lurched. *Oh, please God, not again,* Libby prayed. *Not another murder.*

Libby took another look at the body sprawled out on the floor. Leeza's eyes were staring straight up. Her mouth was opened in an expression of surprise. An arrow was protruding from her chest. And then there was the blood. It was everywhere. On the floor. On Leeza Sharp's no longer white robe. On her nightgown.

No, Libby told herself. This isn't a joke. Leeza was definitely dead. Not mostly dead. Not nearly dead. Dead dead. No doubt about that. No one could survive an arrow through the heart. At least not in real life.

Libby heard the words, "And on her wedding day too," coming out of her mouth. *What a stupid thing to say,* she told herself as Bernie turned towards her. Like it would have been better if it had happened the day after. Well, in a sense it would have been because then they wouldn't have been here . . .

Books by Isis Crawford

A CATERED MURDER

A CATERED WEDDING

A CATERED CHRISTMAS

Published by Kensington Publishing Corporation

A Mystery with Recipes

A CATERED WEDDING

ISIS CRAWFORD

KENSINGTON BOOKS
www.kensingtonbooks.com

Longely is an imaginary community, as are all its inhabitants. Any resemblance to people living or dead is pure coicidence.

KENSINGTON BOOKS are published by

Kensington Publishing Corp.
850 Third Avenue
New York, NY 10022

All Kensington titles, imprints, and distributed lines are available at special quantity discounts for bulk purchases for sales promotion, premiums, fund-raising, educational, or institutional use.

Special book excerpts or customized printings can also be created to fit specific needs. For details, write or phone the office of the Kensington Special Sales Manager: Kensington Publishing Corp., attn: Special Sales Department. 850 Third Avenue, New York, NY 10022. Phone: 1-800-221-2647.

ISBN 0-7582-0686-0

First Kensington Hardcover Printing: December 2004
First Kensington Mass Market Printing: September 2005

10 9 8 7 6 5 4 3 2 1

Printed in the United States of America

For Dan,
Angels come in strange disguises.

Acknowledgments

I'd like to thank DJM for his help when I needed it. It's not often one runs across someone who knows a lot and has the imagination to put it together.

Once again I'd like to thank Hank Nielsen for her help in the recipe department.

Thank you Sarah Saulson for introducing me to the plea-sures of dark chocolate.

And I owe an enormous debt of gratitude to Juno Wright and Tori Evans who have helped me redo my office. It's been an amazing experience.

A SIMPLE BUT ELEGANT MENU FOR LEEZA SHARP'S AND JURA RAID'S WEDDING RECEPTION

Beluga caviar in carved ice sculptures
Foie Gras
Champagne

First course: Marinated Grilled Quail on mesclun greens with cranberry chutney

Second course: Estate-grown asparagus tips with sauce mousseline

Third course: Line-caught wild Copper River salmon served in a reduced champagne sauce on a bed of hand-harvested wild river rice

Wedding Cake: Croquembouche decorated with candied almonds and white roses

Wild strawberries with crème chantilly

Coffee and liqueurs

Prologue

Leeza Sharp inclined her head over the roses the butler had just handed her and inhaled. Not very strongly scented, she decided as she kicked the door shut behind her with the heel of her foot. She strode across the room, pulling the clear wrapping paper and bow off the dozen long-stemmed white roses as she went. She deposited the paper in the trash can, laid the flowers down on the table by the window, and inspected them.

A frown crossed her brow. "Hmm," she said as she reached into the top of the dresser drawer and took out a ruler.

She tapped it against her teeth before lowering it and carefully placed the stem of one of the flowers against the measuring stick. The stem was eleven inches, an inch too short. She'd been right.

Stems of traditional long stemmed roses were supposed to be exactly twelve inches—no more and no less. Leeza gathered up the flowers, wincing as a thorn pricked her. Those should have been removed as well she thought as she threw the flowers in the trash. Altogether an inferior product. This was her big day and she had no use for something that wasn't perfect.

Leeza sucked the side of her finger for a moment. Then, when it had stopped hurting, she reknotted the sash on her white-silk, hand-embroidered robe, took a sip of tea out of the Limoges cup, and nibbled on a piece of brioche. She could hear the rain drumming on the drainpipe as she carefully replaced the cup on the saucer, wiped her hands on the linen napkin, and strolled across her bedroom to stand by the windows.

Even the rain didn't upset her. She wouldn't let it or anything else dent her composure. In three hours her bridesmaids would be descending on her and everything would start. These were the last private hours she would have as Miss Leeza Sharp and she intended to enjoy every single second of them.

From the window she could just see the top of the large tent the workmen had erected yesterday afternoon. Originally she'd pictured the material as sky blue silk with a sprinkling of stars, possibly with a cascade of cobalt crystal beads decorating the entranceway.

She'd wanted her wedding to have an exotic Arabian Nights feel to it. She'd even planned to have Oriental carpets and rose petals scattered over the floor; actually she was still going to do that even though she'd had to rethink the tent.

According to Wedding Planner Number One there'd been a problem with the silk pulling at the seams, something about the tension of the fabric, something the wedding planner hadn't noticed until the last minute, although for the life of her Leeza couldn't imagine why the planner hadn't checked on it before—after all she was being paid to take care of the details. And this had happened one week before the wedding!

Ohmygod. Leeza put her hand to her heart. Just thinking about the tent fiasco—even now—gave her *agita.* And the wedding planner actually had had the nerve to suggest using tape—tape!—to reinforce the seams. This was the planner's idea of problem solving? The whole idea of the tent, of her vision would have been lost.

The planner had been totally useless. The woman hadn't even been able to get an assurance from the editor that the announcement of the wedding would run in the Sunday *New*

York Times. It had taken the PR person Leeza had hired to do that.

Thank heavens for the caterers. At least they had come through. Leeza hadn't known where to turn about the tent. She'd been in absolute tears when Libby Simmons had approached her and told her she thought she could find a local company to make the tent for her. Of course it had been extremely expensive. Four people had worked three twelve-hour days to sew it, but getting one of those ready-made ones from a rental company was unthinkable for her wedding.

Yes, she knew that those places stocked a multitude of styles these days, but that wasn't the issue. The issue was that she wanted a tent that had been made especially for her, for this day. She wanted . . . what had the other Simmons girl called it? . . . A talisman? No. A memento.

Originally Leeza had been upset about the color options available to her. Nothing that she saw captured her attention, but the other sister, Bernie, had assured her that the cream with the very thin pale, yellow stripes running through the material, would look smashing when it was made up. Leeza hadn't really believed her but, because of the time constraints involved in weather-coating the material, she'd finally acquiesced.

But now looking at the tent Leeza decided that Bernie had been right. As she'd promised, the material had held up well. She rather liked the effect of the white against the green of the willows lining the creek. The tent looked like something that would house a medieval gathering and as far as Leeza was concerned it looked festive even in this weather. So did the white rose bushes she'd had planted specially for her wedding day, white being her signature color. The only thing missing were the pennants, but hopefully it would stop raining by twelve so they could be put up before the reception.

Leeza was glad she hadn't acceded to Libby Simmons's initial suggestion to relocate the reception to the house. They were having the ceremony there and that was enough. As she'd explained to her, yes, she knew outdoor wedding receptions were risky, but she'd had her heart set on an outdoor celebration by the water ever since she could remember, and to Libby's credit she had understood. Of course, if Libby hadn't she wouldn't have gotten the job. So what if the weather made the logistics a little more difficult. After all, facilitating her desires was what the Simmons girls were getting paid for.

And at this point they certainly had come through. In fact, they were the only people who had. Wedding Planner Number Two—or was it Wedding Planner Number One? Leeza was beginning to get them mixed up—they'd both looked the same to her with their Palms and titanium covered Macs and their black suits and pulled-back blond hair. Anyway, one of them had suggested another caterer but Eunice and Gertrude Walker, her mother's old friends, had insisted that she try the Simmons girls—and they'd been right. For once.

The sample meal Bernie and Libby had cooked her had been wonderful, especially the béarnaise sauce for the filet mignon, and she couldn't quibble with the menu—simple, elegant, and drop-dead expensive. Bernie, the better dressed sister, had understood exactly what she'd wanted to give her guests—a unique experience that they would talk about for the rest of their lives. Which was why each detail, no matter how small, counted.

Individually the details were nothing, but together they made up the totality of experience she wanted to convey. Leeza had even thought about releasing Monarch butterflies after the ceremony as a symbol of her and Jura's union after one of her friends had told her she'd heard from her friend out in L.A. that that's what all the Hollywood people were doing.

She'd almost ordered them—one hundred butterflies for a little under eight hundred dollars—but Bernie had pointed out that it would be very depressing if the release went wrong, and you had butterflies dying all over the place. Which was certainly true.

For a while she'd toyed with releasing a flock of white

doves, but she really didn't like birds—they crapped all over everything—and so she'd dropped that idea as well. Especially since Jura's brother Joe had started talking about marching down the aisle with one of his falcons sitting on his shoulder. Falcons! How ridiculous was that, Leeza thought as she inspected her nails.

She still liked the deep burgundy she'd chosen. It was a nice foil for the gleam of her nine-carat diamond engagement ring. She'd gotten a manicure and pedicure yesterday afternoon but she had a manicurist on standby just in case she or one of her bridesmaids needed a touch-up.

After all this was her day and she didn't want it to be ruined by something like a chipped nail. Jura hadn't even complained about the cost of that. Actually he hadn't complained about any of the bills. He'd just written the checks, which was one of things she loved about him. Okay. It was the only thing she loved about him.

He certainly left her cold in the sex department. Even with Viagra. Just because he could get it up didn't mean he knew what to do with it. He hadn't heard about G-spots let alone erogenous zones and had no desire to learn about them, but, hey, she could get sex anytime she wanted. She had that base covered.

As she saw it, the advantage of marrying an older, rich man was that he would do anything to keep her happy. Well, almost anything. Like this wedding. If it had been up to his brothers, she and Jura would be getting married by a justice of the peace and having coffee and cake afterwards or some sort of Estonian food—whatever that was. Leeza snorted at the ridiculousness of the idea. Why were some rich people so cheap? Before she came along Jura, Ditas, and Joe used to do their shopping at Sam's Club which was absurd considering what they sold. But not anymore.

Take the salmon they were serving. It was all wild, all troll- (meaning line) caught, not netted, because as Bernie had explained to her netting bruised the fish. And it was all from the Copper River in Alaska. Bernie had explained that this salmon was the best in the world although for the life of her Leeza couldn't remember exactly why.

She thought it had something to do with the Copper River being so long that the salmon were fatter when they started their journey upstream, but she wasn't sure. The real point though was that they weren't serving any of that farm-raised trash which, Bernie had carefully explained to Jura when he had questioned the expense, didn't taste as good. And, of course, it was bad for the environment.

The asparagus they were using were all grown right here on Jura's estate, as were the wild strawberries. And Leeza wasn't even going to mention the ice sculptures or the bowls of beluga caviar they were serving. Personally she really didn't like the stuff, but everyone else did.

If her mother could see her now, Leeza thought she'd be so proud of her. Not for nothing had she scrubbed out other people's toilets so Leeza could have braces and a nose job and good clothes. Leeza could still see her mom beaming when she'd been crowned Miss Butternut Squash. What would she think of her wedding dress? Leeza went over and ran her finger down the boned bodice.

Now some people might think twenty-five-thousand dollars was too much to spend on a dress, but not Leeza. It was clear to her that if you were going to get married on an estate to someone who was worth easily one hundred million, then twenty-five thousand for a dress was nothing percentage wise. And if she did say so herself the white satin and handmade French lace were perfection, as was the veil shot through with real gold and seed pearls.

Leeza studied her reflection in the mirror—not bad for a girl from Missouri—not bad at all. All that work and plastic surgery had paid off: she was marrying rich, which in her humble opinion was what it was all about. In her humble opinion, anyone who said money didn't matter was a fool.

She glanced at the clock on the wall. It was nine o'clock. Where the hell were the Simmons girls anyway? Even though they had brought the tables down last night they still had to set them up. Leeza gently tapped the nails on her left hand on her cheek. It suddenly occurred to her that maybe she should talk to Jura about getting some of his security people to guard the tent before everyone arrived—after all the caterers *were* using thousands of dollars worth of gold rimmed Lenox bone china and Waterford crystal, not to mention the Tiffany silver.

But then guards would look so out of place, and Jura did have them at the gate. He'd added another two, so there would be five altogether checking invitations. No one who wasn't invited would be getting in. Absolutely no one. She didn't mind being gossiped about, but she wanted to control who gossiped about her and where. That's why she'd hired her own public relations person, another thing Jura's brothers couldn't understand.

"A needless expense," both Ditas and Joe had said.

Well, it was too bad that they couldn't understand the importance of being media savvy, but there it was.

No point in thinking about the disagreement—well really more of an argument—they'd had, Leeza told herself. She'd won it like she'd won all the others. What was so bad about wanting everything to be perfect she wanted to know? And speaking of perfect, the hair stylist and her make-up person should be here in another three hours. But what would happen if the plane couldn't land? What would happen if the flight was delayed at LAX? If the limo that was supposed to bring them out from JFK had a flat tire? A wave of panic ran through Leeza.

She should have used someone from the city, but these people were absolute geniuses. Everyone said so. That's why they did all the Hollywood stars. Leeza took a deep breath and calmed herself. No. She'd done the right thing getting them, which was a feat in itself. These people were the best in their field and as her mother liked to say, "you could never have too much of a good thing." Then after the stylist and the make-up artist were done, the dresser would help her maid of honor and bridesmaid into their dresses and everyone would pose for photos.

As she was thinking about the color eye shadow she'd picked out and whether she should change it to something a little bronzier she walked over to the table and reread the wedding announcement that was running in today's *Times*. The paper was creased from being handled but that was all right. She'd made the maid go out and buy three extra copies, which she intended to have laminated. Leeza's lips moved as she read the announcement. Not that she needed to. She could have recited it by heart at this point. It read:

Leeza Sharp, the daughter of the late Monica G. and Lawrence D. Sharp, of Kentworth, Missouri, is to be married today to Jura Raid, a son of the late Mr. and Mrs. Raid of Brooklyn. Minister James will officiate at the ceremony, which will be taking place on the fabled Raid Estate in upper Westchester County.

A beauty pageant winner,—Leeza decided she was glad she'd insisted that go in despite the PR person's objections. She didn't think it was tacky—*the bride, 27, graduated from the University of Missouri with a liberal arts degree in marketing. Working for Raid Enterprises was the first job she acquired upon her move east.*

Mr. Jura Raid, 53, completed a year at Wharton Business School before going to work in the family business, a move made necessary by the untimely death of his parents in an automobile accident. He is popularly credited with expanding the business, Imperial Caviar, into the successful enterprise that it now is.

Jura noted, "I actually saw Leeza in the lobby her first day of work and was instantly attracted to her, but I didn't approach her. Imagine my delight when she turned up in my office two months later."

"Actually," Leeza confided, laughing, "turning up in his office wasn't an accident. I was really attracted to him, too, and so I arranged to swap jobs with one of the women who

worked for him. At first she didn't want to, and I had to bribe her with a month's worth of free coffee and bagels."

Not bad, Leeza thought. Not bad at all. She had just gotten to the part about how the couple was planning a three-week honeymoon on Bali when her cell phone rang. She pulled it out of the pocket of her robe.

"Yes?" she said.

She frowned as she listened to the other person on the line.

"I don't know why I have to meet you. Why can't it wait? No. We've already discussed that."

Leeza tapped her fingers on her thigh while she listened some more.

"Well, I'm sorry, but you're wrong," she told the person on the other end who, judging from the expression on Leeza's face, was saying something she didn't like.

"My make-up and hair people will be coming soon and I have a million little details to attend to before the ceremony. Surely you know that."

As she listened to the answer two little spots of red appeared on her cheeks.

"Fine," she snapped. "I can give you five minutes. At the most."

The person on the other end of the line said something else and Leeza replied, "Hey, be glad I'm giving you that."

"What an idiot," she muttered to herself as she pressed the off button on her cell.

As soon as she had she was sorry she'd agreed to the meeting. It was going to be unpleasant, and she didn't want anything to mar this day, but not going might potentially make the situation even worse. And if there was one thing she'd learned working for Jura it was that it was better to take control of the situation then let the situation take control of you.

She slipped her phone back into the pocket of her white silk robe, slid on her satin mules, and walked out of the room. Hopefully she wouldn't meet anyone on the way to the tent. She didn't want to have to lie about where she was going. It would just be a needless complication and Leeza believed in keeping things simple when she could. Fortunately, no one was around. Jura, Jura's brothers, and his executive secretary, Esmeralda Quinn, who was also Leeza's maid of honor, were all in the main wing of the house preparing for the big day.

"This had better be good," she muttered to herself as she opened an umbrella and stepped out into the rain.

Even though the downpour had become a drizzle, Leeza's feet and ankles were soaked by the time she'd walked down the embankment to the tent. She was so angry she didn't even see the ruts in the grass the tent people had made when they'd delivered the tent yesterday.

What was the matter with people anyway? Didn't they realize how busy she was? Two little dots of color appeared on Leeza's cheeks as she realized the person she was supposed to meet wasn't even here yet. If they were, she would be able to see a silhouette through the tent.

Leeza couldn't believe she was being kept waiting. She tapped her nails against her thigh. This would be the last time something like this would happen. When she was Mrs. Jura Raid things were going to be very different. Very different indeed. And people better start getting used to it now.

On that note she pushed the tent flap open and walked in.

She didn't have time to scream when the arrow hit her, much less get out of the way.

Chapter 1

Libby Simmons stifled a yawn as she regarded the wedding cake that she and her sister Bernie had stayed up almost all night making. She had to admit they'd done a great job. Even if the cake did lean a smidgen to the right, which, hopefully, no one would notice.

The croquembouche was beautiful, a tall, intricate tower of profiteroles, glazed with caramel, decorated with candied almonds and white roses, and balanced on a columned base of nougatine. Leeza would love it. Of that Libby was sure.

As Libby contemplated the cake she thought about how her life had changed since her sister Bernie had returned home. *PB,* as Libby had come to think of the years before Bernie moved back from L.A., Libby would never have attempted this cake. And she certainly wouldn't have attempted making it while drinking Cosmopolitans.

But, although she'd never admit it to her sister, Libby admitted to herself that it *had* been fun staying up all night with Bernie, sipping cocktails, and giggling while they worked. It had been totally worth it—even if she did feel as if she'd crawled out from under a rock this morning.

"The reputation of *A Taste of Heaven,*" she'd pointed out to Bernie after her sister had mentioned baking the cake, "is founded on cookies, muffins, scones, and cheese and carrot cakes, not fancy French wedding cakes."

"So what?" Bernie had countered. "That's like saying Prada can't make shoes and handbags at the same time."

Trust her sister to mention Prada, Libby had thought. But then she'd always been a fashion magazine junkie, unlike Libby and her mom who'd bought their clothes at J.C. Penney.

"You know I'm right," Bernie had continued.

"No, I don't. Maybe Prada can diversify, but we can't. We're a shop, not a multinational company. Catering Leeza's wedding is enough of a stretch." Which was true. Between Leeza's constant demands, running the store, and the high school graduation parties they'd picked up, she and Bernie were working twelve-hour days as it was.

"Anyway," Libby had continued, "she's got Jacques Bonet to make the cake. She doesn't need us." Jacques Bonet being the celebrity pastry chef of the moment.

"Not anymore," her younger sister had gleefully informed her. "You should read the *Post.* He got busted for selling Ecstasy."

"Terrific," Libby had said. "Okay. So, Leeza will find someone else."

"She wants us to do it. I mean how hard can it be?" Bernie asked as she'd whipped out a picture of the cake Leeza wanted. "All the thing is, is tiny custard-filled cream puffs, glued together with caramel, wrapped with some spun sugar and plunked down on some nougatine."

"I know what a croquembouche is," Libby had snapped, offended. "I'm not a culinary idiot."

"I didn't say you were," Bernie had retorted.

Which mollified Libby slightly, even though she suspected Bernie was just saying that so they wouldn't get into a 'thing'. "It's not the degree of difficulty that concerns me," she'd harrumphed. "It's the fact that we're on overload as it is."

Bernie had rolled her eyes, something that never failed to piss Libby off. "You know the trouble with you?" she'd asked.

"No. And I don't care," Libby had responded.

Not that that had stopped her sister Libby reflected because she'd continued on as if she hadn't spoken. "The trouble with you is that you're kakorraphiaphobic."

"What?" Libby had asked. "That's not a word. You made that up."

Bernie had raised her right hand. "Swear it is. It's in *Roget's Thesaurus*. It means fear of failure. Look it up if you want."

"You're bluffing."

"You know I'm not."

Looking at her sister's expression Libby knew she was telling the truth. This, she reflected, was why she'd stopped playing word games with her.

"Okay," she'd told Bernie, "let's get back to the matter at hand. First of all for your information, I don't have a fear of failure. I have a realistic view of how much we need to do. What concerns me about the cake is that it has to be made at the last minute. It can't stay. Which means we'll be up all night making it, and then we still have the reception to get through."

Bernie had grinned. "It'll be fun. You'll see."

"No, it won't."

"Yes, it will. Come on. Remember the all-nighters we used to pull in high school. We haven't done anything like that in a long time."

"I don't know if I still can," Libby had admitted. Much as she hated to say it, one o'clock was late for her now.

Bernie laughed. "Of course you can."

"Well, you should have asked me first," Libby had persisted, trying to keep control of the situation even though she could tell that Bernie knew she was winning the discussion.

"Sorry," Bernie had replied. "I just assumed you'd see this as an opportunity to branch out. Not to mention the fact that we'll be making an extra twelve-hundred dollars."

"Twelve-hundred dollars?" Libby had asked.

"Yes. Which we could use to get new ovens."

"You have to deduct food costs."

"So we'll clear eight-fifty," Bernie had said. "That's still not bad. None of the components are that difficult to make."

Which Libby admitted was true. She ran through the facts in her head. Okay, the ingredients were cheap enough. They had the room and the equipment, except for a decent candy thermometer, which she could really use anyway. And the cream puffs were certainly easy enough. *Pâte à choux* was nothing more then flour, boiling water, butter, and eggs. And the vanilla crème patissiere wasn't a big deal either. They could make that in advance and store it in the fridge.

Libby looked at the illustration more carefully.

"They have cones you can buy to fit the profiteroles around," Bernie had told her as she helped herself to one of the strawberries in the strainer in the sink. "Not that it matters because Leeza wants the cake constructed freehand."

"Considering she wanted a custom-made tent," Libby had answered, "I would have expected nothing less."

"Me either." Bernie popped the strawberry into her mouth, then licked her fingers. "I did some research on the net. A large cake, which is about sixty centimeters wide, is made up of between 240 and 280 cream puffs. That's not so bad."

Libby had to agree that 280 cream puffs were doable.

"Did you know," Bernie went on, "that the traditional way to serve the cake is by hitting it was a sword, with the bridesmaids catching the pieces in a tablecloth. Can you imagine the mess with the custard going all over the place?"

"No. I honestly can't," Libby had replied. Where did her sister get this stuff from anyway, Libby asked herself as she pointed to the base of the cake. "The trick is going to be molding the nougatine into columns."

Bernie had drummed her fingers on the countertop. "We'll figure it out."

Libby wasn't so sure about that, but the more she thought about it the more she was sure that as much as she hated to admit it, Bernie's instincts probably were correct. This was a good business opportunity, and the truth was they were so far over their head already that one more thing probably wouldn't matter.

"Okay," she'd finally told Bernie. "Tell Leeza we'll do it. Except we're not using spun sugar. We'll decorate the cake with sugared almonds and flowers."

"But . . ." Bernie had begun.

Libby had held up her hand. "If she insists on the spun sugar we can't do it. I won't take a chance on the weather."

"Fair enough." Bernie had popped a third strawberry into her mouth. "Sugared almonds are the traditional decoration anyway."

She'd been right to insist, Libby thought as she continued looking at the cake. Given the fact that it was raining, the spun sugar would have dissolved into little droplets by now. The only thing she hadn't factored in was transportation. The cake had to go from the kitchen of *A Taste of Heaven* to the van and from the van to the temporary kitchen she and Bernie had set up on the Raid Estate and from there to the tent where the reception was taking place.

Just the thought of having to move the cake not once but three times—in the rain no less—made Libby reach for one of her chocolate chip cookies. She was supposed to be on Atkins, but there were times when only carbs would do and this was definitely one of those times. Libby was taking a bite of her cookie when Bernie walked in to the kitchen.

"We have to go," Libby told her. "It's almost eight o'clock."

"I'm ready," Bernie said handing her a cup of coffee from the pot she'd brewed for the store. "Here. You're going to need this."

Libby looked at what her younger sister was wearing. She could understand the black hip-huggers and the tank top, but not the shoes.

"You're wearing pink wedges to stand in the kitchen? Are you nuts?"

"Hey," Bernie told her, "I don't comment on your Birkenstocks and you don't comment on these. How's the coffee?"

Libby took a taste.

"Sumatran?" she guessed.

Bernie nodded. "Good isn't it?"

"Very," Libby agreed. The way the day was going she was going to need several pots of the stuff and a bottle of aspirin. She glanced down at her sister's feet again. "How can you wear those to work in?"

Bernie shrugged. "Some people wear flats and *other* people wear heels and wedges. I am one of the *other* people."

"I just hope you don't trip when we carry the cake out to the van."

"Have I ever tripped?"

"No," Libby conceded.

"Well, then don't worry about it."

"But I do."

But then Libby admitted to herself, if truth be told she worried about everything. But if she didn't, she wouldn't have a successful business. Or at least that's what she told herself. She finished the coffee and took a deep breath. It was time to move the cake.

They'd just finished loading it into the van, when Libby heard her dad calling her name. She looked up. Her father was leaning out of his bedroom window on the second floor.

"You be careful out there," he told her.

Libby laughed. He'd been saying that to his daughters as long as she could remember.

"We're catering a wedding Dad, not executing search warrants."

"I'm talking about the aunts."

Libby sighed. "Oh them."

How could she have forgotten about Eunice and Gertrude Walker? They weren't really her aunts; she and Bernie just called them that. They were distant relations, old friends of one of her mother's cousins. Or something like that. Libby could never remember.

It wasn't that they weren't nice. After all, if it hadn't been for them *A Taste of Heaven* never would have gotten this job. No. That wasn't the issue. The issue was that they were nuts. Until she'd met them Libby had thought that Marxists were something that only existed in history books. And if that wasn't bad enough they did things like dye their hair magenta and go back to school to study entomology.

Libby still remembered the time their locust collection had escaped. That had been bad. But their driving was worse. Both of them had gotten their licenses when they were sixty-two. Libby remembered drawing straws with Bernie. The loser got to go with the aunts. "It'll be fine," her mother always said. "They never go over thirty-five miles an hour." To this day Libby could still remember the curses from other motorists as the aunts toddled down the highway. Amazingly, they'd never got any tickets. Finally, it was her father who'd put his foot down. Libby realized he was talking to her now.

"If they ask about me," he was saying, "tell them I've gone to Nepal."

"That wouldn't help. They'd find you there. Courtney will be here if you need anything."

"I'll be fine," her father said.

"Because . . ."

"Just go," her father ordered. "I'm not a total invalid."

"I know," Libby said. And she did know. It's just when she left him like this she got worried. But there was Courtney. And Rob's mom was going to give him lunch so everything would be fine. Libby gave her father a thumbs-up sign and got in the van. A moment later she and Bernie were on their way to the Raid Estate.

"I hope this goes well," Libby said as they headed out of Longely. At this hour of the morning, the only people out on the town street were runners.

"Well, it's got to go better than the high school reunion," Bernie pointed out.

When they'd catered their seventeenth annual high school reunion last year the guest of honor had been poisoned on the dais, which in Libby's humble opinion was not a good advertisement for the shop.

Libby groaned as she remembered. "God was that awful."

"Yes it was," Bernie agreed. "Especially for the poisonee." Then she pointed to a slim woman jogging down the block to the left of them. "There's Bree."

Libby glanced over. "I wish my thighs looked like hers."

"If you didn't eat anything and ran five miles a day they could."

Libby grunted. She couldn't even manage running half a block. She kept on saying she was going to get in better shape, but somehow it never happened.

"You know she's invited to the wedding, don't you?" Bernie said as Bree turned the corner.

"Unfortunately, yes."

This was another thing Libby was not happy about. Bree Nottingham, real estate agent extraordinaire and social arbiter of Longely could spot a water splotch on a glass at fifty yards away. As her mom would have said, Bree gave her the yips and had since kindergarten when she'd spotted the smudge on Libby's blouse and pointed it out to everyone.

"It'll be fine," Bernie consoled her.

"You're right," Libby agreed as she turned north on Ash Street. She desperately wanted to believe her younger sister. "I mean what's the worst that can happen?"

"One of the falcons can escape and attack the wedding cake," Bernie said. "Just kidding," she added as Libby shuddered. "They only go after living prey. But I guess they could use the cake as a perch."

"Why would anyone keep birds like that?" Libby asked.

Bernie tucked a strand of her hair back behind her ear. "I think they're kind of cool in a vicious kind of way."

"Well I don't," Libby said as she darted a glance in Bernie's direction. "That's one thing that Leeza and I agree on."

Chapter 2

As Bernie Simmons watched Jura Raid fishing around in the pocket of his jacket for the key to caviar storeroom, she wasn't thinking about how upset her sister was with her for accidentally knocking the top two tiers off the croquembouche when they'd moved the cake into the kitchen from the van.

After all, it would just take a couple of minutes to glue the tiers back on with sugar cement. No. Bernie was thinking about Jura and Leeza and how Leeza was going to run this guy ragged, not to mention cost him a small fortune. Well, she'd already done that with the wedding.

Actually, Bernie decided, she felt a little bit sorry for Jura, even though she normally didn't feel bad for older guys who married younger women, figuring that they got exactly what they deserved. But Jura wasn't a player like his younger brother, Ditas, who'd hit on her two minutes after he'd met her. Okay. Maybe she was exaggerating. Maybe it had been ten. Bernie made a face as she remembered how Ditas had shaken her hand and then pressed his thumb into her palm and wiggled it around while he told her how good she looked. I mean how skeevy can you get?

In any other circumstance she would have smacked the guy really hard, but given how Libby felt about confrontation she'd managed to keep her hands down by her sides and not punch him out. She would have probably split his lip with her silver and onyx ring anyway, and he looked like the kind of guy who would have had her arrested and brought up on assault charges.

Unlike Jura, who she couldn't imagine hitting anyone, let alone hitting on them. As she watched him continue to fumble around in his pocket she wondered if he'd ever even been out on a date. Probably not. So when someone like Leeza came along it must have been all over for him. Of course, if the story in the *Times* was to be believed it was a mutual thing.

Yeah. Right, Bernie thought. *Mutual my ass.* It was mutual once Leeza realized how much money Jura was worth. No. As her dad had said, Leeza getting Jura had been as easy as shooting fish in a barrel, which Bernie agreed with even though she didn't agree with her dad's phraseology. When she'd pointed out the fundamental illogic of the expression he'd used her father had groaned and reached for the remote. But it was true.

"Think about it," she'd told Libby. "You can't shoot fish in a barrel. You'd have to net them instead. If you shot into a barrel you'd have bullet holes and all the water would run out onto the ground and the barrel would be useless and barrels are expensive."

Libby hadn't looked up from the scones she was making, let alone answered. Even her boyfriend Rob, whom she could usually count on when it came to things of this nature, had told her to get a life. Oh well. It wasn't her fault that no one else she knew was interested in things like this.

But even Libby had agreed with her about Jura being ill at ease around women. How could she not? The two times Jura had met with her and Libby he'd been uncomfortable around them to the point of not being able to look either one of them in the eye. At first Bernie had thought it was them but Jura had been like that with his administrative assistant too. In fact, the only female Bernie had seen him relaxed with was Leeza, who'd cooed and batted her eyelashes at him like she was in some fifties movies.

It was weird. Jura was a big guy and big guys usually own the room. But this guy's posture was stooped which emphasized his narrow shoulders and big ass. Couple that with his pale complexion, and grayish, blond hair and he looked totally ineffectual.

But he couldn't be that ineffectual, Bernie reasoned. Ineffectual men don't run caviar empires that are worth millions of dollars. But maybe he was one of those guys who are better with numbers and figures than with people. Maybe his brothers handled that end of the business while he stayed in the office and emailed instructions to everyone.

Looking at Jura, Bernie wondered if all Estonian people were big and blond with prominent cheekbones and slightly slanted eyes. Somehow, she had thought they were short and dark and Jura was some sort of an anomaly, but his two younger brothers, Ditas and Joe looked exactly like him, except they were much better looking.

When Libby had announced that they'd gotten this job, Bernie had dragged out her old atlas and, ignoring Libby's eye rolling, looked at a map of the Baltics. It seemed that Estonia was quite close to Finland. For some reason, she'd pictured the country as being near Russia—maybe because it had been occupied by Russia until recently.

Bernie was trying to remember exactly what she'd read when she saw Libby dart a glance at her watch and start to nibble on her lower lip. Then her sister brought her hand up to her mouth and switched to biting her nails, which Bernie couldn't help noticing were in desperate need of a manicure.

Libby is flipping out, Bernie thought as she and her sister exchanged looks. And she could understand why. They still had an enormous amount to do. And if she, Bernie, was concerned she could only imagine how crazed Libby was feeling. And being tired and hung over certainly didn't help. In retrospect the Cosmopolitans might not have been such a good idea after all. Next time she'd make chocolate martinis instead.

For openers, she and Libby and Amber, who was coming in her own car, still had to drive the van loaded with all the linen, plates, silverware, and crystal that they were using for the dinner down the embankment to the tent, and offload everything. Which should be lots of fun.

Driving down that embankment was a pain in the ass when the grass was dry. But now the grass was wet and slippery and given that the van was top heavy—well, Bernie didn't want to think of the breakage if the van rolled over. The crystal alone cost fifty dollars a glass and they were using how many of them? Leeza was spending more on tableware for one afternoon than the store made in a whole year.

At least the tables and the chairs were in place. And hopefully the florist would be on time with the centerpieces—white roses and calla lilies. And at least she and Libby and Amber had folded the napkins into swans yesterday and wrapped the chocolate bars in doilies another one of Leeza's brilliant ideas. But they still had to prep the vegetables, clean the berries, and get the fires in the grill ready to go in addition to plating the caviar and arranging the toast points and foie gras.

It will all get done, Bernie told herself. *It always does.* As her yoga teacher used to say: "Negative thoughts lead to negative energy."

And Libby had hired a crack crew to work along with Googie, Stan, and Amber so that was good. Bernie reviewed the day's schedule in her head. The ceremony was taking place at two. Googie and Stan would be arriving at the estate at a little before one o'clock to serve drinks to the arriving guests in the living room, while the rest of the wait staff would arrive half an hour after that to help with the dinner.

The bar would close when the ceremony began and reopen after it was done, probably three-quarters of an hour, at which point the guests would reassemble in the living room and while away the time waiting for the bride and groom to refresh themselves by sipping Cristal and eating beluga and foie gras.

Then when the happy couple emerged, they would lead everyone down to the tent where dinner was being served. *What a production*, Bernie thought. If she and Rob ever got married, she'd go to Vegas and get married by an Elvis impersonator. Well, not really. Her father would kill her. But she wouldn't have a circus like this. She'd have a nice little reception at the house.

No, No, Bernie told herself when she realized what she'd been thinking. *Don't go there. Don't even think the M word. You'll jinx everything if you do.* She forced herself to pay attention to Jura instead.

It was nine o'clock in the morning of his wedding day and Bernie was interested to see that Jura was wearing a beige linen jacket, a pink oxford shirt, a tie, and a pair of immaculately pressed navy pants. Not that she'd ever really been around a guy on the day of his wedding—she just imagined someone in his position would be wearing something a little more casual before he changed into what he was going to be wearing for the ceremony. But maybe this was casual for him. Come to think of it, she'd never seen him in jeans or khakis. If he wore them, he'd probably get someone to iron and starch them.

"Locking the storeroom ensures that no one on my staff is tempted to pilfer," he explained to the girls as Bernie wondered how he got to be like that.

"That's been a problem?" Bernie asked trying to keep her mind off picturing Jura Raid in starched boxer shorts.

Jura shrugged. "Well naturally. After all, these days beluga is going for almost ninety-six dollars an ounce. That's a little under sixteen hundred dollars a pound."

"Amazing," Bernie said. She'd read that in colonial days caviar was known as the poor man's food because the fisherman had given the sturgeons' roe away for free. The fish had been so plentiful in the Hudson River that they'd exported it to Europe. Now, of course, they were all gone, fallen victim to over fishing and pollution.

"Yes," Jura replied. "Of course, people sell beluga for less but they're selling an inferior product. My company only sells the best from the Caspian Sea."

"I thought the beluga sturgeon there were on the CITES list," Bernie said noting Jura's look of surprise with a certain amount of pleasure. Not for nothing was she known as the Internet queen.

He nodded.

"That's why it's so expensive. Every tin we sell has been labeled and authenticated," Jura told the girls as he finally extracted the key from his pocket.

Libby turned to Bernie.

"CITES list?" she asked.

"It's the endangered species list," Bernie explained as Jura Raid fitted the key in the lock, turned it, and opened the door.

A blast of cold air greeted the girls as Jura motioned for them to step inside.

"It's freezing," Bernie said rubbing her shoulders. She'd wished she'd brought along a long-sleeved shirt or a sweater.

"Actually," Jura informed her, "the temperature in here is kept at exactly twenty-eight degrees Fahrenheit, the ideal temperature for storing caviar, which as I'm sure you know is extremely perishable. That is why it must be salted, but salt it too much and you take away the taste. Finding the right amount is an art."

"Interesting," Bernie said who always appreciated facts. What had Rob said to her recently about that? Something about her being like a guy in that regard. No. That wasn't it. She was trying to remember exactly when Libby started talking.

"I feel as if I'm stepping into a bank vault," Libby observed.

"As well you should," Jura agreed. He gestured around the room. "Ounce for ounce this stuff is more valuable than gold."

"Well not really," Bernie heard herself saying. "Gold is almost three hundred and eighty dollars an ounce right now and I believe you said beluga is under one hundred dollars an ounce." She would have said more but she realized that Libby was glaring at her.

Too bad, Bernie thought. So she'd broken Libby's first dictum: Never contradict the customer. So what? Sometimes her sister was beyond uptight. Or maybe Bernie admitted to herself she was feeling a little crabby from lack of sleep. She must be getting older. When she was in her twenties staying up all night would never have bothered her.

"I've never been around so much caviar in my life," Libby exclaimed as Bernie decided she should really lighten up on the Cosmos.

"Normally," Jura answered, "we don't keep this much product in the house, but after all this is a special day."

"It certainly is," Libby agreed in her best customer-relations voice.

Bernie contented herself with looking around as Jura and her sister continued to chat. The storeroom was a small closet-like affair, barely big enough for the three of them to fit in. It was lined in stainless steel and filled from top to bottom with shelves. Each shelf was neatly stacked with tins.

"Each side holds a different type of caviar," Jura explained. He pointed to his left. "For example, this side has Iranian caviar which is really the rarest there is, while this side, "here he pointed to his right, "holds Russian caviar. Our company deals in American caviar as well." Jura pointed out the tins on the back wall. "People buy this because it's cheap, although it's really not that good," he explained in a dismissive tone. "People in this country are trying to farm-raise sturgeon, but I'm sorry to say they really haven't been successful. And in my personal opinion they never will be."

Bernie watched Jura make a millimeter adjustment to his tie before gesturing towards the blue one-pound tins on the bottom shelf. The labels on them read "beluga."

"I want you to serve this," he told her and Libby.

Bernie was just about to ask him how long before serving they could plate the caviar when Ditas squeezed into the storeroom with them. *Great*, Bernie thought as he wiggled in close to her. Just the person she didn't want to stand next to, even if he was really good looking in a big blond kind of way.

"So what are you giving the guests?" he asked his brother.

Jura frowned and made another adjustment to his tie. *He's nervous,* Bernie thought as she watched him, but then she reasoned why wouldn't he be? After all, what groom wasn't on their wedding day?

"We've already discussed this," Jura told his brother in a voice that Bernie decided would freeze water on a ninety-degree day.

"I know," said Ditas.

"Then why are you bringing this up again?" Jura demanded. "As the oldest of this family I have the right to make these decisions."

"That's what you keep saying."

"Because that's the way it's always been."

Bernie thought she saw a flash of hatred radiate from Ditas's eyes but it was gone so quickly she couldn't be sure. Instead he'd plastered a big smile across his face, the kind of smile Bernie had seen on her ex's face when he was struggling to control himself. A second later Ditas winked at Bernie.

"The problem is that my brother is crazy," he told her. "Crazy with love. I told him we should give everyone the American stuff. They won't know the difference. But Jura, he wants to spend millions on his bride. Now if she were you," Ditas leered at Bernie, "I could understand it."

"Thanks," Bernie said as she felt his hand on her thigh. "You're too kind." She tried to move away from him but there was no room.

She could feel herself getting angrier and angrier as his fingers crept across her thigh and closer and closer to her crotch.

You want to play, she said to him silently, completely forgetting about her sister's injunction to always be nice to the customer no matter what. *I'll play.* She smiled at him and put her hand over his.

Ditas winked at her again, which was when she dug her nails into the back of his hand. After all, Bernie reasoned as she watched him grimace in pain, what's the point of having fingernails if you can't use them when you need them.

Chapter 3

Libby ignored Bernie and Amber and concentrated on driving. The van was not happy in the mud, let along going around sharp turns, but since this was the only road that led to where the tent was, this was the road she had to take. And of course she didn't even want to think about unloading.

The only good thing Libby reflected was that it was no longer pouring. The rain had turned to a light sprinkle. She rolled down her window and the smells of early summer, grass, roses, and honeysuckle, came flooding in. It is a pretty site, Libby mused as she took in the creek with its drooping willow trees. She had to give Leeza that.

And she had to admit that the tent did look wonderful. She'd thought Leeza was crazy when she'd insisted on silk instead of something a little sturdier, but the fabric had held up beautifully. When they turned on the lanterns the tent would look . . . what was the word Bernie had used? . . . luminous.

Everything worked, from the freshly graveled (with special stones of course), rose-lined path down to the tent from the house, to the artfully arranged canopies over the path that would protect the guests from the rain. But no matter how pretty it was Libby decided the fact remained that from a practical point of view getting the food down from the temporary kitchen was going to be a logistical nightmare, something she should have given more thought to before she agreed to take the job on.

Why had she taken this job anyway? Libby asked herself for the hundredth time this morning, even though she knew the answer. She could have said no. Despite what Bernie had called her she wasn't afraid of failure. Otherwise they wouldn't be doing this now. She hadn't even thought about failure. Libby nibbled on one of her cuticles. It would have been better if she had.

The truth was she'd gotten caught in delusions of grandeur. She'd lain in bed at night having these fantasies—and not the kind that Bernie had. Her cooking would be so wonderful that it would catapult her into fame and fortune. She would become an icon. Everyone would talk about Libby's scones and Libby's muffins.

For a brief moment she'd fancied herself signing copies of *The Simmons Sisters Cookbook* at Barnes and Noble. And then there'd be the primetime show on the cooking channel. And naturally she and Bernie would be on the cover of *Time* magazine with the headline: CATERERS TO THE STARS. Or something along those lines. Well, she'd been way wrong.

The truth was: She didn't operate well under extreme pressure and never had. This job was keeping her up at night and all the money they were making wasn't worth the anxiety level she was feeling. She really was a small town girl and always would be. Just the thought of what they still had to do made Libby reach for one of the freshly baked chocolate chip cookies in the bag by her seat.

"You guys want any?" she asked offering the bag to Bernie and Amber.

They both shook their heads.

"Suit yourself," she said taking a bite. The hell with Atkins. She'd get back on her diet tomorrow. She needed this now to calm her nerves. Libby sighed as a piece of the bittersweet Lindt chocolate she'd used in the cookie melted in her mouth. *Good choice,* she told herself as she stared at the embankment she was supposed to get the van down. "I don't know about this," she observed.

The van was not the most stable vehicle under the best of circumstances and this was not the best of circumstances. Libby estimated that the pitch of the hill she was supposed to drive the van down had to be about twenty degrees. Okay. Maybe it was fifteen. It didn't matter. It was still pretty steep. She could see deep ruts in the grass where the tent people had parked their rigs, not to mention ruts on the side of the embankment made, she presumed, when the tent people had tried to get their trucks back up. Leeza would pitch a screaming fit when she saw those, Libby thought as she took another bite of her cookie. She was thinking she was glad they weren't her fault when she became aware that Bernie was talking to her.

"You know," her sister was saying, "even if we get the van down the slope, I don't think we'll be able to get it back up. The guy from the tent company told me they almost got stuck yesterday and it's even muddier now."

Libby nodded as another burst of chocolate dissolved in her mouth. "I can see that."

It certainly wouldn't be good if they had to get someone to haul the van back up, that was for sure. Libby closed her eyes at the thought of Leeza's reaction to seeing the store vehicle, with all its dings and dents and rust spots sitting by the tent, ruining the atmosphere she'd spent so much money to create. And Libby didn't even want to think about what Bree Nottingham would say. Just the idea of it gave her a headache. She could hear Bree's expression of pained puzzlement.

"Surely Libby, you made alternative plans," she was imagining Bree saying, when she became aware that Amber was moving besides her. Libby opened her eyes as Amber leaned forward, narrowed her eyes, and stared out the front windshield.

"What do you see?" Libby asked her.

Amber shrugged and chewed on a strand of her hair, a habit Libby detested, instead of replying.

"Well," Libby said, prodding her to answer.

"I was just thinking . . ." She stopped and started again. "You know, last year there was this movie I saw where it was raining and these people were at an estate and then this killer sprang out . . ."

Libby put her hand up. "Okay. That's enough."

"But you asked," Amber protested.

"I know I did but I've been up all night, we have a full day of work to do, and it's not even nine o'clock in the morning. I just can't deal with serial killers right now."

Amber sniffed. "Fine. If that's the way you want to be."

"It is," Libby said firmly. Her request, she felt, was not unreasonable. "Don't you ever watch anything else besides horror movies?"

Amber giggled. "Not when my boyfriend is around."

Bernie grinned. "I can totally understand that."

Libby bit back her retort to Bernie about acting like an adult and said instead, "Come on guys. We're running out of time. We have to concentrate."

"Yes we do," Bernie replied.

Libby watched her sister twist her ring around her finger while she thought.

Finally she said, "I guess we could carry everything down there if we had to."

Libby turned and looked at her. "That would put us way behind schedule."

Plus, call her crazy but the idea of lugging boxes full of thousands of dollars worth of Waterford crystal and Lenox china down a slippery grass slope didn't seem like a remotely good idea. God, she wished yet again that Leeza had allowed them to do the reception inside the house. Even a tent outside in the backyard, if that's what you called a formal flower garden, would have been easier. But no. Leeza had been adamant. It had to be by the friggin' creek, which Libby, if she was honest with herself, was beginning to absolutely hate.

"I can call Stan and Googie," Amber offered, already digging in her pocket for her cell.

"It'll take them almost an hour to get over here," Libby pointed out. She sighed. It was always something. Murphy's Law should be changed to The Catering Law. "But we could get some of the guys from the house to help." There were enough of them around for sure. They'd still be behind, but not as behind.

"I have a better idea," Bernie told her.

"What?" Libby asked reluctantly because this phrase coming from her sister always struck dread in her heart.

"The estate is backed up to a golf course."

Libby nodded, not sure where her sister was going with this.

"And golf courses have carts, right?"

"So?"

"So, I saw one a couple of days ago when I was down by the creek. It's really close by. I'll just run over and borrow it. It'll take me two seconds. Tops. It'll be perfect. We can offload the cartons onto the back. The cart is way lighter than the van so it shouldn't have any problem going up and down the hill. I figure it'll take us four trips, max."

"Let's not," Libby said.

"Let's," Bernie countered.

"We're going to get into trouble," Libby told her sister.

Bernie waved her hand in the air. "It'll be fine. You worry too much."

"No, I don't." Libby gritted her teeth. "I don't worry nearly enough."

"Yes, you do," Bernie insisted. "And you always have."

Libby was rummaging around for a comeback when she noticed that Bernie was bent over. "Are you all right?" she asked suddenly concerned.

Bernie brushed the hair out of her eyes as she looked up. "Sure. Why wouldn't I be? I'm just taking my shoes off."

"And you're taking your shoes off because . . ."

"Because I can run faster."

This was not going well, Libby reflected. She tried a new tack, the voice of authority. After all she reasoned, it had worked for Jura with Ditas.

"As the oldest, I forbid you to do this." So much for that, Libby thought as Bernie made a rude noise before getting out of the van. Time to proceed to argument number two. "What you're planning to do is illegal," Libby protested to her sister's back.

Bernie turned her head. "I'm not stealing anything. I'm borrowing the cart."

"Somehow I always thought borrowing involved the concept of asking."

"I'd ask if I had time. I'm sure the people at the club would be glad to help once they knew the circumstances. Jura is probably a member."

Which, Libby conceded to herself, while probably true had nothing to do with the point she, Libby, was trying to make. Libby thought of one last argument.

"How do you know the cart will still be there?" she demanded triumphantly as Bernie closed the van door.

"Why shouldn't it be?"

"Why should it be?"

"I guess we'll find out," Bernie told her.

Libby shook her head. She couldn't think of anything else to say and even if she could she was pretty sure it wouldn't make any difference because the truth was: once Bernie got an idea into her head it was impossible to dissuade her.

"Great." Libby said to Amber as she watched Bernie run towards the wooden post fence that separated both properties. "Just great." Then she reached in the bag and took another cookie.

"Is doing something like that a felony?" Amber chirped.

"Probably," Libby replied morosely.

"Because one of my brother's friends stole a golf cart and he got caught and they made him go to jail for a year. Do you think they'll do that to Bernie?"

"I don't know."

Libby envisioned the headlines. EX-POLICE CHIEF'S DAUGHTER IN JAIL. Her father would be so pleased. She could see the expression on his face now. She wondered if they'd arrest Bernie before they served the dinner or after. Hopefully it would be after so Bernie could still work. Or maybe they'd arrest her, Libby, for sistericide. Or whatever the hell the correct word was.

Libby looked at her watch for what she knew had to be the hundredth time in the past half an hour. They were already fifteen minutes behind schedule and the clock was ticking. What would happen if Bernie didn't come back? What if she was arrested? What if she couldn't find a cart? A wave of panic swept through Libby. She bit into the cookie. She'd just lost ten pounds and Bernie had made her buy new clothes. Fitted ones. No more loose tee shirts for her. If she went back up to a size fourteen she was going to hold Bernie personally responsible.

Bernie could feel the wet grass and the little rocks digging into the soles of her feet as she ran. It was uncomfortable, not to mention bad for her pedicure, but still better then ruining one of her favorite pairs of shoes. Plus, as much as Bernie hated to admit it, it was hard to run in wedges.

She slipped under the fence that separated the Raid Estate from the Conenus Golf Club and kept going. The cart should be right under the next grove of trees. At least the cart had been there two days ago. She'd spotted it when she'd gone for a hike while Libby had been talking to Leeza. Well, it hadn't been a hike exactly. More like a forced march. She'd just had to get away from Leeza and her demands before she said something she shouldn't.

Please be there, she prayed as she ran towards the trees. It would be horrible if Libby were right. She'd hear about it for the next twenty years. God, it would be just her luck to have someone bring the cart back to the clubhouse.

Bernie stopped for a moment and surveyed the area. She didn't see the cart. It definitely wasn't by the maple. It had been a maple she'd seen it under, hadn't it? Bernie chewed on her inner lip. Now that she was here she wasn't so sure about the locale. The truth was she'd always been a little shaky in the tree identification department. Botany wasn't her strongest subject. She looked again and let out a sigh of relief. There it was half-hidden behind what? A gum locust? Or maybe a hawthorn? Bernie shook her head at herself. *Get a grip, Simmons. Forget the trees. You're becoming like your sister: obsessive.*

As Bernie sprinted towards the cart, she remembered something else. Her heart sank. Golf carts need keys to go. How could she have forgotten that? Man oh man, she hoped the key to this one was in the ignition. Usually they left them in, at least they did in the country club at Longely. It would be just her luck to have it not be there.

But when Bernie got up close she could see that it was. Thank God, Bernie thought as she jumped in the cart and turned the key. Nothing happened. Damn, Bernie thought. Of course. That's why the cart was out here. Because it doesn't run. *Duh,* as the kids in town would say. She tried again. Still nothing.

This time Bernie took a deep breath and put all her energy into visualizing the cart moving. "Third time's the charm," Bernie said to herself. She turned the switch again. The cart moved. Yes. She pumped her arm in the air and let out a whoop. Despite what her father said about New Age gobbledygook her yoga teacher was right. Visualization does work. Bernie took off.

The cart lurched forward. Stopped. Started again. *Relax,* Bernie told herself. After all, this thing was really nothing more than an overgrown lawn mower engine with seats on it. After another minute she got the hang of it. *I'll be back at the van in three minutes flat,* she estimated. Actually it took Bernie five minutes because she had to remove two of the wooden cross pieces from the fence before she could get the cart through.

"Okay, ladies," she said to Libby and Amber as she turned the key to the off position. "I'm wet, but I'm here. Let's go."

Libby and Amber jumped out of the van and ran to the back. Libby threw open both doors and began handing boxes out to Amber, who in turn handed them to Bernie who packed them in the cart. When she had gotten four in she held up her hand.

"I think that's enough."

Libby nodded her agreement as Bernie jumped back in the golf cart and Libby got into the seat next to her. Bernie started down the hill slowly, careful to go around so they avoided the steepest part of the hill. Even so, she could feel the cart wobbling slightly. When they got down they unloaded the boxes near the tent flap and went back for a second trip. And a third. And a fourth. Twenty-eight boxes later, not only was Bernie's back hurting her, but her tee-shirt was wet. So were Amber's and Libby's.

Bernie wiped away a drop of rain that had gotten into her eye. "We should have brought a couple of changes of clothes," she said to Libby.

Libby nodded as she removed another carton from the cart.

"We'll know next time," Bernie continued.

Libby put the carton down. "There won't be a next time. We're not doing this again. Not ever."

"At least not without some more help," Bernie said.

That was another problem with doing a job like this. Hire too many people and you ate up your profit margins, hire too few and you killed yourself and couldn't do a good job. It was a fine line and hard to gauge, but in Bernie's humble opinion Libby consistently understaffed. Which was, let's be honest here, because her sister was cheap.

If Libby had brought along another person they'd be further ahead and she wouldn't be glancing at her watch every two seconds like she was doing now and making herself into a nervous wreck.

"Come on guys," she said to Bernie and Amber confirming what Bernie had been thinking, "let's pick up the pace."

"We're almost done," Bernie pointed out.

"If you want," Amber said to Bernie, "I can go inside and start putting the table clothes and napkins out.

"Good idea," Bernie told her approvingly as she put a finger to her nose to stop a sneeze. Boy she hoped she wasn't getting sick. Summer colds were the worst. "We're lucky to have her," she said to Libby as Amber disappeared inside the tent. In the year she'd spent working with her sister she'd come to realize how hard it was to find responsible employees.

"Yes, we are," Libby agreed.

A second later she and Libby heard a bloodcurdling shriek.

"Or maybe not," Bernie said. "Stop it," she yelled at Amber. "You're not being funny." Bernie turned back to Libby. "You're right. This horror thing is getting out of hand."

She'd just gotten the words out of her mouth when Amber reappeared at the tent flap. She had one hand over her heart and was pointing towards the front of the tent with the other one.

"She's dead," she cried.

"Who?" Bernie cried. "Who is dead?"

"Her." At which point Amber took a few steps and collapsed in a heap on the wet grass.

Chapter 4

When Libby glanced down at Leeza Sharp her first thought was: this is a practical joke. Her second thought was: I don't have time for this nonsense. Her third thought was: Amber and Bernie are dead meat.

"Not funny," she said whirling around to face Bernie. Then she saw the horrified expression on Bernie's face and Libby's stomach lurched. *Oh, please God, not again,* Libby prayed. *Not another murder.*

Libby took another look at the body sprawled out on the floor. Leeza's eyes were staring straight up. Her mouth was opened in an expression of surprise. An arrow was protruding from her chest. And then there was the blood. It was everywhere. On the floor. On Leeza Sharp's no longer white robe. On her nightgown.

No, Libby told herself. This isn't a joke. Leeza was definitely dead. Not mostly dead. Not nearly dead. Dead dead. No doubt about that. No doubt at all. No one could survive an arrow through the heart. At least not in real life.

Libby heard the words, "And on her wedding day too," coming out of her mouth. *What a stupid thing to say,* she told herself as Bernie turned towards her. Like it would have been better if it had happened the day after. Well, in a sense it would have been because then they wouldn't have been here.

"Yeah," her sister said. "She should have eloped."

"Bernie!"

"Well it's true." Bernie tucked a curl back behind her ear. "Weddings never bring out the best in people and that goes double for Leeza."

"She was a pain," Libby conceded.

"Just a pain?" Bernie echoed. "How about annoying, vexing, and aggravating, not to mention galling and grating?"

"Fine. She was impossible," Libby said thinking of all the napkins in the shape of swans they'd had to fold which were now going to go to waste.

"She was a Bridezilla stomping on everyone."

"Even so that's not a reason to shoot someone in the chest with an arrow," Libby said as she reached up and wiped the sweat off her cheeks. Why she had to sweat when she got upset was something she'd never know.

Bernie pulled up her bra strap. The damned thing kept sliding down. "It's as good a reason as any," she noted. There was something about that arrow. Now what the hell was it? She almost had it in her grasp when Amber stepped back inside the tent and the thought vanished.

While Amber still looked a little shaky, Bernie noticed that she'd managed to reapply her lipstick and fix her hair. For the photographers? Bernie thought uncharitably as Amber ran up to her. Because they'd certainly be here as soon as the word got out. She could see the headline in the *New York Post* now. SHOT THROUGH THE HEART AND WHO'S TO BLAME? Or SIMMONS SISTERS CATER ANOTHER SLAY. Bernie shook her head to clear it. She didn't want to think about the last time she and Libby had been involved in something like this. The press had pestered them for weeks.

"See," Amber was saying. "I told you there was a homicidal maniac around here. I did," she told Bernie. "Ask her"—Amber gestured in Libby's direction—"if you don't believe me." Amber began wringing her hands; a gesture Bernie had never actually seen anyone do before except in the theater. "And now we're all going to die."

"Don't be ridiculous," Libby retorted when she heard a crack. *Amber's right, we* are *going to die,* she thought as she dropped to the ground. "Get down," she yelled at Bernie who was looking at her and Amber and shaking her head in disgust.

"Guys get a grip," Bernie said. "That was a willow tree branch breaking."

Libby looked up at her sister from the floor. If the murderer didn't kill her, she would. "It was a gunshot."

"How do you know? You've never heard one," Bernie retorted.

"Neither have you."

"Of course I have. Remember, I've lived in L.A. Besides," Bernie continued, "I saw the branch falling."

"I didn't."

"That's because you were facing the wrong way."

"Just get down," Libby hissed at Bernie.

"And grovel in the dirt for no reason whatsoever? I don't think so." When Libby didn't get up, Bernie said, "You don't believe me. I'll prove it to you."

"Wait," Libby cried as Bernie turned and started to march outside. "Don't go out there."

But Bernie wasn't listening to her. No big surprise there, Libby reflected as she heard her moving outside the tent. For a moment Libby debated staying on the floor but then she decided, no. If anyone was going to have the pleasure of shooting her sister, it was going to be her. Libby jumped up. She'd taken about five steps when Bernie reappeared dragging a willow branch behind her.

"See," she said.

Libby cringed. Bernie would never let her forget this. Ever. "It could have been a gun shot," she countered. "How did you know it wasn't?"

Bernie put the branch over to the side of the tent wall. "I saw it. Anyway, I went with probability. Most violent offenders, despite media reports to the contrary, do not commit multiple homicides. Ergo, it's safe to assume that whoever killed Leeza is not here at the crime scene. At least not now. Although according to what I read he may revisit it at some later date."

"Maybe you should stop reading," Libby said to her sister.

Bernie turned to answer but before she could Amber said, "What about a serial killer? A serial killer could have done this."

Bernie snorted.

"There are less than one hundred of those operating in the United States at any given year so that's highly doubtful. Isn't that right Libby?"

"Oh, absolutely," Libby said, vigorously nodding her head.

In truth, she didn't have the vaguest idea whether what Bernie was saying was true or not, but if agreeing with Bernie calmed Amber down and kept her sister from lecturing Libby was willing to go along. And then for some reason Mrs. Centra, Amber's mom, popped into Libby's head.

Mrs. Centra was so protective of her daughter—smothering was the term Bernie used—that she hadn't let Amber go on a sleepover until she was almost sixteen. Libby couldn't imagine what was she going to say when she found out that it was Amber, her precious flower as Mrs. Centra liked to call her, who had discovered Leeza's body. She'd probably never let her work in the store again Libby gloomily reflected as she suggested to Amber that it would be better if she waited outside.

"Alone?" Amber shrieked. "You want me to wait outside by myself with a homicidal maniac armed with a bow and arrow running around?"

"There is no homicidal maniac. There's a murderer," Bernie interjected. "I thought I explained that to you."

"Like that's so much better." Amber crossed her arms over her chest and planted her feet on the ground. "I'm staying with you guys."

Libby tried again. "Amber," she began. Then she stopped because Amber wasn't paying attention to her.

She was raptly staring at Leeza's body. Libby noticed that Amber no longer looked even slightly upset.

"You know," Amber confided to Libby and Bernie. "I've never seen a dead person before in real life."

"You're lucky. I wish I hadn't," Libby said. I could use a chocolate cookie right about now she decided.

Her mind drifted to her backpack. She usually kept some in there along with a bottle of water, a fifty-dollar bill, and a needle-nose pliers, but this wedding had made her so crazy she'd forgotten to check her supplies to see if they needed to be replenished. Oh well, she thought as she went back to listening to Amber.

"My mom wouldn't even let me go to my uncle's wake because it was an open casket," Amber was saying. Then she wrinkled her nose and indicated Leeza Sharp. "She looks like something from a wax museum, doesn't she?"

"A little," Bernie agreed. "Well, a lot actually."

Libby made herself look at Leeza's body again. Unlike Bernie she was squeamish and always had been. It wasn't the dead part that got her. It was all those bodily fluids oozing out where she could see them that did her in. But now that she'd disgraced herself by acting like a total dweeb and dropping to the floor she felt as if she had no choice but to suck it up.

"What are you thinking?" Bernie asked her.

"I'm thinking," Libby replied, "that Leeza looks like Wendy in Peter Pan."

"Well," Bernie replied, "Wendy was shot by one of the lost boys."

Libby nodded. "Only I don't think this was an accident."

Chapter 5

"For sure there's not going to be any question about the cause of death," Bernie observed.

"Agreed," Libby said.

At least this time no one could even consider blaming her cooking, Libby caught herself thinking. And speaking of cooking, what were they going to do with seventy-five quail, not to mention the asparagus waiting for them in the kitchen? Well, she could always make a cold soup out of the asparagus and freeze that and the quail if necessary.

To make the soup, she'd roast the asparagus to bring out the flavor, then puree it and add some chicken stock, a touch of cream, a dash of nutmeg. Maybe a sprinkling of toasted walnuts on the top. Or perhaps almonds. Libby was thinking that almonds would be the better choice when she realized that Bernie was talking to her.

"Yes?" she said guiltily.

"I was just saying," Bernie repeated, "that this is obviously a homicide."

"It would be hard to shoot yourself with an arrow," Libby concurred. She couldn't believe that she'd been thinking about recipes at a time like this.

"Unless it was in the foot . . . or you had really long arms." Bernie began tapping her fingers against her chin.

"Maybe someone shot her in the heart and then stabbed her with the arrow to cover it up," Amber suggested.

"And they'd do that . . . why?" Bernie asked her.

Amber hemmed and hawed.

"Exactly," Bernie said when she didn't answer. She started twisting her ring around her finger. "So we know this is a homicide and we also know the shooter is left-handed."

"We do?" Libby said.

"Yes we do." Bernie pointed to the shaft of the arrow sticking out of Leeza's chest. "Look at the way the feathers are pointing," she impatiently. "They're pointing to the left of the notch," she went on when Libby didn't say anything.

"So what?" Libby said.

"Well people that are left-handed shoot with the feathers pointing in that direction. Of course," she added, "if you're shooting a crossbow given the way it's fired it really doesn't matter."

Libby just stared at her. "Where do you get this stuff from?"

"Camp. We had to take archery, remember?"

"I didn't."

"You could have if you weren't spending all your time in the nurse's office."

Libby began chewing on one of her cuticles. "Excuse me if I have allergies."

Bernie made a rude noise.

Libby put her hands on her hips. "And what's that supposed to mean?"

"Nothing." Bernie turned back to study Leeza. This was not the time to discuss her older sister's pitiful performance at Camp Min-Nie-Ton-Ka or Camp of the Little Truck as her father insisted on calling the place. "For that matter why use a bow and arrow?" Bernie mused, thinking out loud. "Why not a gun?"

Amber coughed. Bernie looked at her.

"What?" she asked.

Amber nodded towards Leeza's body. "Maybe it's supposed to be like a Cupid's arrow thing," she said hesitantly.

"I mean since she's shot through the heart and everything. It's like about love."

I can't believe I missed that, Bernie thought. Perhaps Amber wasn't such a ninny after all. "That's a really good observation," Bernie told her. "I'm impressed." And she was.

Amber flushed with pleasure.

"So what do you think brought Leeza down here in the first place?" Bernie asked.

Amber nibbled on her lower lip for a moment, hesitated for a few seconds more, and then said, "Well in the movies she'd have gotten a call luring her into the tent."

"Give me a break," Libby grumbled.

"No. Don't be so dismissive. That works," Bernie said to her sister.

"So does the fact that Leeza went for a walk," Libby replied wondering as she did why she was feeling so annoyed. It was like suddenly Amber was Bernie's new best friend.

"In the rain? Please," Bernie scoffed.

"Maybe she came down here because she wanted to make sure the tent wasn't leaking."

Bernie snorted at the idea.

"Leeza? No way. She would have sent one of her staff. Or called us up at six o'clock in the morning and told us to get down here. No. Amber's hypothesis makes sense. Leeza is wearing her nightgown and her bathrobe and she doesn't have any make-up on."

Libby put her hands on her hips. "Meaning?"

"Meaning given that Leeza was the kind of woman who wouldn't go to the bathroom without putting on her mascara first, she would have gotten dressed if she was going for a walk. The fact that she didn't indicates she didn't have time to. That she came down here in a hurry, which means someone called and told her to meet them down here."

"Perhaps you're right," Libby reluctantly conceded. "But for my money that's an awful lot of maybes."

Bernie grunted and tapped her ring against her teeth. "You know what else puzzles me?"

"Maybe you should leave something for the police to figure out, Sherlock," Libby observed.

Bernie ignored her.

"How Leeza was shot."

"What do you mean? She was shot with an arrow."

"And?"

Libby gave her a blank look.

"Well, think about it," Bernie said. "There's nothing here but the tables, right?"

Libby and Amber both nodded their heads.

Bernie began to pace back and forth. "And you can pretty much see anyone who is inside the tent from the outside."

Amber wrinkled her nose. "Okay. And your point is?"

Bernie looked at Libby. "You get it, don't you?"

"Not really."

Bernie slapped her forehead in frustration. "Think. A bow takes times to aim. It's not like a gun. It's not inconspicuous. Why didn't she see her assailant and duck? Why did she come in at all?"

Libby shrugged. "Who knows? Maybe he wasn't inside yet. Maybe Leeza arrived first."

"Then why didn't she see the bow when he came in? I mean he had to have come in. He didn't shoot through the tent. There are no tears in the material."

"Maybe he . . ."

"Or she," Amber interrupted. "The killer could be a female. Those are the worst kind . . . ."

"Whoever," Libby said. "As I was saying maybe he," she nodded to Amber, "or *she* was hiding their weapon under their raincoat."

"But Leeza would have seen him taking it out."

"Not if her face was turned away and she was looking at something else."

"Like what?"

"How the hell should I know," Libby snapped. "I wasn't there. Maybe he left the bow under the table and then bent down and got it and whammo."

"That would work," Bernie conceded.

"Or maybe he/she/it was crouched down when Leeza came in," Libby suggested getting into the spirit of the thing despite herself. "Or maybe she did see him and it was too late."

"I don't know." Bernie glanced around again.

Libby tugged at her sister's sleeve. "Come on. We have to call the police. Anyway we should leave. We've already contaminated the crime scene enough as it is."

Bernie clicked her tongue against her cheek. "Go ahead and call them. There's something I want to check out."

Libby groaned. "There's nothing to check out. Remember we agreed that after the last time we wouldn't get involved in another homicide investigation."

"No," Bernie told you. "You suggested it; I never agreed to it. Anyway, if I recall correctly, you were the one that was hot to investigate the last time not me. You were the one that got me and Dad involved."

"Okay. That's true," Libby allowed. After all it had been her best friend that had been accused of murder. What else was she supposed to do? "But this is different. We don't know these people."

Bernie turned to face her. She had that look of intense concentration on her face that Libby had come to associate with trouble.

"Do you believe in karma?" she began.

"No," Libby told her. "I believe in Julia Child's recipes and the *Joy of Cooking.*"

"I'm being serious."

"So am I." Libby shook her head. "Mother was right. You should never have gone out to California. Then you wouldn't have met Swami whatever the hell his name is."

"It's Mister Gupta and he's my spiritual adviser."

"Whatever," Libby retorted.

Bernie held up her hand. "Don't be so close-minded. I want you to think about what I'm going to say."

"And I want you to think about getting out of here."

"Don't you consider it odd that we're present at yet another homicide?"

"That's exactly what I'm afraid the police are going to say," Libby told her.

Bernie shook her head impatiently. "No. I'm talking about a different plane. I mean maybe this is the reason we got this job. Maybe we're supposed to investigate Leeza's death. Maybe solving homicides is what we've been put on this earth for."

"Maybe she's right," Amber chimed in.

It took all of Libby's willpower not to throttle Amber. "No. No. No." Libby could feel her head begin to throb. She desperately wished she had a chocolate chip cookie. A peanut butter cookie. At this moment she'd even settle for a Fig Newton and she hated those. "Please don't start in with that stuff now. Next you're going to be talking about channeling and astral planes."

"How do you know what I said isn't true?" Bernie demanded.

Libby took a deep breath and marshaled her thoughts. "I don't," she allowed. "But here's what I do know. I know we're standing in front of a dead body. And I know the cops will be pissed if we don't call them."

Bernie waved her hand. "Of course we're going to call them. In a few minutes."

"This is not our responsibility." Libby could hear her voice rising. *Get a grip,* she told herself. Why she always let her sister get to her was something she did not know.

"Just give me a minute," Bernie replied. "That's not too much to ask."

Libby bit her lip. "Okay," she said grudgingly. "Two minutes, but no more."

Bernie grinned and went over to stand besides Leeza's body. Amber was right behind her.

"I mean it," Libby said as she wondered if Amber could get any nearer to Bernie without stepping on the backs of her feet.

"I know you do," Bernie replied. "Let's see," she continued. "The arrow went into her heart. Arrows follow straight trajectories which, allowing for distance, means that it probably came from somewhere over there." She started walking to the back of the tent.

"What the hell are you doing?" Libby demanded. Why had she said yes to Bernie? Every time she did she regretted it.

"Looking," Bernie said her eyes fastened to the ground.

"I can see that. Looking for what?"

Suddenly Bernie's face lit up. "For this." And she pointed to a chair.

Libby hurried over. "Ohmygod," she said as she put her hand to her mouth. "I've never seen anything like it."

"It's a booby trap," Bernie said with grim satisfaction. "See, that's why Leeza walked in here. There was no one waiting for her. I was right. She got a call to come down here and that was all she wrote, folks."

Libby looked closely. Someone had secured a wooden box to the chair and mounted a crossbow on it. "But what set it off?" she asked. "I don't see any wires."

"That," Bernie said indicating the remote control car hanging down from the bow trigger, "is the really brilliant part. Someone started up the car with its remote control device and then that made the wheels go which pulled the crossbow's trigger.

"And since the radius of a remote control device can be a couple of hundred feet, I'd be willing to bet you that whoever did it was probably sitting in the big oak by the creek. They could see everything and Leeza certainly wouldn't be looking up." Bernie stood. "Whoever set this up is very smart. It's very simple. Very elegant. And you can get a remote control car like that in any hobby shop across the country."

"Elegant is hardly the word I'd use, dear."

Libby, Bernie, and Amber spun around at the same time. They'd been so engrossed they hadn't heard anyone coming in. Now Eunice and Gertrude Walker were standing behind them. Their faces were wrinkled and they were so short they barely came up to the Simmons girls' chests. They were both wearing matching dresses made of some kind of pale green gauzy material and had hats on to match. But it was their hair that really made Libby, Bernie, and Amber blink. They'd cut it short, spiked it up, and dyed it turquoise.

"I told Leeza," Gertrude said in a surprisingly strong voice.

"Yes, you did," Eunice agreed.

"I told her this marriage was bound to end in tragedy."

"Why?" Libby asked as she tore her gaze away from Gertrude's hair.

Gertrude looked at her as if she was a moron.

"Because, dear," she explained. "Whenever a proletariat marries into the capitalist upper class, no good ever comes of it."

Libby couldn't help it. Maybe it was the stress she was under. But before she could stop herself, even though her mother had taught her never to be rude to the elderly, the words "Give me a break" fell from her lips.

Eunice fixed Libby with a gimlet eye. "My dear," she said in a frosty tone, "despite what you so obviously think, Marxism can be used to explain personal as well as economic issues. Bernie, I hope you can see that even if your sister can't."

Bernie just grunted. Ordinarily, she would have said something about it being Leeza, the poor downtrodden proletariat, who had been acting like the Wicked Witch of the West, but now she had other things on her mind.

Like she'd just remembered that she'd seen a whole bunch of bows in a room in the estate.

Chapter 6

Sean Simmons hung up the phone and turned to his friend Clyde Schiller.

"That was Bernie," he told him.

"So I gathered." Clyde patted his ample midsection then took another bite of a piece of Libby's homemade cherry pie. He sighed with pleasure. He was never happier than when he was visiting his ex-boss and eating his daughter's food. "Cap, you're lucky Libby is a good baker. If my wife cooked even a quarter as well, I'd die a happy man.

"The touch of cinnamon in the filling is inspired." Clyde picked up a cherry with his fork and waved it around before plopping it in his mouth. "You don't find these in pies anymore. Most people use that nasty, gummy canned stuff. Where'd she find the sour cherries?"

"Turlington has some trees out on his farm. She gets them from him." Sean studied his hands for a moment. They were shaking less today. Or maybe he just wanted that to be the case. Sometimes, the doctor had said, cases like his went into remission.

"Bernie checking up on you?" Clyde asked.

"Not exactly." Sean pursed his lips for a second while he thought about what his daughter had just told him. What was it with Bernie and Libby anyway? They were like lightning rods for disaster. "She called to tell me there's been a homicide at the Raid Estate."

Clyde raised an eyebrow. As a veteran police officer first down in the Bronx and now in Longely, he'd mastered the art of understatement a long time ago. "No kidding."

"No kidding," Sean repeated.

He could tell from Clyde's expression that his friend was thinking the same thing he was about his daughters and the way murders seemed to follow them wherever they went. Like Bo Peep and her sheep. Or whatever that nursery rhyme was. If Rose were alive she'd probably be blaming him for that, Sean gloomily concluded. Not that she'd ever have come out and say it directly mind you.

But she hated it when he'd talked about his cases at the dinner table, hated having his gun in the house. It brings bad luck, she'd said. And she'd always been after him to work at something more respectable. Even the fact that he was chief of police hadn't changed her opinion. But the truth was he'd enjoyed being a cop. Always had. He'd enjoyed being where the rubber hit the road. He hadn't realized how much he'd enjoyed it until he'd had to quit.

"Amber was the one who found the body," Sean added as he watched Clyde center his plate, one of Libby's better ones, on the tray table in front of him.

"That's too bad." Clyde dabbed at the corners of his mouth with his napkin. "Mrs. Centra won't be pleased."

"No, she won't," Sean readily agreed thinking unhappily of the call he was most likely going to get from Amber's mom when she found out. For some reason he couldn't get it through her head that he wasn't the chief of police anymore. "I don't like the new one," she kept saying. Then he brightened as an idea struck him. Maybe he could pretend to be asleep. After all, being an invalid should be good for something.

He tapped his fingers on the arm of his wheelchair while Clyde speared another cherry with his fork and conveyed it to his mouth. After a moment of silence Sean continued.

"According to Bernie, the bride caught an arrow in the heart. She walked into a booby-trapped crossbow someone set off with a remote-control device."

"Very fancy, not to mention an interesting choice of weapon," Clyde observed after he'd swallowed. "A crossbow, huh? Well, that's got to narrow the field considerably. Except for some hunters, not many people have those things around. Most people use guns." Clyde absentmindedly tapped his fork on the plate. "The whole setup sounds real elaborate, definitely not the kinda thing you see in your average, everyday homicide."

"For sure," Sean agreed. "If I remember correctly, the fanciest we ever got around here was when Mrs. Quinn spiked her old man's tomato juice with arsenic and prune juice."

Clyde laughed. "It was the prune juice that got me. It's hard to believe someone would drink something mud brown."

"He was color blind."

Clyde nodded his head. "That's right. I forgot." He savored his next bite of pie for a moment before speaking. "Don't forget the guy that put ground glass in his boss's sugar bowl. Put the glass through a blender twenty times till it was fine as sand."

"Yeah. But his boss never drank it, he'd switched to Sweet 'n Low, so it doesn't count."

"But he was still indicted," Clyde said. "So it does count."

"I'm not going to argue with you." Sean stifled a yawn. He hadn't slept well last night. Maybe Libby was right about not sleeping in the wheelchair.

Clyde frowned. "Raid, huh?"

"That's what I said."

Clyde ate the last of the pie then put his fork down and loosened his belt a notch. "Didn't I just read about them in the *Wall Street Journal*? Three brothers. Run a caviar business. The paper called them the caviar barons."

"That's them," Sean said.

Clyde reached back and scratched underneath his collar.

Why his wife kept insisting on putting starch on the collars of his polo shirts he would never know. "Your daughters are moving in some high-class company."

Sean grunted. "It depends on the definition you give to high class."

"That's a rather dyspeptic view."

"Nice word," Sean told him. "Bernie would approve."

"She ought to. I got it from the *Learn a Word a Day* calendar that she gave me last Christmas. But you're right. I'm glad I don't have to deal with those people," Clyde said. "In my experience taking statements from the rich and famous is never anything but a pain in the butt. They think they own everything and everybody."

"Maybe because they do," Sean said. He studied a squirrel scurrying across the cable wire outside his window for a moment before continuing. "The girls wouldn't even have this job if it weren't for the Walker sisters. I told Rose those women are nothing but trouble. Have been ever since I've known them."

"Aren't they the anarchists?" Clyde asked.

"Marxists," Sean corrected.

"What's the difference?"

"I'm not sure," Sean admitted. "I keep forgetting." Of course, Bernie would know. So would his wife for that matter. If she were alive he could have asked her.

Clyde frowned and waved his hand impatiently. "Never mind. It doesn't matter. My question is what are the Walker sisters doing with people like the Raids? I would have thought they would have steered clear of people like that."

"They're related to the bride in some distant way," Sean replied. "And they were friends with the groom's parents. I think they shared a railroad flat on the Lower East Side with them at some point or other."

Libby had explained it to him, but he'd be damned if he could remember what she'd said. That kind of family stuff—who was related to whom—didn't interest him a whole heck of a lot.

Now it was Clyde's turn to grunt. Both men remained silent as they imagined the scene that must be unfolding at the Raid Estate. Sean stared out the window for a few seconds, before turning and facing Clyde again. Suddenly he was tired of his bedroom, tired of the view out his window, tired of hearing everything second hand, tired of relying on his daughters—they should be relying on him.

He was especially tired, if he was being honest with himself, of being at the mercy of his daughters' whims, especially the most recent one. He didn't need any strange female traipsing in and out of his bedroom, thank you very much. He'd loved his wife, but now she was gone and as far as he was concerned that part of his life was over and done with.

"Do you think you could get this wheelchair downstairs?" he asked Clyde impulsively, surprised at the words that were coming out of his mouth.

"Don't see why not," Clyde said. "That's what you have that riding seat contraption for."

"I'm thinkin' maybe we should take a drive over to the Raid Estate and see what's what."

This time both of Clyde's eyebrows shot up.

"What's the big deal?" Sean said.

"The big deal is that people have been trying to pry you out of this place for three years, and you've flat out refused to go."

Sean shrugged. "My girls need my help."

Clyde chuckled. "No, they don't. They can do just fine without you. They already proved that." Then Clyde stopped speaking. A look of comprehension crossed his face. "This isn't about them, is it? You're just using them as an excuse."

Sean began studying his bedspread.

"If I recollect, isn't Ina Sullivan supposed to be coming over to make you a late lunch?" Clyde asked him.

Sean tried to look as if he didn't know what Clyde was talking about. "How should I know? My daughters set things like that up."

"Ina's a nice lady," Clyde said.

Sean kept his gaze fixed on the bedspread and away from his friend's face. "I never said she wasn't."

Clyde smoothed what was left of his hair down with the palm of his hand. "The girls are going to be pissed."

"Libby's been trying to get me out of the house for three years. She'll be happy."

"No she won't."

"Okay. She won't," Sean allowed. "Let me worry about that. Are you going to help me or not?"

Clyde studied his old friend for a moment then slowly said, "I'd like to Cap, but I don't know if this is such a good idea for me with the chief feeling the way he does about you. What if Utley doesn't appreciate my being there and tells Lucy? You know what people are like when it comes to jurisdictional issues."

Sean made a dismissive motion with his hand. "Oh come on. Don't be such an old lady. It's not as if you're there in any official capacity. You're just helping me out and I'm just a civilian, a concerned father come to check on the health and well-being of his daughters after the terrible discovery they made."

Clyde scratched his neck.

"I guess maybe you're right."

"You know I am."

"But I still think you should have lunch with Ina. Despite what you think, you could use some female companionship."

Sean put up his hand. He wasn't going to discuss this with Clyde. Or anyone else for that matter. He didn't discuss his illness and he didn't discuss his feelings. "Fine."

"You'll do it this month?" Clyde asked.

"Now you're my mother?" Sean demanded.

Clyde shrugged. "Take it or leave it."

Sean cursed to himself. Clyde had him and he knew Clyde well enough to know that unless he agreed to his conditions Clyde wouldn't drive him.

"All right. I'll have lunch with her this month."

Clyde grinned. "Okay then." He got up and stretched. "Let me just call the missus and tell her where we're going. Lucky for you I'm driving her minivan." He patted his hair down again. "Well, I guess this murder has one benefit."

Sean looked momentarily confused.

"Like what?"

"It's getting you out of the house."

"Somehow," Sean said, "I don't think the victim would see it quite that way."

Chapter 7

"Aren't you going to take down what I said about the crossbow?" Bernie demanded of the policeman standing in front of her, blocking her view of Leeza's body.

He frowned.

Bernie put her hands on her hips.

"Well, aren't you Officer Fisher?" she repeated.

Instead of answering, Officer Fisher closed the pad he was taking notes on and ostentatiously put it in his trouser pocket.

Well that's a clear no, Bernie said to herself.

"Listen," he told her. "This isn't Longely, this is West Vale. You keep to your catering and let us do the investigating and we'll all be happy."

"Hey," Bernie protested, "I'm just trying to help."

Officer Fisher crossed his arms across his chest. Bernie could see that his shoulders were damp from the drizzle outside.

"Thanks anyway, but somehow," he said, "I think we can manage just fine without your assistance. We don't need civilians mucking things up."

"Is that a fact?"

"Yes it is. We do things by the book here in West Vale."

"Maybe you should get a new book," Bernie told him.

Officer Fisher nodded towards Libby who was tugging on

Bernie's arm and telling her to come on. "You should listen to your sister." He made a shooing motion with his hands. "Now you be a good girl and run along and get the coffee going. Make yourself useful. I'll send someone to tell you when you can leave the premises."

Bernie's eyes narrowed. She began tapping her foot. "Excuse me, but did you just tell me to make myself useful?"

Officer Fisher stuck his face in Bernie's.

"You have a problem with that?" he demanded.

"I always have a problem with . . ." but before she could get the rest of the sentence out of her mouth Libby had dragged her out of the tent. Bernie shook off her sister's hand.

"Leave me alone," she spat. Then she turned on her heels and started marching back towards the tent. "He wants coffee," she announced to Amber and Libby. "I'll give him coffee."

"No," Amber and Libby cried simultaneously as each one of them grabbed one of Bernie's arms and held on.

"Let go of me," Bernie demanded, struggling against their grip.

Libby clamped down harder on her sister's wrist. God, Bernie was strong. "Not until you calm down. Can't you see he was baiting you? I need you with me, not off in a cell on some obstruction of justice charge."

"That's because you're afraid I won't be there to help peel the tomatoes," Bernie retorted.

But even before the words had flown out of Bernie's mouth she knew her sister was right. Being in jail would suck under any circumstances, but it would especially suck tonight. She had plans involving Rob and some really hot underwear she'd bought yesterday.

"Now that's not true and you know it," Libby answered.

"No, I don't." Bernie sighed. "Okay," she conceded. "It's mostly not true. All right. All right. It's not true at all."

Libby peered at Bernie's face. "You promise you won't run in there if we let you go?"

Bernie nodded.

"Say it," Libby ordered. She'd learned long ago to her cost that unless Bernie said it it didn't count.

"Okay. I promise I won't assault Officer Fisher."

"Or say anything stupid."

"Or say anything stupid. There. Are you satisfied?"

"Yes, I am." Libby and Amber loosened their grip.

Bernie rubbed her wrists. "You didn't have to grab me so hard."

"Then don't flip out," Libby said. She trimmed one of her cuticles with her teeth. "Officer Fisher is right about one thing, though," she said to Bernie.

Bernie glared at her. "And what would that be?"

"No matter what. Wedding. Funeral. Murder. People need to eat. Thank God," she added. "Otherwise we'd be out of a job."

As Jura and Esmeralda Quinn, Leeza's maid of honor walked into the kitchen, Libby was thinking that the condition of the place was a good indication of Jura's lack of concern for the people that worked in it. As her mother used to say, if you want to know about a man or a woman look at how they treat their wait staff.

Jura had mountains of money to spend on the wedding, he'd probably spent millions on furnishing his house, and yet it was perfectly obvious to Libby that he hadn't spent a penny on upgrading and modernizing the kitchen. No doubt because he never set foot in it.

No wonder the cook was so grumpy, Libby thought. If she had to work here every day she'd be more than grumpy. She'd be suicidal! The place probably hadn't been touched in twenty years. At least. The walls were dingy, the lighting inadequate, the white enameled sink was chipped, and the old Viking stove needed a good steam cleaning.

Libby couldn't even discern the original pattern on the linoleum floor, let alone see out of the window by the sink. And she wasn't even mentioning the fact that the counters were too low and the refrigerator should be in the Smithsonian. It wasn't even frost free for heaven's sake. It still had to be defrosted.

"Here," Jura said.

Libby looked up at him as he plonked down two tins of caviar on the counter. He was wearing the same expression and clothes that he'd had on when she'd seen him in the caviar cooler.

"I want you to serve the sevruga directly out of the tin," he instructed her. "The less movement the caviar experiences, the less chance of bruising the eggs. You can accompany the sevruga with toast points, butter, and a little sour cream, but that's it. No chopped hard-boiled eggs. Especially no chopped onions.

"Those are an abomination." Jura's voice rose. "And I refuse to allow something like that under my roof. Also you may use the goose liver pâté we had earmarked for the post-wedding ceremony reception to make sandwiches with. No sense letting good food go to waste because of an unfortunate event. The devising of the rest of the menu I will leave up to you."

Unfortunate event, Libby thought. *Now there's an interesting way to refer to the murder of your wife-to-be.* As she regarded him she decided that she'd seen people manifest more emotion over the death of their pet hamsters then Jura was showing over the death of his bride. Of course maybe he just hid his emotions well. Or maybe this is the way they reacted in Estonia, never mind that Jura was born in the United States.

Maybe she was being judgmental, an emotion her mother had always warned her she had to guard against. Maybe Jura had really been upset when he'd gotten the news. Maybe he'd broken down and cried. Libby found herself wishing she'd been there when the security guards had told him about Leeza's death, so she could have seen for herself. Then she quickly quashed that thought. *My God*, she reflected, *if I'm not careful I'll become infected by the Bernie bug.* Bad enough to have one person in the family creating chaos. They didn't need two.

Still, she had to admit that Jura's reaction was strange. So, for that matter while she was on the subject, was everyone else's. These people, all of them family members or members of the wedding party, were milling around in the place that had been set up for the post-wedding ceremony libations and from what Libby could see from the kitchen no one, except for Ditas and the Walker sisters, seemed terribly concerned that the bride was, to use her mother's phrase, no longer among them.

Everyone else was chatting away. Joe, Jura's youngest brother, was busy talking to one of Leeza's bridesmaids, who was smiling and giggling, while another bridesmaid was batting her eyes at one of the security guards.

Libby decided that, despite the fact that Joe was definitely the smallest of the three brothers and had brown hair and brown eyes instead of blond hair and blue eyes, there was still a marked family resemblance. He had the same cleft chin and the same thin lips as Jura and Ditas, who was staring out the window.

Judging from the expression on his face, he seemed extremely upset which struck Libby as strange because he hadn't impressed her as a man that cared much about anything. And then of course there was the maid of honor, Esmeralda Quinn.

A woman that her mother would have described as plain as a sack of potatoes, she was presently doing an excellent imitation of a limpet by gluing herself to Jura's side. Looking at her even Libby had to concede that Bernie was right. One should never underestimate the power of a good haircut and properly applied makeup. She was imagining what her sister was going to say when they got home—something along the lines of "What was she thinking?"—when Esmeralda gave a fluttering little cough.

"One doesn't see many chartreuse maid of honor dresses," Libby heard her sister say.

Libby sighed. How did her sister do it? If she had said

that Esmeralda would be insulted. Maybe it was Bernie's tone? She always felt like such a clod next to her.

Esmeralda tittered. "Is that's what it's called? I keep forgetting."

"The word for the color derives from the drink of the same name," Bernie informed her. "It's a liqueur flavored with angelica and hyssop made by the Carthusian monks at their monastery near Grenoble, France."

"Fascinating. I had no idea." Esmeralda smoothed down her skirt. "Frankly I don't think it's my best color."

"Well, not many people can wear it," Bernie said truthfully. Actually, she couldn't think of anyone who could. While she was on the subject, the drink wasn't too great, either. It tasted like cough medicine.

"Leeza," Esmeralda dabbed at her eyes with the crumpled up Kleenex she was holding in her hand before going on, "said it brought out the pink in my complexion."

More like the yellow Bernie thought. But in reality the color was the least of the issues with the dress. The thing might have worked on a beautiful sixteen-year-old with a great body but on a fortysomething woman it was a disaster.

The rucking on the bodice made Esmeralda look even more flat chested than she already was. Add to that the form-revealing bottom which merely served to emphasize Esmeralda's pot belly and wide hips and you had something close to an act of sartorial cruelty.

Esmeralda dabbed at her eyes again. "I wanted to wear something a little more . . . conservative, but Leeza insisted I get this dress. She said I had to start showing off my assets, otherwise I'd never get anyone interested in me. Now I can hardly wait to get out of it." Esmeralda let out a small sob. "Just looking at it reminds me of Leeza."

And not in a good way I'm betting, Bernie thought. Personally she would never have gotten into something like that for any reason. Leeza must have hated her, Bernie reflected. What other motive could she have had for talking Esmeralda into wearing something so unflattering?

But why had Esmeralda acquiesced? That was the other question. Obviously she knew what she looked like. Did she feel she had no choice? She must have. But why? Even though Esmeralda wasn't a great beauty, when Bernie had last seen her sitting at a desk in Raid's office dressed in a business suit she'd looked moderately acceptable. Now she looked like a clown.

As Esmeralda dabbed at her eyes one last time and dropped her hand to her side, Bernie realized she had a tic going underneath her left eye, something she hadn't seen when she'd been sitting behind the desk. "I don't want to talk about my dress anymore," she told Bernie. "It's just too painful, isn't it, Jurie?" Esmeralda said as she brushed an invisible speck of dust off of Jura's jacket.

Jurie? Bernie thought as Jura nodded absentmindedly and began opening thc can of caviar he'd brought in with him. Now that's interesting. At the office, it had been, "Yes, Mr. Raid. No, Mr. Raid. Right away, Mr. Raid."

As Bernie was thinking about the implications of what she'd just heard and seen, Esmeralda turned and faced Libby.

"If it wouldn't be too much trouble I was wondering if you could put Splenda on the table instead of any of those other artificial sweeteners," she told her.

"I don't think there's any in the kitchen," Libby replied.

Esmeralda's face fell. "Oh my. I can't eat anything artificial. It's bad for my gallbladder."

Libby put on her best customer smile. "Perhaps I can call someone from the store and they can bring it to the gate and the guards can relay it to us."

"Don't bother," Jura said. "She doesn't need the sugar."

"Really?" Bernie said as Esmeralda cringed.

Libby shot her sister a warning glance as she watched Esmeralda begin to pull at the hairs on her eyebrow. *Okay,* she thought. *So now we know for sure that the man's a total asshole and Esmeralda has no spine.*

"Is there anything else I can get you?" Libby quickly asked Esmeralda, trying to forestall a comment from Bernie.

Esmeralda gave her a tremulous smile and put her hand back down by her side.

"If it's not too much trouble, I'd love a half-decaf, half-regular, skimmed milk cappuccino."

"I'll manage something," Libby assured her. Surely they had to have an espresso machine around here somewhere.

Esmeralda dabbed at her eyes again. "Thank you so much. And oh yes, Theodora, that's the tall, thin, woman in the yellow taffeta dress, would like decaffeinated tea with a slice of lemon on the side and make sure Jura's coffee is decaf as well. Otherwise the poor man will be up all night, won't you, Jurie?"

Jura gave her a brief wintry smile, took the lid off the tin, and opened a drawer beneath the counter and took out a small horn spoon.

"One never samples caviar with a metal spoon," Jura explained to Libby, pointedly ignoring Esmeralda. "In fact, you never put caviar anywhere near metal. It has a disastrous effect on the taste. The interaction of the metal and the roe is most unpleasant, but then I'm sure you already knew that."

"Actually I do," Libby said even though she could tell that Jura wasn't really interested in her answer.

In truth she would have said that even if she didn't know anything. The man was absolutely insufferable. She couldn't help thinking that Leeza and he had deserved each other.

"Actually," Bernie chimed in. "Some people claim that metal—well not silver as much—affects the taste of anything it touches. It can even change the color of some food as it cooks. Witness the effects of cooking tomatoes in an aluminum pan, and I won't even go into the controversy over aluminum and Alzheimer's disease." She didn't even pause for breath before going on.

"And as for spoons—now that's a really interesting subject. Some author, I forget who, wrote that spoons are the Ur eating utensil, if you will. I don't think forks were used until the seventeenth century, whereas spoons have been around for almost three thousand years. They've been found in various digs. Some were made of clay, others of bone and shell. So you see," Bernie pointed to the spoon Jura was holding, "you're continuing a tradition that goes back three millennia. It's really amazing when you think about it, isn't it?"

Jura blinked several times in rapid succession. "Fascinating," he finally commented as he turned his attention to the tin of caviar.

Libby watched as he dipped his spoon in the can and drew out a small mound of glistening dark gray eggs. Then he closed his eyes, slowly raised the spoon to his lips, and tipped the contents between his lips. He rolled the eggs around in his mouth and took a bite.

His eyes flew open. He reached for the tin and examined it. A slow line of color crept up his face. He whirled around and strode out of the kitchen. The swinging door almost hit Esmeralda in the face as she ran after him.

"Jurie, Jurie," she trilled, "what's the matter?"

If Jura answered her Libby didn't hear it. Instead Jura called for his two brothers.

"Ditas," he yelled. "Joe. Come here this instant. I have discovered something most disturbing. Perhaps you can explain this to me."

Chapter 8

Libby turned to Bernie. "What was that all about?"

"I don't have a clue." At which point Bernie went to the door and peeked out into the living room.

Jura was huddled in the far corner of the room with his two brothers. He was waving his arms up and down, while his younger brother Joe was rocking back and forth on the balls of his feet and Ditas was shaking his head from one side to another. All three were ignoring Esmeralda.

"He seems really upset," Bernie commented. "In fact this is the most emotion I've seen from Jura since we've arrived."

"I think he's really creepy," Amber said, bending down to retie her shoelace. "I wouldn't marry him no matter how much money he has."

"Obviously, Leeza didn't share your opinion." Bernie went back to the counter. "I wonder if they signed a pre-nup?" she mused as she reached for the spoon Jura had used, washed it off, dipped it into the can, and took a taste.

"This stuff is not good," she said after she'd rolled the eggs around in her mouth. "I bet these are paddlefish eggs instead of sturgeon roe. Either that or the sevruga is actually a lower-grade caviar. Or the tin has been incorrectly stored, compromising the product's quality. Caviar spoils very quickly.

In any case, one thing is for sure. The sevruga doesn't taste the way it's supposed to."

"What would it mean if it was paddlefish eggs?" Libby asked.

Bernie started tapping her fingers on the counter. "Oh a difference of seven dollars an ounce versus sixty-five to seventy dollars an ounce. At least that's what the prices were the last time I looked. Paddlefish is way cheaper because it's domestic. Actually I think there's a lot of virtue in getting something local versus something from far away. However, there's more cachet attached to getting some from Russia or Iran . . ."

Libby held up her hand. "Please, no lectures now."

"Sorry," Bernie told her.

Libby took the spoon from Bernie and tasted the caviar. She wrinkled her nose. "It's very salty."

"Exactly," Bernie said. "With the good stuff when you crush an egg between your teeth you should get a burst of a clean, briny flavor. It's almost like having a taste of the ocean in your mouth. It doesn't taste like this."

"How do you know?"

Bernie shrugged. "I used to eat it out in L.A. all the time. It's great diet food. High in protein. Low in carbs. Lots of minerals. Spoon it on scrambled eggs and you're good to go. It's the perfect meal."

"Caviar as a diet food. Why didn't I think of that?" Libby said.

"If you were rich you would," Bernie replied.

Amber looked in the can. "I don't care how rich I was, I'd never eat that stuff. It looks gross."

Libby handed her the spoon. "Here, taste it."

Amber put the spoon down and moved away. "Fish eggs, I don't think so."

Libby stared at the tin. "I guess we shouldn't serve this."

Bernie indicated a skinny looking ginger tabby that had magically appeared next to her feet. "I bet she would like it." And she scooped a half a cup of roe out onto a small plate and put it on the floor for the kitty.

"Jura's going to love that," Libby observed.

"Well, it's just going to spoil," said Bernie. "And anyway, he's not here."

Libby watched the cat eat for a few moments while she pondered what she could put out for people to eat that she could pull together fairly rapidly. She started opening and closing kitchen cabinets. There wasn't much in the way of food there.

"Well one thing is clear," she said to Amber and Bernie when she'd finished with her inventory. "Jura and his brothers don't eat at home a lot."

"So what now?" Bernie asked.

Libby thought for another moment. "Open-faced sandwiches."

Bernie wrinkled her nose. "Sandwiches?"

"Yes," Libby said firmly. "Sandwiches."

For openers, they were easy to make and they had other merits as well. Sandwiches were really comfort food. They had the merit of being familiar, they were homey—everyone's mom had made them sandwiches when they were a kid—and they were filling, which was good because Libby had observed over the years that death tended to whet people's appetites. And most importantly, you could make them out of anything.

Aside from the goose liver pâté Jura had asked her to serve, Libby had spied some fairly decent looking tomatoes on the far counter. She figured she could combine them with the mozzarella she'd seen in the fridge. Hopefully the cook wasn't planning to serve the tomatoes and the cheese later in the week. But if she were, she'd have to get over it. This was an emergency.

Of course the sandwiches would be better if the tomatoes were local instead of hothouse, but even so they wouldn't be bad. Mozzarella and tomatoes had to be one of the better combinations going.

Now she needed a third thing. Libby tapped her fingers on the counter while she weighed her options. Finally she decided on asparagus and smoked Gouda. That would look good and the smoky taste of the Gouda would make a nice foil for the sweetness of the asparagus. They could decorate the platters with the grapes in the fridge and they'd be all set.

Libby bit at her fingernail. "Okay we just need something for dessert."

"We can always serve the wedding cake," Bernie suggested.

"Ha. Ha. Talk about bad taste."

"Somehow, I don't think the people here are going to care."

Amber spoke up. "I saw some cookies in the pantry if that'll help," she said as the kitty scampered away.

Libby nodded.

"Good. Amber you go get them, I'll start on the sandwiches, and Bernie you make the coffee. I saw it in the top cabinet to the left of the window."

Bernie nodded. "You want to use this?" she asked after she'd located it. "It'll just take me a couple of minutes to go get our stuff out of the garage."

Libby shook her head, as she dug into her backpack. "Don't bother." She didn't know why but all of a sudden she was overwhelmed with an urge for a chocolate chip cookie. As she looked for it, she decided maybe she was feeling this way because Esmeralda and Jura reminded her of the way things had been between herself and her ex-boyfriend, Orion. Even now, thinking about how she was always running after him made her flinch.

Finally she found the cookie at the bottom of her backpack. Perhaps I should save it, she thought as she took it out. But then she decided no. Eat it now. As she bit into it and her mouth was filled with the flavors of vanilla, chocolate, and sweet butter, she could feel her body relaxing. Suddenly she had a flash of insight. *This is how an addict feels,* she told herself. *I am addicted to sugar. I have to do something.* But then she pushed that thought to the back of her mind and concentrated on the present. Specifically what kind of coffee to serve.

"Use the stuff you found in the cabinet. It'll be faster," she told Bernie after she'd taken another nibble of her cookie. Over the years she'd learned that most people in America were used to drinking something that was more akin to brown-colored water, than coffee. What counted was getting it made and getting it out there. Taste was secondary.

"It's sad, really," Libby said to her sister when Bernie came back from setting up the coffee urn in the living room, "that Leeza doesn't seem to have had any friends."

"Maybe that's because she was such a bitch," Bernie replied.

Libby lifted her head up. "You shouldn't say things like that."

Bernie snorted. "Why not? It's the truth."

"You're not supposed to speak ill of the dead."

"Why? Because they'll come back and haunt you?"

Amber stopped rubbing cloves of garlic over slices of French bread. "They will?" she squeaked.

"Jeez," Bernie told her. "It was just a figure of speech. All I'm saying is that I've never understood why when someone dies they automatically turn into a saint."

"Maybe it's because they can't defend themselves," Libby replied.

"Why do you always have to be so namby-pamby?" Bernie asked.

"And why can't you use normal words?" Libby demanded. She patted the tomatoes she'd just washed dry, placed them on the cutting board, then picked up a knife, sliced one tomato, and put the knife down. "I have to say though that Jura seemed more upset about the caviar than he did about Leeza."

"Exactly." Bernie got out the creamer and began filling it.

Libby picked up her knife again and looked at the tomatoes. She didn't want to think of where this conversation was leading. She had enough to worry about. Like when were the police going to let them out of here. Like the muffins she had to bake for tomorrow morning for the store. Like what would they do with the food and the cake? Like would Jura pay her the rest of the money he owed her? At least she'd gotten most of it up front.

"I don't suppose anyone's seen any basil?" she asked.

Bernie and Amber both shook their heads.

Libby sighed. She was just thinking that the tomato and mozzarella sandwiches would have to get made without it when Bernie's cell phone rang. "That has the most annoying ring," she said to Bernie as she retrieved her phone from the counter and placed it to her ear.

"Hi Ina," she said. "How's lunch going?" There was a pause and then she said, "What do you mean he's not there?"

"Who's not there?" Libby asked.

Bernie turned her face from the phone to answer. "Dad. He's gone."

"Gone?"

"Exactly what I said. Ina went upstairs with his tray and no one was there. Alice said she heard a noise on the stairs and when she looked out the window she saw Clyde loading Dad into his minivan."

Libby could feel her chest constrict. She should have saved the cookie.

"Relax," Bernie told her. "I'm sure everything is fine."

Libby knew she was being ridiculous. She knew that Bernie was right, but her father hadn't left his bedroom since he'd gotten sick three years ago because he'd refused to be seen in his wheelchair. She told herself there had to be a reasonable explanation for his disappearance, but offhand she couldn't think of one.

Chapter 9

Twenty minutes later, Sean and Clyde were at the back kitchen door watching Amber, Libby, and Bernie working. There had been a few minutes there Sean reflected when it looked as if the police weren't going to let them through the gate, but good old Clyde had played the concerned parent card and ended up convincing them to let them in. Sean was just thinking about how lucky he was to have a friend like that when Libby turned around and spotted him.

She ran over. "Where the hell have you been?" she demanded.

Sean threw his arms out and put on his biggest smile. Always take the offensive when possible. When it wasn't, play dumb. "Hey, what's this? I thought you'd be pleased to see me."

"Pleased to see you? Pleased to see you?" Libby cried. "We've been worried sick. Ina called and told us you weren't there."

Clyde sighed. "Told you we should have waited around, Cap. Guess she didn't get the message on her answering machine."

"Evidently." Bernie took the kitchen towel she had slung over her shoulder and wiped her hands. "Ina was very upset."

"She said that?" Sean asked.

"No. But I could tell from her voice."

"That's too bad." Sean hoped he looked properly contrite. "She's a nice lady."

"Yes, she is," Bernie replied. "What am I going to tell Rob?"

"Tell your boyfriend the truth. He'll understand."

"I'm not sure he will." Bernie took a deep breath and folded her arms across her chest. It was weird but she felt like the parent. "Now what are you doing here?"

Sean looked his daughter straight in the eyes and lied.

"I came to make sure you girls were okay. Your dad was worried about you."

"Really?"

Sean looked in Clyde's direction. "Isn't that so?"

"Sure is, Cap."

Sean decided that Bernie looked unimpressed. When Bernie put her hands on her hips and leaned towards him he realized he should have tried something else.

"That is a load of BS, and you know it," she told him. "At least if you're going to lie put some effort into it. You're Irish for heaven's sake. You ought to be able to do better than this."

"Now you're maligning your ancestors." Sometimes doing indignant worked, but Sean could see from the expression on Bernie's face that it was having no effect on her, either. Not that he was surprised. Of the three women in his life, she was the one who was hardest to fake out, the one least likely to defer to him, the one—unfortunately—most like him.

"Don't try and change the subject," she told him.

"I'm not."

"Oh yes, you are. You always do."

"How can you say that?" Sean protested.

"Because it's true. If you didn't want to have lunch with Ina that badly why didn't you tell Libby or me when we made the arrangements?"

Sean decided he'd rather have his teeth pulled without Novocain than continue with this discussion.

"Look," he said. "I thought that you'd be glad I finally got out of the house, but if you want me to go back home . . . ."

Bernie lifted her hands in the air and dropped them. "Don't do your poor me, humble pie act with me," she told him."

Sean turned and appealed to his eldest. "Libby," he said.

Libby sighed and went over and planted a kiss on his forehead. Sean grinned. Libby could never stay mad at him for long. Just like his wife. "So tell me what's going on?"

Bernie glared at him, but Sean could tell she was thawing.

"Come on," he told her. "You know that you want to."

Bernie wavered for another second, but it was obvious to Sean that was just for show.

"Fine," Bernie said and she and Libby filled him in.

"Alex Fisher?" Sean said when Libby and Bernie were through with their recital.

"You mean Officer Fisher?" Bernie asked.

Sean nodded. He and Clyde exchanged glances.

"What about him?" Bernie said.

Clyde stroked his chin. "Let's just say he's not real fond of your dad."

Libby looked towards the living room. She really had to get another pot of coffee going so she could refill the coffee urn. "Why's that?" she asked.

"Because your dad ticketed him for indecent exposure."

"He was taking a leak outside of R.J.'s," Sean said, chuckling as he recalled the incident. "As he'd just given your uncle a speeding ticket in West Vale, I decided to return the favor."

Bernie tapped her ring against her teeth. "Well, that explains a lot," she said.

"It certainly does," Sean agreed. Things, he decided, were on the upturn.

"Dad," Bernie began, "as long as you're here, I was thinking . . ."

Never a good sign, Sean knew. "Yes?" he said in a cautious voice.

"I was just thinking that you might want to see the arms room and kinda check things out."

"Don't listen to her," Libby told him. "You shouldn't be going there."

"Sure he should," Bernie replied.

"And why would I want to do that?" Sean asked.

"Hum." Bernie laid a finger on her cheek. "Let's think. Because you owe me for standing Ina up. She's a very nice lady."

"I'm not sure I agree about owing you."

"Really?" Bernie said.

"Yes, really," Sean replied although he wasn't sure that he liked the smile playing around his daughter's lips.

"Fine then. If you want to stay here I'll just nip into the living room and tell the Walker sisters you've arrived. I'm sure they'll want to speak to you."

Sean looked at his daughter in horror. He'd known they were here; but, in his haste to get away from Ina's ministrations, they'd slipped his mind.

"That's blackmail."

"No. It's creative motivation," Bernie replied complacently.

"You wouldn't."

"You know I would."

"Don't I get a say in this?" Clyde asked.

"No, you don't," Bernie told him. "You shouldn't have helped him run away from Ina. That was rude."

"But . . ." Clyde began but before he'd gotten the next word out of his mouth Sean interrupted him.

"I'll do it," he told Bernie.

Libby looked dismayed. Sean was sorry he was upsetting her, but he knew there was no appealing to Bernie once she an idea in her head. She would tell the Walker sisters he was here, and the idea of listening to a polemic on Marxism and the evils of the capitalist West, not to mention a cross-examination of his personal life, was more than he could bear right now, even for Libby's sake.

"All right," he told her. "What am I looking for?"

"Crossbows and arrows." And Bernie described the arrow embedded in Leeza Sharp's chest.

"Sounds like a carbon one to me," Sean said.

"Whatever. You're looking to see if there are any there that match that one."

"And why do you care?"

"Because I'm curious," Bernie said. "Isn't that enough of a reason?"

Sean had to allow as how it was. Certainly that motivation had operated in his professional life more than he would like to admit.

"And, oh yes," Bernie said flashing a defiant look at Libby. "I'm coming along with you."

"Can you tell me where the room is that they keep the weapons in?" Bernie asked the burly man hurrying down the corridor. She'd gotten her and her dad lost, which given the way the mansion was laid out was fairly easy to do.

The man made a miniscule adjustment to his uniform jacket before replying. "The arms room is in the second corridor, third door to the left."

"You work here?" Bernie asked him.

The man gave a slight bow. "Yes, Madam. I am Mr. Jura's personal assistant. Are you one of the hunting party?"

"Yes," Bernie lied thinking as she did that this guy could bench press lots of pounds.

"Because you're quite early. In fact, Mr. Ditas did not expect anyone until tomorrow after the ceremony."

"Our transportation arrangements got confused," Sean told him. "Ditas knows. I e-mailed him."

The man looked at Sean but didn't say anything. It was the look of a person used to assessing people, Sean decided. A cop look.

"What's your name?" Bernie asked him.

"Vladimir, Vladimir Meyers."

"Well, Vladimir, you've been very helpful, but I think we can manage on our own from here on out."

Vladimir bowed his head to indicate he'd heard, then turned and hurried off in the direction he'd been going.

"You think he believed us?" Bernie asked her dad after Vladimir had rounded the corner.

"No. I think we should pick up the pace."

Bernie nodded her agreement. "Hunting, huh?"

"You ask me, someone's gotten an early start."

"True enough," Bernie replied. She moved her ring up and down her finger. "What I want to know is why would an Estonian have a Russian working for him considering what Russia did to Estonia?"

"From what you told me about Jura that might be the point," Sean told her.

"You might be right," Bernie conceded as they moved in the direction Vladimir had indicated. She pointed to the portraits lining the walls as they went by. "Do you think there's a Decorate a Castle company in the phone book? You know, you just call and they bring over all the family portraits, crests, everything a social climber needs?"

Sean laughed. "I can't imagine living in a place like this."

"Me either," Bernie agreed.

Five minutes later they had finally located the arms room.

"This room is like something out an English country house," Sean said looking around.

He hadn't spent time watching Public Television for nothing. There were plaster busts dotted around the room and trophies hanging on the wall that ranged from deer to tiger heads.

"Well these people definitely hunt," Bernie observed.

"They most certainly do," her father agreed as his eyes took in the rest of the room.

The windows were flanked by heavy drapes and the walls were painted a dark green and hung with weapons, both new and old. These people had everything from old silver-plated

Remington rifles, antique Smith & Wessons to AK-47s, Glock 9mms, and .22s.

"The hell with hunting. These people are serious weapon collectors," Sean observed. "You could arm a small military force out of this room. I'm surprised they don't have rocket launchers around some place."

Bernie pointed off to the far wall on the right. "I think what we want is over there, beyond Homer's bust."

Sean headed off in that direction on his motorized wheelchair.

He stopped when he was about a foot away and gazed up at the wall. The cross and compound bows were neatly arranged in a horizontal line. There were no gaps, which meant none of them were missing, although that didn't mean that someone hadn't used one from here and replaced it with a similar one. Unfortunately there was no way to tell by eyeballing. The arrows might be a better bet.

"You know, Bernie . . ." he was saying when he heard footsteps. He turned around just as Officer Fisher entered the room.

"Well, well," he told Sean when he saw him. "You've definitely made my day."

That was fast, Sean thought as he took in the gleam in Alex Fisher's eyes. *Vladimir must have gone straight to the cops.*

Chapter 10

Libby glanced at the clock on the wall. She couldn't believe it was only ten o'clock. It felt like two in the afternoon, possibly because this was the first break she'd had since she'd opened the doors at seven-thirty this morning. The store had already sold out of scones, and they were nearly out of muffins. Nothing like a little murder to bring in customers, she reflected. At least this time she'd known enough to bake extra.

Boy, she would have given anything if she could have closed up shop and gone back to bed. But that was not going to happen. Libby looked at the clock again. The minute hand had scarcely moved. She had nine more hours to go. It was going to be a long, long day.

And on top of everything else—thanks to Bernie—her eyes felt as if they had grit in them. Libby began rubbing them, then stopped herself. It felt so good, but she knew it would only make them worse. What she needed were some eye drops, which, unfortunately, were in the bathroom upstairs, meaning she'd have to climb a flight of steps to get them.

Libby took another sip of her coffee while she debated whether or not it was worth the trouble. After a moment, she decided it wasn't. Her eyes would just have to go on stinging. What with everything that had happened yesterday it was a little after midnight by the time she'd left the West Vale police station. Clyde had told her to go home, but she couldn't. The only good thing was that one of Clyde's buddies was a judge and he'd come out to the courtroom.

When she'd gotten home she'd gone straight to bed, but she was still so angry all she'd done was toss and turn. Then, just when she was drifting off to sleep her alarm had rung.

Somehow she'd managed to drag herself out of bed and stumble down to the kitchen to do what she'd been too tired to do the night before: put the chickens up for the chicken salad and grill the tuna for the salad nicoise. Then she'd started in on the homemade mayonnaise but for some reason the eggs and oil had refused to emulsify and after remixing it, she'd been forced to throw out the batch and whip up a new one.

Next she'd cooked and peeled the new potatoes for the potato salad, blanched the string beans for the bean and tomato salad, and baked the quail originally intended for the wedding dinner, and after that she'd tackled the raspberry and blueberry scones and baked the lemon ginger, carrot, and chocolate chip muffins. By the time she was done she would have given anything to have crawled back into bed.

Libby added another spoonful of sugar to her coffee and stirred. Her sister could go without much sleep, but she'd always needed at least seven hours, ten was even better, and yet between last night and staying up the night before to finish the wedding cake she hadn't gotten more than two hours sleep in the last two days.

When she thought about it, it was a miracle she hadn't cut or scalded herself this morning. Of course, she could have woken Bernie up and gotten her to help. But then she would have had to have talked to her and Libby hadn't been ready to do that yet. By seven o'clock this morning though, she'd been forced to concede she would have to—not that her sister knew that Libby wasn't speaking to her since Libby hadn't informed her of that fact, which was good because it relieved Libby of the humiliation of asking Bernie for her help.

Libby took a bite out of one of the peanut butter cookies that had just come out of the oven, noting, as she washed it down with another swig of coffee, that it had been baked about two minutes too long. No doubt about it: Family relations were a bitch. But she'd have to ask Bernie. She didn't have a choice.

That was the problem with having a shop like this, Libby reflected. It was impossible to do it on your own. You needed at least one other person to cover for you. Because it didn't matter what you felt like or how little sleep you had, short of a death in the family, or a catastrophic illness you had to open the shop on time the next morning, and you had to have an adequate amount of product to sell.

And the product had better be good. Her mother had impressed that fact on her. If it weren't, people would stop coming. And once they got out of the habit of patronizing your store, they didn't come back. That's why everything at *A Taste of Heaven* always had to be perfect. Always.

Actually, Libby decided as she rearranged the almond croissants in the display case, if you thought about it, owning this store was almost like being married. If you weren't fully committed to the relationship, it wouldn't work out. And even after putting years into the relationship you never knew. Look at what had happened to her and Orion. She'd never have thought he'd end up marrying someone else. Hopefully she and the store would do better.

Libby sighed and looked at the clock again. Bernie had gone to the farm to get the free-range eggs about an hour ago. She was wondering when her sister would get back so she could start in on the curried egg salad when she saw Bree Nottingham, real estate agent extraordinaire, coming through the shop door.

As Libby watched her advancing to the counter she became painfully aware of the fact that she'd been too tired to go back upstairs and put her make-up on and that she was wearing a T-shirt that showed off the roll of fat around her middle. But then Bree had been making her feel fat and unattractive since the fourth grade. Maybe it was because even back then Bree had worn the equivalent of a size four and she had worn closer to a size fourteen.

"So," Bree cooed when she got close enough, "I understand the Simmons family had some excitement yesterday."

Here we go again, Libby thought. "You could say that," she replied.

Bree got her wallet out of her bag, which Libby couldn't help notice thanks to Bernie's fashion tutelage, was the new Louis Vuitton.

"You can't imagine what I felt like when I got to the estate gate and heard the news about Leeza. It must have been so much worse for you and your sister finding her like that," she said. "*I* would have fainted."

"Fortunately, *I* didn't," Libby replied. In her book, almost didn't count.

Anyway, her father always said never to show weakness in the face of the enemy. All she wanted to do was forget about yesterday; and, even if she did want to talk about it with somebody, Bree Nottingham was the last person she'd want to talk about it with.

Bree extracted a five-dollar bill from her wallet then put the wallet back in her bag. "I hear the sandwiches you served were very good, although the coffee left something to be desired."

Libby sighed. Screw up once and you never stopped hearing about it. She hated to admit it, but Bernie had been right about getting their coffee from the garage instead of using the swill in Jura's house.

"I hope you're not using the same type here in the store," Bree continued.

"Not at all," Libby told her pleasantly. "Jura asked us to use his." When cornered, lie. "Would you like some of ours? We just got a new shipment in on Friday."

Bree formed her lips into an O while she thought. "I suppose," she said after a moment of reflection. "Make it one third French decaf, one third French regular, and one third hazelnut if you don't mind." Then she leaned forward and concentrated her gaze on Libby's shirt. "Is that a spot?"

Libby looked down to where Bree was pointing. Sure enough. She had a blue dot on her white T-shirt. She must have gotten that when she made the blueberry scones. Unbelievable.

"Do you have any hard boiled eggs?" Bree asked.

"In the back," Libby replied. She had exactly two, the yolks of which she'd been planning to use for her mother's short bread cookies.

"Good. Because I'd like one." Bree patted what in Libby's opinion were nonexistent hips. "I'm on Atkins now and I've already lost five pounds."

Where? From your skeleton, Libby thought.

Bree tapped an immaculately manicured nail against her tooth for a moment. Then she said, "And can you cut it in half, and sprinkle on some *fleur de sel* and a little cracked fresh pepper. You should try Atkins. It's a miracle."

Libby hoped she was smiling not gritting her teeth. "I am," she replied although she had to admit she was honoring it more in the breach these days. Well, really she wasn't doing it at all.

"Good. Because it would be perfect for you. You really don't need any will power for this."

Libby took a deep breath and pictured throwing Bree through the plate glass window. But then she reminded herself that despite the pleasure it would be bad for business, not to mention that getting the window replaced would cost a small fortune. And then there would be the lawyer's fees. So instead Libby went to get Bree her coffee.

As she did Bree added, "I'm surprised the reporters aren't here after yesterday."

"They've already called," Libby conceded. She'd told them neither she, her sister, or her father had anything to say. She'd said the same thing to the media people swarming around the estate last night.

"They were reporting the story on CNN."

"I've been too busy to have the TV on," Libby lied.

Bree sighed. "Bride killed on her wedding day. Shot through the heart. My dear, the story is simply too good to resist."

Libby handed Bree her coffee.

"I have to say," Bree said after she'd taken a sip. "Bad luck seems to follow you and your sister around. At least the murder is in West Vale instead of Longely this time," Bree went on. "Although it would have been better if it wasn't in this geographical locale."

"I agree," Bernie told Bree as she came sailing through the door. "It was so inconsiderate of Leeza to get herself murdered in the town next door." Bernie took off her sunglasses and hung them from the neck of her T-shirt. "Next time I arrange a homicide, I'll be sure and have it somewhere in Alaska. After all, we wouldn't want you to lose any commissions."

"That's not what I meant," Bree protested.

"Then what did you mean?" Bernie asked her as she handed Libby the three-dozen eggs she'd just gotten from the farm.

Nothing ever fazed her younger sister, Libby thought as she put the eggs on the counter. She always managed to have the right comeback. And she always look so pulled together no matter what. She didn't have a stain on *her* shirt. And if she did, she would have made it into a fashion statement. Sometimes Libby just hated her.

Bree emptied a packet of Splenda into her coffee and stirred. "I'm just making the factual observation that there's been trouble in town ever since you got here."

"You can't blame her," Libby blurted out.

Both Bree and Bernie looked at her. Libby felt herself shrinking into her T-shirt. Why was she trying to defend her sister anyway?

Bree said to Libby, "I wasn't blaming your sister for anything. As I said, I was merely making an observation." Then Bree turned back to Bernie. "I was just about to say to Libby that I understand you and your father ran into a little problem last night."

Bernie smiled back. "Not at all."

"Oh. That's funny. I'd heard you two were arrested."

"No. It was just a mix-up," Bernie assured her.

"So Marvin didn't have to come up with bail money? That's what he told me when he was pounding on the door at ten o'clock at night. I mean really. I can't believe he doesn't have an ATM card?"

Bernie had two thoughts. The first one was: what was Marvin thinking of choosing Bree to ask for money. The second was: given the expression on Libby's face the sooner she changed the topic of conversation the better.

"You know how overly dramatic Marvin can get," Bernie told Bree. "But of course that's why we love him."

"Dramatic would hardly be the adjective I'd use to describe Marvin," Bree replied.

Bernie plowed on. "That's because you don't know him the way we do. Nice bag by the way."

Bree patted it the way you would a puppy. "I got it when I was in Paris two weeks ago," she informed her.

Right, Bernie thought. Maybe it was a real Louis Vuitton, but if she had to bet, she'd lay money that Bree had picked it up from a street vendor outside of Bloomies. The woman was notoriously cheap. She was always haggling over the price of everything. "So how do you know the Raids anyway?" she said instead.

Bree took a sip of her coffee and put her cup down on the counter. "I sold them the house they're living in. Or I should say estate."

"I've never been in a place that big," Libby observed.

"I've sold bigger, but it is large, isn't it?" Bree agreed. "It was originally built by an Anglophile who wanted to live on an estate modeled on one built by a Lord Chesterton-Wilkes that he'd seen when he was over in Devon. Hence the layout.

"Then after Jura closed on the place he decided he wanted a hunting preserve conveniently situated for weekends—I guess the three brothers got tired of flying off to Louisiana—so he ended up buying several hundred acres to the south and building his hunting lodge there. It must be nice to have that kind of money. I've never been there," Bree confided, "although I don't agree with hunting. Even those dreadful birds . . ."

"Falcons," Bernie said.

"Anyway, as I was saying," Bree continued, "the birds that Joe insists on carrying around on his arm freak me out. I was so nervous sitting there going over the contract with those things looking at me. But given that, I'd still like to see the place. I understand from the article about it in *Design* it's amazing. All the political higher-ups come there to shoot." Bree patted Bernie's arm. "Not to change the subject or anything, but is your dad all right?"

"Why shouldn't he be?" Bernie demanded.

"Well, he hasn't been out in almost three years and then with everything that happened yesterday . . ." Bree's voice got lower. "You know sometimes stress can trigger an episode in someone with his condition."

"He's fine," Bernie repeated. "Just fine."

"Good. Glad to hear it," Bree patted Bernie's arm again, took her egg from Libby, and left the store.

"Well, he is fine," Bernie said to Libby once the door had closed.

Libby just glared at her.

"In fact, I think he enjoyed having Fisher arrest him. It gives him something to stew about."

Libby slammed the creamer down. Half-and-half slopped over its sides. The fact that she knew what Bernie was saying about her dad was true just made her madder.

"Having to call Marvin to post bail for you guys was one of the more humiliating things I've ever had to do."

"Then you've led a very sheltered life," Bernie replied. "Handing out ads while dressed as a banana was the most humiliating thing I've ever had to do."

Libby turned her head away. "Don't think you can turn everything into a joke."

"Oh come on, Libby," Bernie said. "Lighten up. You did Marvin a favor. How often does he get to play white knight coming to the rescue?"

"He was asleep when I called. I had to wake him up."

"So what? He likes you. What difference does it make?"

"It makes a difference to me," Libby told her. "I don't like airing our dirty laundry in public."

Bernie moved her silver and onyx ring up and down her finger as she considered her sister. It always amazed her how conservative Libby was becoming.

"What are you looking at?" Libby demanded.

"I was just thinking that you have to give people a chance," Bernie told her.

"That's easy for you to say," Libby said as she wiped up the spilled half-and-half.

Bernie watched her for another moment before she spoke.

"I guess you're still mad at me," she said.

"Good guess." Libby went over to the sink, rinsed the sponge out, squeezed it, then put it back in its holder before speaking. "All I know," she finally said, "is that I'm just glad Mother isn't alive to scc what happened last night."

"Don't be silly."

"She would have been furious."

"For about ten minutes." She went over and gave Libby a hug. "Come on," she said. "Look at all the business you've been doing today. Everyone wants to know what happened."

"That's a terrible way to look at things," Libby told her.

"But true," Bernie pointed out.

"Well, maybe a little," Libby conceded.

Chapter 11

It was a little after seven at night and R.J.'s was nearly empty when Bernie entered the bar. In another hour it would be crowded with hooting and hollering postgame softball players, but right now there were only ten people in the place.

Glancing around Bernie realized how glad she was to be back here. She'd had enough of the L.A. esthetic. If she never saw another piece of chrome and black leather or ersatz Tudor it would be okay with her. There was no there there.

Bernie inhaled. Yes. It was good be home. She couldn't believe she was saying this but she even loved the scent of Pine-Sol and chicken wings that seemed to linger in the air here. She loved the pictures of Longely from days gone by hanging on the walls. She loved the crunch of discarded peanut shells as she walked by the tables. She loved the old-fashioned dartboard. No electronic one here.

Okay, maybe the place was a dive, but it was her dive and that, in her humble opinion, was what counted. Besides, unlike the places she'd hung out in when she'd lived in L.A., the people at R.J.'s weren't pretentious. Or maybe, Bernie decided, ostentatious would be a better word choice although affected might do just as well.

Heaven knows she liked her Manolos and Jimmy Choos

and Lulu Guiness bags as much as the next girl, but she didn't think of owning them as a matter of life and death. Well maybe she did a little she admitted to herself, but not to the extent that some of the other women did and she definitely couldn't get behind the whole car deal.

Having a car that cost more to lease than your apartment made no sense to her at all. And then there was the plastic surgery thing. That was huge. Especially in L.A. Everyone she knew, from secretaries and script girls on up to producers, were always getting something done and that had kind of freaked her out as well.

And even if she'd wanted to—she wouldn't have minded a little lipo on her thighs if she were being honest—even she, the person who could spend five hundred dollars on a pair of shoes, wasn't going to take out a loan so she could fork over three thousand dollars so she could look a little better in her jeans. Although, Bernie mused, given the interest rates right now maybe she should have. As she was debating the question her eyes fell on Rob.

One of the things Bernie loved about him, besides the fact that he was gorgeous, funny, smart, and fantastic in bed was that he was always on time, unlike her previous boyfriend Joe who was always at least a half an hour late, if not more. In fact, Rob was altogether too good to be true.

She was still waiting to see his fatal flaw emerge. She knew he had to have one. After all, she liked him, didn't she? What bigger proof was there than that? Or maybe Bernie was beginning to think it was her. Maybe she just wasn't used to nice men anymore. The only thing she did know was that if things didn't work out with Rob she was going to take a vow of celibacy. Well, not really. But she was definitely going to lay off of men for a while.

"So how's my little jailbird tonight?" Rob asked when she hopped up on the barstool next to him.

Bernie gave him a kiss. "Tired. Very tired."

Rob grinned. "I know something that will wake you up."

She punched him in the arm. "No. That will put me to sleep."

"Either one is fine with me. I promise I'll be a perfect gentleman while you're unconscious. He he." He leered and twirled an imaginary mustache.

Bernie grinned at him. "You're impossible."

"I was hoping you'd say that."

"Sorry, but I have to go home tonight. Libby is still mad at me," Bernie told Rob as Brandon materialized in front of her.

"God are you sunburned," she said to him. "Your face is bright red."

He smiled. "It goes with my hair."

"I didn't realize you were going for the monochromatic look. What were you doing?"

"I was out on a boat with Sam. I can't take the sun. Us fair-haired Irish are a woodland lot."

"Since when is Mazurski an Irish name?" Rob demanded.

"You mean it's not?" Brandon said as he pushed a full stein of beer across the bar towards Bernie. "It's on the house," he told her.

"You do this for all the miscreants that come in here?" Rob asked Brandon as Rob tousled Bernie's hair.

"Nice word," Bernie observed. "Did you know it comes from Old French and originally meant heretic?"

"Fascinating," Brandon replied. "Simply fascinating. I'll have to write that down somewhere to share with the rest of the guys. They'll be thrilled. No. The only miscreants I give free drinks too are my old classmates. The rest have to pay."

"That's rather arbitrary," Bernie said.

"That's because I'm an arbitrary kinda guy and no," Brandon held up his hand, "please don't tell me the derivation of the word."

"I wasn't going to." Bernie took a sip of her beer. "Nice. What is it?"

"Brooklyn Lager. Actually consider this a bribe." Brandon planted his elbows on the bar. "I want all the gory details."

Bernie had just gotten to the part about Fisher walking in on her and her father and accusing them of mucking up the crime scene and how he'd had to call a special van to accommodate her dad's wheelchair so they could cart him off to jail when Marvin walked through the door.

"Hey," Rob shouted lifting his glass, "it's the man of the hour. Come on. I'll buy you a beer."

As Marvin came towards them, Bernie couldn't help thinking about what a good couple Libby and Marvin would make. They had the same body type, the same outlook on life, and most importantly Marvin had liked her sister since grade school.

Plus, he was smart, nice, hard working and it didn't hurt that he was going to inherit his dad's business. So what if he needed to lose a few pounds. So did Libby. And as for him being a funeral director, at least he'd never get laid off. Now, if she could only convince Libby to loosen up a little and give Marvin a fair try.

Everyone would benefit. Libby would be happier and if Libby were happier then she and her dad would be too. Maybe she'd chill out a little, Bernie thought, remembering how her sister had flipped out last night. In truth, not that she'd ever say this to Libby, but maybe if she got a little more sex—correction: any sex—she'd freak out a little less.

Marvin readjusted his glasses and sat down on the other side of Bernie.

"I called Libby and asked her to meet me but she said she was going to bed. She sounded angry. I hope it wasn't anything I've done."

Bernie reached for the peanuts.

"Why would she be angry at you? You saved the day last night. If it weren't for you, Dad and I would still be in jail. Libby just gets cranky when she's tired."

"Oh," Marvin said. He took his glasses off, fiddled with them, then put them on again.

Bernie made to slide off the stool. "You want me to go get her for you because I will."

Marvin shook his head. "She doesn't want to."

"So what?"

"She was really very specific."

Bernie leaned over and patted Marvin's shoulder. "Let me give you a word of advice. Don't listen to my sister. She doesn't know what she wants."

"Yeah," Rob put in. "Just go over to her house, barge into her bedroom, and drag her off into the woods. Her dad would really like that."

Bernie poked Rob in the ribs. "Hey buddy, no one is talking to you. Don't listen to him," she told Marvin.

"She really is tired," Marvin protested.

"So what?" Bernie countered. "Sleep is a waste of time. Last offer. Do you want me to go get her? Because just say the word and I will."

Marvin shook his head.

"Sure?" Bernie asked.

"Positive," Marvin said as Brandon put a stein in front of Marvin.

"On the house," Brandon informed him.

"It's amazing your boss hasn't fired you yet," Rob told him.

"Hey, if it wasn't for me half of these people wouldn't be in here," Brandon pointed out. "So he can swallow a few freebies. Swallow." He slapped the bar. "Get it?"

Rob just snorted and shook his head.

"Anyway," Brandon continued, "when beer's on tap it's hard to tell exactly how many have been sold. That's why in my bar I'd just serve the bottled stuff."

"You thinking of opening one?" Rob asked.

Brandon glanced around to make sure no one was looking at him then nodded as Marvin took a sip of his beer.

"Foam," Bernie said, pointing to his upper lip.

Marvin hastily wiped it off. "Here's something that's interesting," he told Bernie, Rob, and Brandon. "My dad just told me that the police released Leeza Sharp's body. We're doing the burial."

Bernie ate another peanut and dropped the shell on the floor. "What about her family?"

Marvin shrugged. "I don't think she has any. At least I didn't see any next of kin listed on the paperwork. Jura's already contacted my dad about the funeral arrangements."

"Why didn't he use the funeral home in West Vale?" Bernie asked. "They have one, right?"

Marvin took another gulp of beer and wiped his upper lip off with the back of his hand.

"I'm guessing because they're way more expensive and he doesn't want to spend any money."

"Go on," Bernie prompted.

"I really shouldn't. I probably shouldn't have said as much as I did," Marvin replied.

"Tell us," Bernie urged. "You know you want to. We'll be discreet."

Rob almost choked on his beer.

"Well I can be when the need arises," Bernie said as she watched Marvin trying to decide what to do." She stroked his arm. "Come on, Marvin. I'm sure Libby would want to know."

She watched Marvin take another sip of his beer. She could tell he was weakening. A moment later he began to talk.

"Okay," he said in a low voice. "But you can't tell anyone. Except for Libby."

"We won't," Bernie promised as Rob rolled his eyes. "Ignore him," she told Marvin as she poked Rob in the ribs.

"Hey, that hurt," Rob complained rubbing his side.

"It was meant to," Bernie told him. "Go on," she urged Marvin.

Marvin fiddled with his glasses for another moment and licked his lips. Finally he said, "Let's just say that the casket he picked is one step up from a pine box. Plus he's having her cremated."

Bernie grabbed another handful of peanuts and began cracking the shells and throwing the nuts into her mouth one at a time.

"All that money he was going to spend on the wedding and nothing for her funeral. Interesting."

"Some people think that funerals are a waste of money," Marvin pointed out. "Not that I agree of course. But maybe he's one of them."

"Maybe," Bernie agreed.

"And he's another interesting thing. He wants Leeza dressed in her wedding dress."

"How romantic," Rob said. "Very Edgar Allan."

"I don't get it," Brandon said.

"He means Edgar Allan Poe," Bernie explained. "You know, he wrote poems about being in love with dead girls. Like Tom Petty."

Marvin smiled. "*Annabelle Lee.* Yeah. We read it in high school." He threw open his arms and declaimed, "And so, all night-tide, I lie down by the side/Of my darling, my darling, my life and my bride . . ."

Bernie clapped as Brandon waved his hand.

"You would remember something like that," he told Marvin.

"Meaning?" Marvin demanded.

"Meaning nothing," Bernie told him. "Brandon was just pulling your chain."

Brandon nodded. "It's true, man."

Bernie tapped her fingers on the bar while she thought. "The thing is," she said slowly, "Jura never impressed me as the romantic type. In fact, he impressed me as just the opposite. Maybe, the impetus for his actions isn't romantic. Maybe he just wants to get rid of everything having to do with the wedding."

"And why would he want to do that?" Rob asked.

"Because he doesn't want to think about it anymore," Marvin observed.

"Well, he certainly wouldn't if he killed her," Bernie said.

Rob looked at her. "Don't go there."

"Where am I going?" Bernie protested.

"You can stop that wide-eyed innocent bit you're doing because it doesn't work."

"I'm not doing anything. I'm just speculating."

"Good. Because you're leaving this case to the professionals, right?"

"Right," Bernie repeated.

"You promise? No cross counts."

"I promise," Bernie said, raising her right hand. "At least for the time being."

She was too tired tonight to go into the whole thing about how solving crimes was her karma.

Chapter 12

Three weeks later Sean Simmons was sitting in his bedroom typing on his computer at two o'clock in the afternoon when he heard a knock on the downstairs door. A moment later, he heard footsteps coming up the stairs and Libby popped her head into his room.

"You're not going to like this," she said.

"Like what?" Sean asked quickly turning off the monitor before he turned to regard his eldest daughter.

In truth he really didn't want her to see what he was working on. Not that he was doing anything wrong mind you. He just hadn't told Libby about the letter he was in the midst of writing because he was pretty certain she wouldn't approve, and why cause problems if you didn't have to? Why subject yourself to one of those emotional scenes Libby had a habit of throwing if you could avoid it?

He was as willing as the next man to listen to what someone had to say, but he preferred that it be presented to him in a logical fashion. He didn't think that was too much to ask. But Libby was like Rose in that regard. She could never manage to talk dispassionately. She always had to bring feelings into it, and then she got mad when he walked out.

All he was doing here was looking for justice. What was so bad about that? On the advice of his attorney—well really he'd had to coax Paul a little bit to get him in back of this—he was in the midst of drafting a letter to the West Vale District Attorney informing him of his intent to lodge a wrongful action suit against Alex Fisher and the West Vale Police Department for the false arrest and imprisonment of him and Bernie.

Sean figured there was time enough to let Libby know about the lawsuit if it came to anything. Who knew? Maybe it wouldn't. Then he'd have to listen to her blather on about how concerned she was that he not stress himself out, but not before it was necessary.

Anyway a man needed some stress in his life, something to butt up against. Otherwise you might as well be a sack of potatoes sitting on the shelf. And he had to say he was enjoying anticipating the look on Alex Fisher's face when he was served with the papers. He only wished he could be there to see it.

"The Walker sisters are here," Libby said, interrupting his train of thought.

"The Walker sisters?" Sean repeated hoping he hadn't heard correctly.

Libby brushed a piece of lint off her T-shirt. "That's what I just said."

Sean groaned. They were the last people he wanted to talk to. "I thought they were in Sumatra." Or was it Bali? He forgot. Well actually, he didn't care.

"I think it was South Dakota."

Sean waved his hand in the air. "Same thing."

"Not exactly," Libby pointed out.

"Frankly, I don't give a hoot if they've just come back from the Arctic Circle. Can't you put them off? Tell them I've had a relapse, and I'm on my deathbed. Better yet, tell them I've died."

"You know what they're like. They'd want to see your corpse," Libby told him.

Sean had to agree that unfortunately Libby's assessment was spot on.

"Can't *you* talk to them?" he asked.

"They want to speak to you. They said it's urgent."

Sean licked his lips. That wasn't good. Heaven only knows how but the last time they'd said something like that they'd convinced his wife, Rose, to keep a twelve-foot Burmese python for them. Just for a couple of weeks, they'd said. Naturally the two weeks had stretched into two months.

And of course the damned thing had escaped just like he'd predicted it would. And of course, Rose had gotten hysterical just like he'd predicted she would. He'd wasted two whole days looking for the snake when he should have been out patrolling the town. He'd taken the house apart. Nothing. Then the thing had turned up next door. To this day he didn't know how that had happened.

But there it was wrapped around the toilet bowl when his neighbor Mrs. Peabody had gone to take her morning pee. He could remember her shrieking. He'd thought a murder was being committed. Then when he'd gotten there, having busted through her screen door he might add, he'd thought she was going to stroke out on him.

Lucky for him she hadn't. But that vision of Mrs. Peabody with her undies down around her ankles had stayed with him. Unfortunately. He couldn't look the woman in the face after that. He wouldn't have claimed ownership of the damned thing, if Rose hadn't been in back of him shaming him into it.

"What would I have told Eunice and Gertrude when they got back?" she demanded when they'd gotten home.

Well that had just opened the door to all sorts of comments he'd been married long enough to know better than to say, so he'd kept his mouth shut. With a great deal of difficulty, he might add.

Libby coughed. Sean shook his head to clear it.

"You want me to bring up tea or coffee?" she asked him.

"Coffee," Sean said bowing to the inevitable, "and some lemon bars." From what he remembered of the Walker sisters they didn't eat sugar, so he'd have them all to himself.

A moment later, the Walker sisters came into his bedroom.

He blinked his eyes. The last time he'd seen them, which was not more then three weeks ago when Alex Fisher was carting him off to jail, their hair had been turquoise. Now it was green. Why would anyone do that to themselves he wondered as they took seats on the sofa opposite him.

He watched as they both tucked their skirts under their thighs and sat down in unison. They'd been living together for so long, Sean reflected, that they were like an old married couple. In fact, they looked so much alike it was hard to tell them apart.

Especially since not only did they have the same hair color, they were both dressed in the same clothes, in this case long black skirts and bright pink T-shirts, with the logo *We Kick Ass* printed on them. The only difference between the two women as far as he could see was that Eunice had brown eyes and Gertrude's were blue.

"So what can I do for you ladies?" he asked them.

"I hope we didn't interrupt," Eunice said.

"Not at all," Sean lied.

He watched as Eunice looked at Gertrude and Gertrude looked at Eunice.

Finally Eunice said, "You start, Gertrude."

Gertrude smoothed down her skirt again and coughed into her hand. Sean didn't say anything. He waited. It was something he'd become good at in his years on the force. He'd learned in his first year that most people couldn't deal with silence. Eventually they talked just to fill the void.

"I know you don't like us very much," Gertrude began.

Sean opened his mouth to deny it, but Gertrude put up her hand to stop him.

"We're too old for lies at this stage of our life," she told him.

Speak for yourself, Sean thought. He wheeled himself a little closer to the sisters.

"Go on," Sean told Gertrude. Never admit; never deny. That was his motto.

Gertrude coughed again. "I know you think we're strange.

I know you don't approve of the way we dress or the color we dye out hair. I know you think we imposed on Rose over the years. I know you never forgave us for the snake."

"That's not true," Sean protested.

Gertrude snorted. "Even back then," she told him. "You could never could hide what you were thinking very well. That's one of the things Rose loved about you."

Sean looked away. The last thing he wanted to do was discuss Rose with them. Or anyone for that matter.

"And I know you'd prefer that we not be here now," Gertrude continued.

Did they overhear what I was saying to Libby, Sean wondered. Boy, he hoped not.

"And we wouldn't be," Eunice continued. "If we really didn't need your help. And since you are family . . ." Eunice let her voice drop off.

"That would be stretching it," Sean said.

Eunice gave him what Rose had called "The Look" and even though Sean knew it was ridiculous, he felt guilty. "All right. Why are you here?" he asked.

He watched while Eunice and Gertrude exchanged another set of looks. A moment later, Gertrude took up the conversational banner.

"You know," she began. "Marx . . ."

Sean cut her off. "Please not that," he said. "Don't rehash that stuff."

Gertrude opened her mouth and shut it. As Sean watched her casting around for another way to start he wondered where the hell Libby was with coffee and cookies. A shot of Jameson in his coffee would also help, but it was too late to ask for that now.

"Fine," Gertrude finally said. "At least grant me the premise that the rich have more privileges than the poor."

"Agreed," Sean said wondering where this was going.

"And that since they operate in a closed strata unlike, let us say, people in the middle class, what they do tends to be shielded from society at large."

Sean reluctantly nodded his head again. His work had taught him the truth of that statement—after all that's why he'd gotten fired—so he couldn't argue with that either, much as he would have liked to.

Gertrude patted her hair down. "And when I say society, I mean its public institutions such as social services, the courts, and the judicial system."

Can you just get on with it, Sean was thinking when Libby came in bearing a tray laden with coffee, mugs, sugar and cream and, Sean was glad to see, not one but two kinds of cookies.

Not that he really had to ask the Walker sisters why they were here. Two minutes into the conversation and he'd had a pretty good idea where it was leading. He just wished they'd speed things up. Of course he could bring that about, but that was a last resort.

Usually he found it more useful to just let people chat. It was amazing what you could find out that way. And that was what he intended to do here—if he could stand it. For the next five minutes or so he watched Libby serving everyone.

"Very nice, dear," Gertrude said after taking a sip of her coffee. "I hope you made this from fair-traded beans," she said lowering her mug.

"Actually, no," Libby said. Now she knew where Bernie got her nitpicking abilities from.

"Do you know what fair-traded beans are?"

Libby nodded. "Coffee harvested by co-ops."

"If you know, then you have no excuse," Gertrude told her sternly. "Coffee workers are horribly exploited by large conglomerates." She took another sip and put her cup down. "But we're not here to talk about that. We're here to request some help from your father."

"And what do you want him to do?" Libby asked Gertrude.

Sean was amused to see Gertrude pick up her spoon, stir her coffee, then put her spoon down and take a sip. All for dramatic effect, Sean thought. *She's good,* he decided. *Better than I thought.*

"Well, dear," Gertrude began, "it's been a little over three weeks since Leeza Sharp has been killed, and the West Vale police, despite our daily urging, have made no progress whatsoever that we can see in this case. In fact, they are teetering on the brink of declaring Leeza's death a misadventure."

"They wouldn't," Sean said, despite his resolution to remain silent. "Not with the booby trap that they found."

"They're thinking about it," Gertrude told him. "Although I don't understand how they can be given the situation.

Gertrude smiled and Sean realized she'd got him, too. She was almost professional caliber. No wonder Rose had had trouble saying no to the sisters. But then Rose was a civilian. He wasn't. He knew how things worked. Prided himself on it, in fact.

"Evidently," Gertrude continued, "the booby trap is being considered a practical joke gone bad. At least that's my understanding though I might be mistaken. The officers I've been talking to have been less then communicative. In fact, I've had better conversations with the baboons at the San Diego Zoo."

Nice one, Sean thought.

"So," Gertrude went on, "you can see why my sister and I are of the opinion that the police department of West Vale isn't interested in finding the person that murdered Leeza Sharp, which coincidentally leads us to believe it has to be one of the brothers because if it were a servant, the police would be on him like white on rice. As far as we can see, the only thing the police department is interested in doing is making sure that the whole thing goes away. Bad for property values."

"That sounds like Bree," Libby said.

"Well she's right," Eunice said. "Just look at the funeral," she continued.

"Or lack thereof, " Gertrude added.

"That has nothing to do with the police," Sean pointed out.

"That's true," Eunice conceded. "It doesn't. I'm mentioning it because my sister and I feel the way it was conducted is emblematic of the way Jura felt about his bride."

"It was disgraceful," both women said together. "There wasn't even an obituary in the papers."

"Nothing," Eunice said. "And even though I'm opposed to lavish funerary displays as a means of conspicuous consumption, still one should do something."

"Okay," Sean said. "Now here's my question to you: Why do you care so much?"

"Because," Eunice began, "when the worker is exploited . . ."

"No, no." Sean waved his hand. "Don't give me that. I want to know what your personal stake in this is. Why do you really care about what happened to Leeza Sharp."

Sean watched while Gertrude and Eunice exchanged yet another set of looks.

"I guess that's fair." Eunice finally conceded. "I suppose . . ."

Gertrude finished the sentence for her. ". . . we feel responsible since we were the people that got her her job."

"You did?" Sean asked. Now that surprised him.

"Well," Gertrude said, "Leeza wrote and told us she was coming when she moved out east. As old friends of her mother we felt an obligation to assist in any way we could."

Eunice leaned forward. "The first job we heard of was in Harlem," she told Sean. "But Leeza didn't feel comfortable working with people of color."

"Naturally we were horrified," Gertrude confided. "But we try and keep our opinions to ourselves."

"Naturally." Sean hoped he was managing to keep a straight face. "And I must say you do a wonderful job of it."

Gertrude gave him a sharp glance before continuing on.

"So," she said, "when we heard of this position opening up in Raid Enterprises, we told Leeza. We never dreamed things would turn out this way."

"We really blame ourselves," finished Eunice. "If it hadn't been for us, Leeza would be alive today."

"That's a pretty big stretch," Sean commented as he picked up a lemon bar, broke it in half, and took a bite.

"Well," Gertrude said, "even though Eunice and I believe in the concept of personal responsibility we also believe that Leeza was in an injurious environment and since we put her there we have to take responsibility for that."

"We should have known better," Eunice said. "A firm that deals in a luxury item. We should have known something unsavory was bound to occur."

"Okay," Sean said to the sisters after he'd swallowed. "And what do you ladies want me to do?"

By now he'd have to be a moron not to know, but he wanted Eunice and Gertrude to say it because over the years he'd observed that the asker was always one down on the askee. It was like saying, "I love you." You never wanted to be the first one.

"Obviously," Gertrude said, "we want you to find out who killed Leeza Sharp. We're willing to pay all expenses. And a fair wage. We don't believe in people working for nothing."

"Of course we'll want an accounting," Eunice said. "Once a week will be sufficient, I believe."

Sean raised his eyebrow.

"I'm shocked. Simply shocked. Are you suggesting a capitalist concept?"

"Just because we're communists doesn't mean we're fools," Gertrude answered.

"And once you find out, we'll take it from there," Eunice added.

"That's absolutely out of the question," Libby said. At the same time Sean replied, "It will be my pleasure."

Chapter 13

It was now ten o'clock at night and Sean reflected that he and his daughters, his eldest daughter to be precise, had been arguing since the store closed. That was two-and-a-half hours or one hundred and fifty minutes. Way too much time for him.

Four years ago he would have left and taken a drive in his car and come back when Libby had calmed down. But now he was trapped in this dratted chair. And his daughter knew it too, blast her hide.

"No," Libby said again. Sean watched her as she paced back and forth from the window to the door, pausing every now and then to take a chocolate chip cookie from the plate sitting on the night table. "We don't need to get involved."

"You know," Sean told her for what he was sure was the fiftieth time, "even though, admittedly I have a few problems, I think I'm still capable of making my own decisions."

Over the years he'd found that the best way of arguing with Libby was to pick one or two statements and just repeat them over and over again. Eventually the sheer repetition wore her down, but tonight she was hanging on. She was becoming more and more like her mother every day, Sean unhappily reflected.

"Then you're making a bad decision," Libby informed him.

Bernie took a last sip of her Cosmopolitan and put her glass down.

"Hey, stay out of it if you don't agree with Dad," she told Libby. "You don't have to participate in this if you don't want to. We're not asking you to."

Sean threw his youngest daughter a grateful glance as Libby whirled around to face her sister.

"I'm sorry," she told her. "But what you fail to grasp here is that this will have an impact on everyone in the family."

"No it won't," Bernie told her.

"Really?" Libby put her hands on her hips. "Then answer this. Who is going to be doing the work in the store while you're running around playing Nancy Drew? Who is going to be driving Dad around?"

"Who was working in the store before I came back?" Bernie challenged. "You should think about Dad and what he wants to do."

"I am thinking about him," Libby said. "And don't you dare suggest otherwise."

Bernie snorted. "Yeah. Well, he's had more fun being arrested with me than he's had sitting up here in this room."

Oh, oh, thought Sean. Things were not going in a good direction here. If he didn't do something now he'd have the girls not speaking to one another for the next week which would be inconvenient at best and downright unpleasant at worst.

"Time out," Sean said before Libby could reply. Then he grabbed Libby's hand as she made another pass around the room. "I want you to come and sit down next to me," he ordered. The principle of dealing with an angry daughter or a drunk was the same, he reflected. Divert the attention to something else. Give the person a new focus.

Libby sat down reluctantly, as Sean knew she would. After all he'd reasoned, how could you say no to a request like that from your dad, especially if he's crippled.

"Now I want you to calm down and listen to what I have to say," Sean told her.

He watched his daughter bite her lip.

"I just don't want you to get worse, that's all," she told him. "You know what the doctor said about stress."

"Yeah, I do. If I listened to him I'd just shoot myself now and get it over with."

"That's a terrible thing to say," Libby told him. "Terrible."

Sean patted Libby's hand. "Don't think I don't appreciate everything you've done for me for the last three years. You know I couldn't have gotten along without you." Libby nodded her head and Sean could feel her hand relaxing under his. "But once I got out, I remembered how good it feels."

"You got yourself arrested," Libby told him. "Did that feel good?"

"I will say it was interesting being on that side of the equation."

Libby pursed her lips. "So you're saying that Bernie's right?" she asked.

"I didn't mean that," Sean quickly replied. He wasn't getting drawn back into a discussion on this topic. Not if he could help it.

"Then what did you mean?" Libby asked.

"That at least I wasn't sitting at home watching the Home Shopping Network. Even if that arrest thing was a slight miscalculation on my part," Sean admitted. "But it doesn't obviate what I said."

"Obviate?" Libby repeated.

"Rule out," Bernie explained.

"Whatever," Libby told her sister.

"Well, excuse me," Bernie snapped.

Sean coughed. Both girls turned to look at him.

"The truth is," he quickly continued, "I realized that I enjoyed being back in the game. And I also think Leeza Sharp deserves better than she got."

"Even if she was a grade-A bitch," Bernie interjected. "Well, she was," Bernie said in answer to her father's glare.

"Okay. She wasn't a very nice person. Is that better?" she asked.

"Marginally," he replied. Talk about not helping the cause. He turned back to Libby. "Now," he said, "I appreciate your concern and I appreciate everything you've done for me, but I am going to do this. And you can help me or not. Either one is fine with me."

Sean watched as Libby got up and snagged another chocolate chip cookie. He watched as she stared out the window for a moment while she thought about what to do. He reflected that even when she was little, she'd always taken a long time to make decisions; buying ice cream with her had been a nightmare, unlike Bernie and himself, who tended to decide things with the snap of a finger.

"Maybe you would be better staying out of this," he said to Libby's back. "Especially if you're not comfortable."

She turned around. "No. I'm in."

"Are you sure?" Sean asked. He couldn't figure out why, but for some reason it meant a lot to him that Libby was joining him on this.

"I'm positive."

"Can I ask what made you change your mind?"

Libby clicked her tongue against her teeth. "I guess I'd rather be with you guys," she indicated her father and sister with a nod of her head, "no matter what. Even if I don't agree with what you're doing."

Sean nodded. "Fair enough."

"What I don't understand though," Libby continued, "is how we're going to pull this off. We have no legal authority whatsoever."

"We managed last time," Bernie pointed out.

"Yeah, but last time we knew all the players," Libby replied.

"We still do," Bernie protested.

"Yeah, but they don't shop in our store. They all live in a different town."

Sean grinned. "That's what's going to make this fun. The

challenge. After all, anyone can investigate a crime if they have a badge."

Bernie swung her leg off the chair she was sitting in and stood up. "I'm going to go get a bottle of Cristal. We should have a toast."

Cristal, Libby thought. They couldn't afford that. Libby looked at her sister suspiciously. "Where did you get a bottle of Cristal?"

"Where do you think?"

Libby wiped her hands on her T-shirt. "Don't tell me this."

"Then don't ask."

"But how?" Libby was mystified. When had Bernie had the time?

"I put it in the car before Dad came."

"I can't believe you stole a bottle of Jura's champagne."

"Oh don't look so scandalized," Bernie told her. "They had more then enough. Anyway, it's not as if they needed it for the guests."

"Don't you have any ethics?" Libby asked her.

"Not where top of the line champagne is concerned," Bernie cheerfully replied.

"Good, isn't it?" Bernie asked as Libby sipped her champagne.

"Very," Libby reluctantly agreed.

Bernie raised her glass. "A toast to Simmons and Daughters. Long may we prosper."

"I'll drink to that," Sean said.

Sean, Bernie, and Libby clinked glasses, then drank down the champagne. Sean carefully set his glass on the nightstand in front of him. Despite what his doctor had told him alcohol seemed to steady his hands not make them shake more.

"How are we going to go about this?" Libby asked.

"I've been giving some thought to that," Sean said and he sat back in his wheelchair and began to talk. "Usually when you investigate a crime you look for motive, means, and opportunity, agreed?"

"Agreed," Bernie and Libby said in unison.

"In this case we know what the means are."

Bernie and Libby nodded their heads again.

"So the first thing I'd like to know is who had access to the weapons? Who can shoot a compound bow?"

"Crossbow," Bernie said.

"I stand corrected," her father answered. "Though my question remains the same."

Bernie tucked a ringlet of blond hair back behind her ear. "All right. From what Bree said and what we saw, I think we can safely surmise that the three brothers are proficient with weapons."

"I concur," Sean said. "And," he continued, "it seems to me that almost anyone could have had access to the room where they keep the weapons. I didn't see a lock on the door. Did you?"

"No," Bernie said. "I didn't." She worked her onyx ring up and down her finger.

Sean nodded his head approvingly.

Bernie picked up the conversational thread. "Actually we don't even know that the arrow and the bow came from the estate. It could have come from the hunting lodge. Which would imply premeditation."

"The whole thing was premeditated," Sean pointed out. "You don't rig something like that up on the spur of the moment."

"No," Bernie said, "you don't. But why Leeza's wedding day?"

Sean wheeled his chair back and forth. "Probably because whoever did it knew she'd be in the house. And then we come to the remote control car. Since they're mostly purchased in toy stores or hobby shops or electronic shops, if I were working this case I'd send people to canvas the vicinity to see if anyone had recently purchased a similar model. However, that would be too labor intensive for us."

"Especially since you can purchase them on the Internet," Libby pointed out.

"Good point," Sean said. He couldn't believe he hadn't thought of that himself.

He looked out the window. His neighbor's cat was busy stalking a robin. The cat was almost there; he had another inch to go when the robin flew away. Reminded him of a few of his own cases Sean thought as he turned his mind back to the business at hand.

"So what we have at the moment," he recapitulated, "is multiple suspects and no good, that is efficient, way to track their movements. That being the case it seems to me at this moment, the most fruitful thing we can do is concentrate our resources on trying to find out who had a motive for killing Leeza Sharp. Can we agree on that?" Sean asked.

"Sure," Libby said.

"Ditto," Bernie echoed. "However, I would like to note that if Leeza Sharp acted the same way with everyone else that she acted with us, everyone is going to have a motive."

"I guess that's what we're going to find out," Sean said.

"What if everyone does?" Libby asked.

"We'll worry about that when we come to it," Sean told her. "Now anyone have any suggestions about how to accomplish this task?"

"Teacher, teacher." Bernie waved her hand up and down. "Pick me. Please. Please. Please."

"All right," Sean conceded. "Maybe I was being a little didactic."

"Ya think?" Bernie told him.

"Do you have an idea or not?" Sean asked her.

"Do ants love peonies? Of course I do. I thought I could go see Esmeralda, Raid's administrative assistant, and tell her we have a big job and want to place a big order with her." Bernie slipped her ring off and on her finger. "Lunch in a nice place is always a good way to get someone to talk."

"She looked pretty loyal to me," Libby noted.

"That's what I'm counting on. Poor Jura," Bernie dabbed

away fake tears. "Such a tragedy. Thank God he has you to rely on, you to protect him." She dropped her hand and re-arranged her hair. "And, of course, you and I can always go back to the Raid Estate and try and talk to the kitchen staff."

"They weren't very friendly when we were there before," Libby reminded her. "In fact they were fairly awful."

"Except for the cook," Bernie said. "She seemed a little on the disaffected side."

"Maybe we should try the shopkeepers instead," Libby suggested. "Sometimes they hear things."

Sean nodded his approval. "Good thinking, but before you do that why don't you find out what Marvin has to say about the funeral."

"There wasn't one, remember."

"That in itself is significant. Find out if anyone showed up at the crematorium. Who took possession of the remains. That kind of thing."

Libby frowned at her dad. "You think you're clever don't you?"

"What are you talking about?"

"You know."

"No, I don't," Sean protested. And he didn't.

"Then why did you suggest I talk to Marvin?"

"I suggested you talk to Marvin because you know him and he might have seen something of interest." Sean scrutinized his daughter's face. She was wearing an expression he couldn't quite read. "Is there something here I'm missing?"

"Forget it," Libby said. "Just forget it."

"Seriously," Sean said.

Working with his daughters, he was beginning to realize was going to be way more difficult then working with his men had been.

"She thought you were trying to fix her up," Bernie explained.

"Why would I do that?" Sean asked, totally mystified. He didn't even like Marvin. At all. He was also not pleased to see Bernie was looking at him the same way Rose had from time to time when she was alive. "You know what?" Sean said. "Can we forget the personal stuff and please stay on task here."

Libby didn't reply which Sean thought was a good thing. He was feeling pretty pleased with himself at having regained the conversational upper hand when Bernie started in.

"Stay on task?" Bernie repeated. "Boy, that's a guy phrase if I ever heard one."

"Really?" Sean said. "That's interesting. Because the phrase was invented by a woman."

"Name her," Bernie challenged.

Sean grabbed the first name that swam into his head. "Bess Peterson." There had to be hundreds of thousands of Bess Petersons out there. For all he knew, maybe one of them had coined the phrase.

Bernie stared at him and he stared back. If I can't face off my youngest daughter he thought, it's time someone put me out of my misery.

"All right," Bernie finally conceded.

"Good," Sean replied. He always believed in being magnanimous in victory.

Bernie grinned. "Even though I don't believe a word of what you said."

Sean grinned back. "Any more suggestions?"

"I was thinking that someone at the golf club might know something," Bernie said. "After all they are right next door to the estate. Maybe someone saw something. Maybe the brothers are members."

"Could be." Sean gnawed on his cheek for a moment. Did he know anyone who was a member there? No. But Paul did. Maybe he'd be willing to arrange a meeting.

"Libby," he asked, "do you have any of that ginger cake left?"

"I have two in the freezer, why?"

"I need them to soften up Paul."

"I thought he liked my brownies."

"He does, but he loves your ginger cake." Sean looked at his daughters. It almost felt like old times. "Okay gang," he told them, "let's get to bed. Tomorrow we're going to hit the streets—metaphorically speaking."

Chapter 14

Libby looked at Marvin from across the bench.

"Take a picnic lunch," Bernie had told her. "And don't pack anything too exotic or show-offy," she'd warned Libby. "Marvin likes simple."

"How do you know?" Libby had demanded.

"Because he's a guy and most guys like simple food," Bernie had answered her. "And while we're on the subject, don't you dare go out of the house wearing those sandals. The rest of what you're wearing is bad enough."

Libby had looked down at her feet. "What's wrong with my shoes?" she'd objected. "They're comfortable."

She'd had them for three years now. She loved them even if the color had changed to a nondescript mud color and the soles were close to nonexistent.

"Exactly. Just wait a minute." And Bernie had rushed up the stairs and come down a moment later with a pair of her shoes. They were orange-suede wedges. Not something Libby would ordinarily wear. Well, ever wear.

"Try these on," Bernie had ordered.

At first Libby had resisted, but then she'd caved in the way she always did when Bernie insisted. As she'd studied herself in the mirror even she had to agree that the wedges made her legs look longer and thinner.

"It's just Marvin," she'd protested as she'd bent down to unfasten Bernie's shoes.

"I know. But I want you to wear them anyway."

"Why?" Libby had asked.

"Because change is good," Bernie had told her.

"That's not an answer."

"Then do it for me. And remember your questions," Bernie had told her as she pushed her out the door.

Well, the shoes definitely made her walk differently, Libby had thought as she'd caught glimpses of herself in the shop windows as she walked down Oak Street with picnic basket in hand. They slowed her down. She wasn't sure that she liked the way wearing these shoes made her hips swing from side to side. She'd couldn't stride. It felt . . . well it felt . . . weird.

But Libby did have to admit that she had liked the way Marvin's eyes had lit up when he'd seen her coming down the path to the swan pond. She also had to admit that Bernie had been right about keeping the food simple because Marvin was really loving her cooking, which made her feel good. There was nothing better in her opinion than having someone enjoy what you made for them. It was like being an author and getting a good book review.

After a lot of going back and forth, she'd finally decided on chicken salad sandwiches. The base was egg bread, which she'd made that morning and lightly spread with French mustard. The chicken salad, one of her favorite recipes, was composed of fresh poached chicken, homemade mayonnaise, finely chopped celery, just a hint of minced red onion, and a few walnuts thrown in for contrast. Then she'd added just a pinch of kosher salt, so you got little bursts of flavor. It was a simple recipe, but boy was it good. The ingredients were the key.

She'd also brought along a Chinese cucumber salad, which she'd composed out of the seedless, edible-skin kind of cukes. She'd used a small paring knife to strip alternate stripes of skin off the cucumbers. Then she'd sliced them moderately thickly. When she was done each slice looked like a pinwheel. To those she'd added a touch of sugar, a little fresh ground pepper, a small amount of rice wine vinegar, a little sesame oil, and a few frozen peas for sweetness. The contrast with the chicken salad—the smooth versus the crispy—always worked well.

She knew Marvin liked dessert so she'd brought along two brownies, which were still warm from the oven, and two coconut cookies that had chocolate kisses in the middle, plus a fruit salad composed of fresh-picked berries and mangoes. She'd also packed two thermoses in her basket. One was filled with fresh-squeezed lemonade and the other with coffee. The meal wasn't bad if she didn't say so herself.

"Have another half a sandwich," she told Marvin.

"I'd love to but I couldn't." He patted his stomach, which pooched over his belt "I'm trying to lose some weight."

"More lemonade?" she asked while she thought, *Damn. I should have said, 'Marvin, you don't need to lose any weight. You look fine just the way you are.'*

Marvin shook his head. "I'm great."

While Libby was trying to decide whether or not, given his diet status, she should offer him dessert she watched Marvin fiddle with his glasses, then smooth down the creases in his khakis. His nose was peeling.

"I couldn't believe it when you called me," he finally said.

"Well," Libby told him, "I wanted to do something nice for you after what you did for me."

Marvin blushed slightly and started fiddling with his glasses again. "It was nothing. I would have done it for anyone."

As Libby watched him she thought that maybe Bernie was right. There was something endearing about Marvin. He was sweet in a little boy kind of way. The thing was she was used to Orion, her last boyfriend. He'd always taken charge. She'd never had to worry, but Marvin was so quiet. Libby never knew what to say. Or do.

Ever since seventh grade Marvin had always just been

there. Around her. Waiting. Looking at her. Expecting her to do something. But she never knew what.

It was unnerving. She and Marvin sat in silence for a while. It was just beginning to get awkward when Libby remembered one of the questions Bernie had told her about when you get stuck on a date with nothing to say.

"I have a question for you," she said.

"Yes?" Marvin looked slightly scared.

Libby found that she was unaccountably beginning to enjoy herself. "Okay. This is it. If you could have one of these super powers, which would you pick: Would you want to fly? Have super-strength? Read people's minds? Or have X-ray vision?"

"Read people's minds," Marvin said promptly.

"Why?"

"Because then I'd know what you were thinking."

"Marvin," Libby wailed.

Marvin's forehead turned red. "I'm sorry if I embarrassed you," he told her.

"You didn't," Libby lied. This wasn't going the way she'd planned. Not at all. Bernie would have come up with some clever retort, and she was such a dweeb. She could never think of what to say. "Here." She pushed the brownies and the coconut cookies over to him. "Have some. I baked these just for you."

Marvin brightened. "Coconut and chocolate are one of my favorite combinations."

"Mine too," Libby said.

"I'm not supposed to, but I will if you will."

"Deal."

Marvin reached over and took a coconut cookie. Libby watched him take a bite. He smiled.

"These are wonderful," he told her.

"They're not bad," she admitted as she ate half of hers. "It's the cream cheese in the dough."

"My dad says I have to lose weight," Marvin said as he

ate the rest. "He says I don't present a very good image to the public. Of course, he still runs ten miles a week."

"You look fine," Libby surprised herself by saying. She'd never liked Marvin's dad anyway. Not since he'd yelled at her at lacrosse practice in eighth grade. She'd gotten so flustered she hadn't played since then. "Everyone deserves a treat now and then." Then she surprised herself even further by saying. "I'm making this low-cal, whole wheat, corn muffin at the store. You should come by and try one. They're really very good."

"I'd love to," Marvin said. "Maybe tomorrow."

"That would be great." Well she *had* been thinking about making those muffins. She guessed now would be as good a time as any to try them out. The question was whether she should make them with low-fat buttermilk or low-fat yogurt. Maybe she'd try both and see which came out better.

"You know," Marvin said, "my dad said he'd heard that your dad had been hired to help investigate Leeza Sharp's murder and that you two were helping him and that's why you invited me out to this lunch."

Suddenly Libby felt terrible.

No. She felt worse than terrible.

She wanted to crawl under a rock.

"He told me not to come," Marvin said.

"Marvin . . ." Libby began but before she could say anything else Marvin interrupted her.

"He said if people knew I was helping you we'd lose business. And I told him he was wrong so we got into a big fight."

"Oh Marvin, I'm so sorry," Libby told him as he watched two swans glide across the pond.

"It's okay." Marvin turned to face her. "We fight about everything anyway these days. He says he wants me to take over the business but every time I suggest something he doesn't like it."

"My mother was like that too," Libby confided.

"Was she?" Marvin asked. "I didn't know that."

Libby nodded. "I don't like to talk about it much. Everyone says, 'Oh it must have been so nice working with your mom. You were so lucky.' But it wasn't all nice."

Now it was Marvin's turn to nod. "I guess it's hard. Somebody runs something for a long time they don't want to give anything up. Maybe," he reflected. "I should have gone off like my brothers."

"Sometimes I think that, too," Libby said thinking of Bernie.

Marvin slapped his hands on his thighs. "But we didn't."

"No, we stayed," Libby agreed.

"So there you go. Now what do you want to know?"

Libby picked up a brownie, broke it in half, and gave one of the pieces to Marvin.

"Maybe your dad is right," Libby told him. "Maybe you shouldn't talk to me."

Bernie will kill me if she could hear what I'm saying, Libby thought but she didn't care. She didn't want Marvin to lose business because of her or hurt him in any way. If it came down to it, somehow or another she'd find another way to get what she needed to know.

"No. No. I want to," Marvin protested. "I think my dad is dead wrong about this. And anyway, maybe this sounds awful, but I think what you're doing is a good thing and I'd like to help if I can."

"It is a good thing," Libby agreed. Suddenly she was glad she was assisting.

"Not that I have anything that interesting to tell you."

Libby divided the next brownie in half and handed a piece to Marvin.

"So who was at the service?" she asked him.

"There really wasn't one," Marvin said as he ate the brownie.

Libby poured him a cup of coffee and handed it to him.

"Really?" Libby said.

"Yes, really," Marvin said. He took a sip. "You know you

make the best coffee, Libby. But then everything you do is good."

Libby felt herself beaming.

"It was very sad, really," Marvin said. "I collected Leeza Sharp's remains. And Jura had already brought over her wedding dress, so I put it on her. I mean I tried to make her look as good as possible. I thought she would have wanted that."

Libby nodded.

"You know," Marvin reflected. "I got the feeling that if Jura could have gotten away with just wrapping her in a shroud he would have. He kept on talking about what a waste of money it was buying something that was just going to burn up. But it really is a mark of respect, you know."

Marvin took another sip of his coffee.

"Jura kept looking at his watch the whole time we were getting the casket ready to be placed in the crematorium. He was talking to this woman next to him, who kept on patting him on the arm . . ."

"Esmeralda Quinn?"

Marvin nodded. "I think that was her name. He even took a couple of calls on his cell. I mean he couldn't wait to get out of there. As if the whole thing were an imposition on him. The only person there that seemed remotely upset was that brother of his with the short hair."

"You mean Ditas?"

"I think."

"The middle-sized one?"

"Yeah. That's him," Marvin said. "In fact he was the one that took delivery of the cremains. Jura didn't want to have anything to do with them. How's that for cold?"

"Pretty good," Libby said as she divided up the last coconut cookie and dished out the fruit salad.

"You know," Marvin said as he took the dish of fruit salad out of Libby's hand. "There is one other thing."

Libby waited.

"This is going to sound weirder than it actually is." Marvin speared a piece of mango and ate it. "People bury things with their loved ones. Like favorite golf clubs, photos. That kind of stuff."

"Like the Egyptians," Libby said.

"Exactly."

"Go on," Libby prompted.

"Well," Marvin said, "Jura insisted that we put a crossbow in Leeza's coffin before we closed it."

Libby leaned forward.

"Did he say why?"

"He said she liked to hunt. It was her passion."

"It was evidently someone else's too," Libby observed.

Chapter 15

Bernie looked down at the page in her hand that she'd ripped out of the store Yellow Pages. Libby would have killed her for doing that—if she'd seen her. She was so OCD. But she hadn't and taking the page with her was easier than copying out a list of all the stores in New York City that specialized in caviar. Well, actually there weren't that many shops. Six to be exact.

Bernie could hear Libby telling her she could have gotten the list off the computer. Which was true. But then she couldn't have caught the earlier train and that would have meant she wouldn't have had time to stop at a copy store and get new business cards made up.

She would have done the business card thing last night, except she'd just come up with this idea this morning when she'd been brushing her teeth and she figured that as long as she was going into the city anyway, it seemed silly not to try and combine two tasks into one trip.

Bernie checked her watch. She had an hour and a half left before she had to meet Esmeralda Quinn at the restaurant. That should be enough to cover at least one, possibly two of the stores on her list, both of which were within a ten-block radius of each other.

The first shop, *Caviar and Nothing Else*, was only eight

blocks away from Grand Central Terminal, so Bernie headed there first. A burst of hot, humid air hit her as she stepped out onto Lexington Avenue. Bernie loved New York but not in the summer time. Then it was sticky and smelly, and she could practically feel her hair frizzing up as she walked down the street—a good reason in her opinion why she'd never live in Florida. But at least she reflected, she was wearing a mint green silk tank top and a matching green and light blue print short silk skirt. Even if she felt hot, she didn't look it—which was a good deal of the battle.

Half an hour later Bernie had arrived at Caviar and Nothing Else, the line at the copy shop being considerably longer then she had anticipated. She paused for a second to consider the window display, which consisted of a tin of caviar sitting on a black velvet draped pedestal that was surrounded by a variety of fancifully carved ivory and horn spoons suspended from the ceiling on wires. Something like that wouldn't work in Longely, Bernie decided as she opened the door and walked inside. Too minimalist.

A burst of freezing cold air greeted her. This is why people get sick she thought as she marched up to the counter and handed the clerk behind the counter one of the business cards she'd just had printed. It read: Bernadette O'Brien. Travel/Food Writer for the *Los Angeles New Times*. Well she *had* worked there. And O'Brien *was* an Irish name, even if it didn't happen to be hers.

"Could you tell your manager I'd like to speak to him," she told him the sales clerk behind the counter.

"Can I say what this is about?" the clerk asked.

"Yes. I'm writing an article about holiday gifts and I was thinking of mentioning your store."

The clerk nodded and departed. Now Bernie knew that some people, such as her sister, would have discussed what she as about to do with her dad, but Bernie figured, why bother? All she was doing was acting on a hunch. The worst that could happen was that the manager would refuse to speak to her, and the best that could happen was that she'd glean some information that she didn't have before.

Okay, maybe she was diverging from the agreed upon plan, maybe there was the small problem of misrepresentation, but so what. That's what doing the kind of work her dad was doing involved. How else was she going to find out something? It had been her experience in the food industry that if you wanted to find something out you talked to the vendors and retailers. They were always the first to hear the gossip, the first to know if something was going wrong. She had to assume the same principles obtained here.

As she waited for the manager she took stock of the shop. Whoever had designed it had done an excellent job. The place screamed money. The walls were painted a rich golden hue. A big vase on the far side of the counter was filled with a variety of expensive, exotic blooms and just enough common flowers to show that whoever had done the arrangement understood the concept of juxtaposition.

The display case in front of her was filled with artfully arranged tins of Russian, Iranian, and American caviar as well as cunning ramekins of various types of pâté and small piles of quail eggs. A second display case was stocked with a variety of jewel-like fresh fruit tarts, which had been placed on white polished pebbles making them look like expensive pieces of art.

Bernie was wondering if they could do something like that at *A Taste of Heaven* when the manager came out holding her card in his hand. He was cuter then Bernie had expected. And younger. And hipper. He'd shaved his head and was sporting a goatee. Her father would have hated him. He disapproved of excess facial hair.

Bernie smiled at him and he smiled back. They shook hands.

"Paul," he said. "Paul Nelsen."

"Bernie," she said. "Bernie O'Brien. I know that you're probably very busy," she cooed. "But if I could just take a few minutes of your time for an article I'm writing about Christmas presents."

"Let's go in the back and talk," Paul Nelsen said.

"Love to," Bernie replied. Twenty minutes later, she left with his cell number, a small tin of caviar, and the information she'd come to find out.

Bernie looked around Shamus's as she waited for Esmeralda to join her. It was a little after one-thirty in the afternoon and the place was just beginning to empty out. She'd chosen it, partly because it was close to the office building Raid Enterprises was housed in, and partly because she'd read a review of it in *Food Works* and wanted to try it out.

Somehow the idea of combining the words, haute, fusion, Irish, and food together in the same sentence let alone the same place seemed somewhat problematic, but—hey—she'd been wrong before and the place *had* gotten a rave review.

Not, Bernie knew, that that meant anything. After all, people had always been trying to bribe her in subtle and not so subtle ways to say good things about their places when she'd been writing restaurant reviews out in L.A. She'd always said no, but that wasn't true of some other people that she knew. Like her ex, Joe, for instance.

Of course, she thought as she ordered a sidecar from the waiter, Libby was right. She could have scheduled this meeting with Esmeralda Quinn in a coffee shop or the equivalent. There was no reason to be eating in a place this expensive. Except that it was fun and the sisters were picking up the check. Plus, Bernie had a feeling that a coffee shop wouldn't have packed the same clout with Esmeralda as this place did. She'd certainly sounded impressed when Bernie had told her where they were meeting.

Bernie was perusing the menu and wondering what thin-sliced maple-glazed corned beef combined with avocado and Indonesian cold slaw served on a bed of radicchio would actually taste like when Esmeralda walked into the room.

Bernie blinked twice.

Esmeralda had certainly done more than a little bit of work in the appearance department since Bernie had seen her at the Raid Estate. She definitely wasn't Miss Dowdy anymore.

For openers, Esmeralda had dyed her hair blond and spiked it up. Then she'd changed her make-up. She was now wearing eyeliner and mascara and a fair amount of blush and lip-gloss.

She'd also lost a lot of weight—probably Atkins or some kind of liquid fast. And her boobs definitely looked bigger. A lot bigger. Bernie had to admit that she looked pretty good in the black slip dress she was wearing. As Esmeralda came towards her Bernie had the oddest feeling that somehow or other she was metamorphosing into Leeza Sharp. But that was ridiculous, Bernie thought. Really silly.

"Wow, you look fantastic," Bernie said to her.

Esmeralda smiled. "Why, thank you. I'm trying."

"Well, whatever you're doing it's working."

Esmeralda smiled again. "I'm sorry, but I can't stay too long," Esmeralda said as she placed a black leather portfolio on the table. "Jura needs me." Then she sat down and began to unzip the portfolio.

A waiter appeared next to her. "I'll just have water," she told him. "No ice and a slice of lemon." Then she opened the portfolio and took out a catalog, and handed it to Bernie.

"You must be very busy," Bernie said to her.

"You have no idea," Esmeralda said. "I'm doing my own job, plus Leeza's. Jura doesn't want to replace her yet. I can understand why, but . . ." And her voice trailed off.

"These things are so hard," Bernie said. "You look as if you could use a drink."

Esmeralda shook her head.

"It'll help you relax a little."

Esmeralda shook her head again.

"Just a little one," Bernie urged. "It's good to go off your diet once in a while."

"I suppose you're right," Esmeralda conceded.

Bernie summoned the waiter and pointed to Esmeralda. "Bring her what I'm having," she told him. Then she said to Esmeralda. "What made you change your hair color if you don't mind my asking."

Esmeralda bit her lip. "You're going to think I'm silly."

"No, I won't," Bernie assured her.

Esmeralda looked away. "Well I did it as an homage to Leeza. I just felt as if I had to do something and then—well one thing led to another. I almost feel as if she's beside me urging me on."

She'd been right, Bernie thought. Very weird. Kind of like some of those tribes that eat their enemies.

"What a wonderful idea," she told Esmeralda.

Esmeralda bobbed her head. "I'm glad you think so. I had my doubts, but Jura seems to think it's a good idea." *I bet he does*, Bernie thought as Esmeralda indicated the catalog with her chin. "I've taken the liberty of circling some of the items you might be interested in. Usually we don't sell retail." She stopped talking as the waiter returned with her drink. Her eyes followed his movements. The moment he set it down she reached over and took a sip. "My, this is good," she said.

Bernie nodded and pretended to read the catalogue.

"So," she said when Esmeralda had taken another healthy sip of her side car, "how is Jura holding up?"

Esmeralda sighed and took possession of the menu the waiter handed her. "He's taking this very hard."

"I'm sure he is," Bernie said thinking of what Marvin had told Libby about Jura's conduct at the funeral.

"He's so grief stricken. He couldn't even bear the thought of a funeral."

"Ah," Bernie said, "I can understand how Leeza's death must have been a terrible shock."

"You have no idea," Esmeralda said. "And now he's relying on me more than ever."

"Well, you seem to be bearing up pretty well," Bernie noted.

"I'm trying," Esmeralda replied. "But it's hard. I feel as if I have to be available to Jura night and day."

Bernie managed not to make the obvious comment as Esmeralda glanced at the menu.

"At least you have the funeral behind you," Bernie said instead.

Esmeralda nodded.

Bernie regarded her for a moment as she took another sip of her drink. "It must be very difficult for you to deal with everyone."

Esmeralda looked startled. "Why do you say that?"

Bernie shrugged. "I've just found from my own experience that in family businesses when something goes wrong with one member of the family it has an impact on everyone else. Everyone is so tightly intermeshed. That's why when there's a fight in a family business it's so nasty."

Esmeralda lowered the menu.

"Well I have to say that Joe and Ditas aren't making things any easier."

"That must be horrible for Jura."

Esmeralda took another sip of her drink. "You can't imagine how terrible. First poor Jura loses his bride-to-be and now his brothers aren't speaking to each other."

"So he must be relying on you more and more," Bernie commented.

"I feel as if I have to be there for him," Esmeralda said as the waiter came by. "He has no one left he can talk to."

Bernie ordered the corned beef special while Esmeralda ordered a hamburger topped with portobello mushrooms and caramelized onions served on two pieces of toasted sourdough bread.

"So why isn't anyone talking to each other anymore?" Bernie asked.

Esmeralda shook her head. "It's nothing important. A business disagreement. It's just that the three of them are so intense."

"That must make your work very difficult," Bernie said.

"I'll say." Esmeralda took another sip of her side car and put the glass down. "I try and keep everything running as smoothly as possible for Jura, but sometimes it's so problematic.

"Jura's brothers don't understand what an enormous amount of pressure he's under. Naturally he's going to be a little sharp sometimes. Even Leeza never understood—though she should have." Esmeralda scowled for a moment.

"So why is Jura under so much pressure?" Bernie asked.

"Because," Esmeralda said, "Jura is the one that determines whether the product he's buying is good or not. The business stands or falls on his palate. It's a terrible responsibility. His brothers just don't have the same ability to taste that Jura does. He really is amazing in that regard."

"Well," Bernie said slowly, "like I just said, family owned businesses can be problematic in the best of times."

Esmeralda looked at her.

"People argue. I know my sister and I do. I've heard instances where brothers and sisters even steal from each other."

"No one would ever do something like that at Raid Enterprises," Esmeralda protested.

Somehow Esmeralda didn't look convinced, Bernie thought as she went on with her lunch.

Chapter 16

Sean shifted the phone from one hand to another as he watched Libby walking around his room and tidying things up. She was like her mother that way he thought. Everything had to be in place, whereas his younger daughter could walk over a pile of laundry that was sitting in the middle of the floor and just keep going.

"That was Bernie," Sean said after he'd hung up.

"So I gathered." Libby removed an empty glass off his nightstand and put it on her tray. "What does she have to say about Esmeralda?"

Sean took a bite of one of the ginger bars that Libby had just brought up for him to try.

"Even more interesting than that," Sean said after he'd swallowed, "is what she has to say about two stores that she visited. Evidently both of them are thinking of discontinuing carrying Raid products because recently the quality has been inconsistent."

Libby set the tray down.

"Stores? What stores?" she asked.

Well that was a mistake, Sean told himself as he watched the edges of his daughter's mouth turn down.

"I thought she was just going to talk to Esmeralda."

Sean began backtracking as Libby put her hands on her

hips and began tapping her foot on the floor. This he knew was not a good sign.

"She was. I think this was a spur of the moment idea."

"Well she better catch the 4:15 out of Grand Central," Libby huffed. "That's all I can say. Amber has to leave by five o'clock tops. Which means I'm going to have to be out front selling instead of in back cooking."

"I'm sure she'll be back in time," Sean reassured her although he thought the odds were that she wouldn't be.

Sometimes, he reflected, talking with his two daughters was like walking through the proverbial minefield. Actually, he'd rather walk through a minefield. At least there, if you paid attention, you could see what to avoid. With Bernie and especially with Libby, who could tell? All this emotion.

When the girls were younger he'd tried to run the family like his unit. So many warnings for talking back or fighting or crying. After five warnings he'd told the girls he'd put them on report. Hey, it worked with his men.

But before he could even explain what being placed on report entailed Bernie had rolled her eyes, Libby had burst into tears, and Rose had just shaken her head and walked back into the kitchen.

Maybe if he changed the subject?

"These bars are excellent."

"I'm using candied ginger from Jamaica. Bree Nottingham said they were too spicy."

"Not for me," Sean remarked.

"You like to eat habañero peppers whole," Libby reminded him.

"That disqualifies my opinion?"

"I didn't say that."

But Sean could see the frown on Libby's face melting. He watched as she went over and began to even up the stack of magazines on his dresser. Then she turned on the window fan. The sound of whirring filled the room. Finally, she came over and plunked herself down on the edge of his bed.

"Bernie could have told me," Libby said.

Sean sighed, started to reach out to his daughter, realized that his hand was shaking, put it back on his lap, and ignored it. Give this friggin' thing he had an inch—he refused to even mention its name. Name something and you called it into existence—and it would take over his whole life. As it was, he realized he'd been paying far too much attention to it over the last three years.

"She doesn't mean to be inconsiderate," Sean explained to Libby for what he was sure was the two hundred thousandth time. "She just gets an idea and goes ahead and does it. She's been like that since she was two."

"I know what's she like," Libby said as she pushed the tray with the glasses away from the edge of the table with the tip of her finger.

Sean watched for his daughter for a moment. She looked halfway between sad and thoughtful.

"What are you thinking about?" he asked.

She shook her head. "Nothing."

"Come on," Sean urged.

Libby sighed. "It's just that . . ."

"Just that what?"

Libby shrugged. "Nothing important. It's just that sometimes I wish I could be like Bernie. You know. Not think things through. I don't know why, I just can't do it."

"And I wish I was a tom cat so I could pee on the police chief's front door. Every day."

Libby laughed. For a few moments Sean and his daughter sat listening to the fan.

Finally Libby spoke. "You know what Bernie said about the stores canceling their orders?"

"Possibly canceling their orders," Sean corrected.

"Okay, possibly canceling their orders. It made me think about what happened in the kitchen when Jura tasted the caviar."

"He stalked off and started yelling at his brothers, correct?"

"Right," Libby replied. "The caviar was pretty bad. Even Bernie said so and she knows better than I do."

"I'd forgotten about that incident," Sean confessed. "I don't know how I could have done that."

He ate another piece of one of Libby's ginger bars. He knew he shouldn't, but they were so good they were impossible to resist.

"This opens up all sorts of interesting possibilities," Sean mused as Libby tucked a lock of her hair back behind her ear.

"Doesn't it though." Libby wiped her hands on her jeans and began picking flour out from underneath her nails. "Maybe someone is switching product around. You know packaging one thing and selling it as something else. Osetra for beluga. Or paddlefish for sevruga."

Last one, Sean vowed to himself as he took a last bite of his ginger bar. "The old bait and switch. It's heart warming to know the old scams never go out of style. The question as I see it is: Where did this happen? In Russia or here? Then the second question would be: How frequently is this occurring? And the third question would be: Who is responsible?"

"I was just thinking," Libby slowly said. "That if this were happening with a certain frequency you could ruin the name of the company, and in this kind of business, your name is your guarantee. If you don't have that, you don't have anything. I mean look at what would happen if I started serving bad food. *A Taste of Heaven* would be out of business in a month. Of course we don't know that this is happening."

"We don't," Sean agreed. "You're right. But for the moment let's assume it is. Then we're back to our first question. Where is this happening? In Russia? Here? Is actual caviar being switched or are empty tins marked Beluga being filled with an inferior product. To do that you'd need to buy the tins."

"Anyone could do that," Libby observed.

"Yes, they could," Sean agreed. "But it would be easier for someone in the company." A picture flashed though his mind of his mother canning tomatoes. "Of course you'd have to have a machine that seals tins. Not that that would be too hard to get."

"They sell them in most big home-store type places," Libby pointed out.

Sean thought about the Raid Estate. The place was enormous. Someone could set up a canning operation there. Hell, someone could put a herd of llamas in the garage and no one would be the wiser.

"But what about the inventory?" Libby asked. "You can't just have extra cans showing up or going missing. They must have a computer program to keep track of that."

"Good point. Which means," Sean said after a moment's thought, "either whoever is doing this is reselling the original product to someone and then refilling the tins, thereby making even more money, or someone in the company is fiddling with the books."

"If it's taking place at Raid Enterprises," Libby said.

"Yes," Sean said. "If it's taking place at Raid Enterprises. But something tells me it is. Something tells me this has to do with the Raid family."

"Why do you say that?" Libby asked.

"Just an old cop's gut talking."

Libby nodded remembering how her father had always known when she'd done something wrong when she was a kid. Then she thought about Jura's expression of surprise when he'd tasted the caviar.

"Well, if it is a family thing I don't think Jura is in on it."

"Which leaves his two brothers."

"Or it could be someone else in the company," Libby pointed out.

"Also true," Sean agreed. "But in the meantime we should go speak to Joe." When he'd run cases he'd liked to start with the principals. For him reading their faces always proved more illuminating than reading a crime scene.

"And Ditas," Libby added.

"Definitely Ditas," Sean concurred. "Definitely Ditas. Almost sounds like the name of a song. I can see someone tap dancing to it."

"Me, too." Libby laughed. Then she broke off a piece of one of the ginger bars and ate it. These are very good, she decided. Using candied Jamaican ginger had kicked them up a notch. "So how does Leeza come into this?" she asked her dad. "After all that's what we're supposed to be investigating, isn't it?"

Sean stroked his chin.

"Maybe Leeza was involved in the caviar scam."

"And he found out and killed her?"

"It's possible," Sean replied. "Not that we have any proof. And she would need other people to pull this off."

"Maybe she was teamed up with Jura's brother Ditas," Libby pointed out. "He seems to have been the only one that cares that she's dead."

"Maybe." Sean wheeled his chair around so it faced the window "Or maybe Ditas was doing it and Leeza found out and was going to expose him to his older brother and he killed her to silence her."

Sean stopped talking. He could see waves of heat rising from the street. Things were too diffuse. He couldn't get his hands around anything substantive, yet. But his gut told him that the more he and his daughters dug, the more likely that they'd find what they were looking for, even if they didn't know exactly what it was yet.

Over the years he'd found that's the way these things proceeded. You just went out and talked to people and got these random pieces of information and eventually they all came together and made sense. He always thought that it was like doing a gigantic jigsaw puzzle. First you made the frame and then started fitting the pieces until eventually you came to the center.

That's why he was going over to the West Vale Country Club this afternoon. To hopefully hear what some of the club members had to say about the Raid brothers. Maybe that would shed some light on the situation.

"What else did Bernie say?" Libby asked when her father didn't say anything else.

"That Esmeralda now has blond hair and implants. Big ones."

"How big?" Libby asked.

Sean blinked. Bernie had said watermelon size but he wasn't going to repeat that to Libby. "Big enough."

"She was all over him at the house," Libby mused.

"So Bernie told me."

"Maybe now that Jura's free she's decided to make a move . . ."

"And," her father continued, "Esmeralda knows that Jura liked Leeza . . ."

"So why not try and copy some of the elements," Libby finished. "After all, they worked before."

"Exactly," Sean said, beaming at his daughter. She was definitely coming along.

"I wonder if she helped Leeza out of the picture," Libby said.

Sean summoned up a picture of Esmeralda in his mind. He'd caught a quick glimpse of her before Fisher had bundled him off. She hadn't struck him as someone who could engineer a booby trap, but that didn't mean anything. Over the years he'd ceased being surprised by the talents people managed to summon up when they needed them.

"She's not on the top of my list," Sean said. "But she's definitely there."

"I don't know," Libby said. "As a motive I think love beats out money any day of the week."

"It certainly equals it," Sean allowed.

Chapter 17

"It's good you got the elevator installed," Marvin told Sean as he loaded Libby's dad's wheelchair into his car. "Libby said it was really tricky getting it put in because the stairs are so narrow."

Sean grunted as he carefully maneuvered himself into the front seat of Marvin's Outback. Marvin stuck his head in the door.

"Here," he said handing Sean one of *A Taste of Heaven*'s takeout bags. "Libby said to give these to you. She said they were for the trip."

Sean peeked inside. Libby had packed a dozen assorted bar cookies in there. Sometimes his daughter was a little much.

"It's only a half an hour drive," Sean said. "We're not going to Alaska."

Marvin shrugged and closed the passenger side door.

"I could have gotten it," Sean snapped.

As Marvin winced Sean wondered how the kid had managed to survive up till now. He'd been here all of five minutes, and Sean was already annoyed with him. He'd been expecting to go with his friend Paul, but at the last minute Paul had gotten hung up in court and had to cancel.

Since Bernie was still down in the city and Libby had to

mind the store, she'd suggested Marvin. Given that he was the only possibility Sean had agreed. He didn't know why the kid rubbed him the wrong way, he just did. Maybe it was because he was always trying too hard. He was always just there. Like a sack of flour. Looking like he'd flinch the moment anyone said boo.

But then Sean reflected he'd never liked the kid's father either. But for different reasons. And there was the fact that Marvin's father wasn't real fond of him. Maybe because he'd caught Bob coming out a motel with one of his neighbor's wives.

But that wasn't why Sean didn't like him, even though he didn't have much use for a man that cheated on his wife. No. It was that Bob had always impressed him as a cold sonofabitch. At least you couldn't say that about Marvin. If anything, he cared too much.

Sean took another gander at Marvin. His glasses were slipping down his nose, and his belly was tugging at his tee shirt. If this guy had to run a mile he'd probably drop dead from a heart attack. He'd never make the force.

Why Bernie was so interested in hooking up Libby with Marvin was beyond him. It's true Marvin was nice enough. And he was intelligent. Admittedly if he weren't, he never would have gone to Cornell. But he didn't know how to hold a hammer or cut down a tree or even replace a washer in a leaky faucet.

Okay, maybe those things weren't that important—it's true you could always hire a plumber or a carpenter—but things just threw the guy. No, Sean thought, he wouldn't want him covering his back out in the field.

On the other hand, Marvin was better than Orion. He wouldn't walk out on his daughter. That was a big plus. But it would also be nice if Marvin weren't such a lummox. He couldn't even get into his car without hurting himself, Sean reflected as he watched Marvin bump his head on the doorframe.

Sean shook his head while he regarded the spectacle of Marvin trying not to wince in pain. Unbelievable.

"So," Marvin said way too brightly for Sean's taste. "Ready to go?"

Sean nodded.

"You know, your daughter is a very good cook," Marvin said as they pulled out of the driveway onto Ash Street.

"Car! Car!" Sean yelled as Marvin almost sideswiped an oncoming Ford Explorer.

Marvin braked and Sean fell forward.

"Sorry," Marvin said.

Sean could see a trickle of sweat working its way down Marvin's forehead. "It's okay," he told Marvin as he silently cursed Paul. "Just watch the road."

"Right. Right," Marvin said and started up the car again.

Sean watched him as he inched out onto the street. "You could go a little faster," he finally said. At this rate they'd get to West Vale tomorrow afternoon.

Marvin nodded and stepped on the gas. The Outback sprang forward.

"Not that fast!" Sean cried as it looked as if the Outback was about to climb up the ass of the Toyota Land Cruiser in front of them.

"Sorry," Marvin repeated as he slowed down.

"Better," Sean said. He leaned back in his seat. It was going to be a long trip. They'd driven two blocks and despite himself Sean kept looking at Marvin. He was griping the wheel so tightly his knuckles were practically white.

He was starting to remind him of a guy called Jitters. Jitters (he never had found out his real name) was a Vietnam vet that had turned up in town one day, stayed for a while, and left. Well, maybe Marvin wasn't as bad. He was still functional. All you had to do with Jitters was yell "Incoming!" and watch him dive to the floor. Some of the guys had thought it was real funny before Sean had put a stop to it.

"You can relax your grip on the wheel," he told Marvin

even though he'd sworn he wouldn't say another word about his driving.

Marvin nodded. Then he turned his eyes toward Sean. "Listen . . ." he began but before he could get any further Sean pointed to the street.

"Concentrate on the road, please."

Nothing annoyed him more then someone who drove and looked at his passengers at the same time. He'd seen too many accidents happen like that. And that was especially true for someone like Marvin whose motor coordination skills were—to be charitable—down in the bottom quarter.

But maybe he was being harsh, Sean reflected. After all Marvin probably wasn't used to talking and driving at the same time. Most of the people he transported were dead.

"You mind?" Sean asked, gesturing to the CD player.

"Not at all." And Marvin reached over and clicked it on.

Strains of a Mozart sonata poured out. *At least the kid has good taste in music,* Sean thought as he turned and looked out the window. He had to give him that.

As Marvin drove through Longely, going exactly thirty miles an hour, Sean thought about how when he was chief of police here he used to know every inch of this town. Every friggin' nook and cranny. But not anymore. There had been a fair number of changes in three years. Some big. Some small.

For example, Dobb's ice cream stand on the corner was gone. They'd made the best coffee ice cream and hot fudge sauce he'd ever tasted. Now a small boutique selling really expensive children's clothes stood there. Then the diner on the corner of the next block was out too.

He'd liked going there in the morning to get bacon and eggs and hash browns. Now the place was under new management and everything there was three times the price. And the coffee. My God what a production. They had five different kinds that changed daily. Who wanted to decide whether you wanted it from Guatemala or Sumatra at seven o'clock in the morning? Not him.

But that was the way it was. All the old places were closing up and being replaced by new, expensive, yuppie stuff. Like hardware stores with fancy garden hoses and fireplace screens that cost three hundred dollars a pop.

If this kept up pretty soon he wouldn't be able to afford to live here. But on the up side the value of the store had gone up. When he and Rose had purchased the place, they'd paid almost two-hundred thousand dollars. Now they could probably get double that. If not more.

Sean snuck a quick look at Marvin as they drove out of town. He seemed to be doing a better job paying attention. When they were almost in West Vale, Sean decided he'd chance some conversation.

"So I heard you were in charge of Leeza Sharp's funeral," Sean said.

Marvin nodded but kept his eyes glued to the road. "Yes, Mr. Simmons."

"It's Sean."

"Okay, Mr. Simmons."

"Sean."

"Right. Mr. Simmons. I mean Sean."

"So tell me about the funeral."

"I already told Libby."

"Well, tell me."

As Marvin pushed his glasses back up the bridge of his nose for what Sean was sure was the tenth time in as many minutes he wondered why he didn't fix them. All it took was a mini screwdriver. Hell, they sold kits to do that in the hardware stores. They were even right by the checkout counters in supermarkets and mini-marts.

Marvin hemmed and hawed.

"Go on," Sean prompted.

"There's really nothing to tell," Marvin said after another moment's hesitation.

"Is this classified information I'm asking you?"

Marvin let out a nervous little laugh.

"No. But there wasn't actually a service."

"Is that normal?"

Marvin bit his lip.

"Well?" Sean insisted. Marvin looked so miserable Sean almost felt sorry for him.

"Not really," Marvin stammered. "Most people have something."

"Something." Sean repeated the word then paused. It was a trick he'd learned when talking to suspects. "Can you think of why Jura didn't have a service?"

"Well, clergy cost money," Marvin blurted out. He put a hand to his mouth. "My father would kill me if he heard me saying that."

"Don't worry about it," Sean told him as he could see the muscle jumping under Marvin's right eye.

Great, Sean thought, *now he's developing a tic and Libby's going to blame me for it.*

Marvin gave Sean a quick glance before looking at the road again.

"He says I shouldn't talk about our clients. He says that it's bad for business."

"That's true," Sean agreed. "Up to a point. But we're trying to solve a homicide here, so I don't think the same rules apply. Do you?"

"No," Marvin stammered. "I guess not."

"I'm glad we're on the same page," Sean said as he watched the twitch under Marvin's eye. "So what happened?"

"Just what I told Libby. There was no viewing. Jura chose an inexpensive casket. It was one of our least expensive," Marvin confided. "He had me dress Leeza up in her wedding dress, and I put a crossbow in the casket and a butterfly pin . . ."

"Butterfly pin?" Sean said. "You didn't say anything about a butterfly pin to Libby."

"I thought I did." Marvin turned to face him.

"Road!" Sean yelled as Marvin started drifting into the oncoming lane.

"Sorry," Marvin said. "I don't know what's the matter with me today."

"No problem," Sean lied.

He took a deep breath and told himself to calm down. He was sorry but Bernie was wrong. The kid was a basket case. The idea of Libby driving around with this guy filled him with terror. His daughter had to be able to do better than this.

"Well, if you did say anything about a pin to Libby, she forgot to tell me," Sean informed Marvin once he was sure Marvin's eyes were on the road.

"It was a small pin," Marvin said.

"Is that strange?"

Marvin shrugged. "Maybe a little."

"How come?"

"Well people usually do that when they're burying people, not cremating them."

"Interesting. Did you put anything else in the casket?"

"No. Just the pin and the crossbow."

"What was the pin like?"

"It was made out of enamel. I don't think it was very expensive. Of course I'm not really that good with jewelry."

"Why do you think Jura did that?" Sean asked Marvin who was slowing down to read the street sign.

"Like I told Libby, most people do it because they want to send along their loved one's favorite things with them into the next life."

"You said most people." Sean pointed to the left. "Go that way."

Marvin did.

"You don't think that was the case here?" Sean asked after they were on Lodi.

"I don't know," Marvin said.

"If you had to say."

Marvin licked his lips. "I really don't know."

Sean stifled his next comment about Marvin not knowing much of anything and reminded himself to be nice. He didn't want Marvin's tic getting any worse. And Bernie and Libby liked him, and he was doing him a favor driving him to the country club.

"If you had to take a guess what would another reason be?"

Marvin considered his answer for a minute. Then he said, "Well getting rid of something would be the only other reason I could think of."

And what better way to dispose of something than by burning it, Sean thought. What better way, indeed.

Chapter 18

Sean was still pondering what Marvin had said when they pulled into the parking lot of the West Vale Country Club. For some reason he'd expected a building with an antebellum facade, but this was some piece of junk. The front was all glass.

"Frank Lloyd Wright's son built it," Marvin explained before Sean could ask. "It's a landmark building."

"It looks like a glass box to me."

Marvin looked slightly scandalized. "It's in all the books."

"Good for it," Sean said as Marvin headed towards a handicapped parking space. He noticed that Marvin's tic was gone. "Park in the second row," Sean told him.

Marvin looked at him. "But . . ."

"Second row," Sean repeated. He was damned if he was going to use those handicapped parking spaces. That was like announcing to the world that he'd lost it. He knew other people would tell him it was stupid to think that way. That convenience was what mattered. But that was too bad. That was the way he felt.

For a moment Sean thought Marvin was going to say something, but he just nodded, kept going, and turned into the second row of cars. At least the kid had some sense, Sean thought. He'd just about to tell Marvin to turn into the parking space on the left when Sean saw a West Vale police car heading towards them.

"Here we go," he said as he made Alex Fisher behind the driver's wheel.

Marvin glanced over at him. "What do you want me to do?" he asked Sean.

"I want you to stop the vehicle and let me handle this."

Sean watched as Marvin put the car in park. The police car kept coming. And coming. He could hear Marvin hyperventilating next to him. He didn't even want to think about what his tic was doing.

"Take a deep breath. Don't worry. It'll be fine," Sean told him.

"Maybe I better back up," Marvin suggested.

"Stay where you are," Sean barked as he watched Alex Fisher close the distance between them.

He wasn't about to let Fisher intimidate him. No way. Still, Fisher wasn't slowing down. Just when Sean thought he'd made a mistake the patrol car squealed to a stop. The vehicles were so close their bumpers were almost kissing. Any closer and they would have been locked. A moment later the door opened and Alex Fisher stepped out.

The man's watched too many movies, Sean thought as he watched Fisher strutting towards them. Who did he think he was trying to impress? If Fisher was putting this performance on for him he was wasting his time. This was strictly stuff for civilians.

Fisher had a big grin on his face as he leaned in Sean's window.

"Snappy driving," Sean told him.

Fisher smirked. "Can't get enough of this town, can you?"

"Apparently not," Sean said. "Anything I can help you with?"

"Yeah. You're on private property." Fisher pointed to a sign on the near side of the lot. "It says: NO TRESPASSING ALLOWED. MEMBERS ONLY."

"I can read," Sean informed him, "unlike some of the other inhabitants of this town. We have an appointment here."

Fisher's smirk widened. "Not anymore you don't. That's been canceled."

"Really?"

"Yes. Really."

"Mind if I call up and ask?"

"Be my guest."

Sean took out his cell and went through the motions even though he knew that Fisher was telling the truth. He wouldn't take a chance on having his bluff called. The guy he was supposed to be speaking to wasn't there. Neither was Paul. *Wonderful*, Sean thought as he dropped his cell into his lap.

Fisher's smirk had turned into an out and out grin.

"So I suggest you gentlemen leave," he informed Sean. "Otherwise I might be forced to run you in for loitering."

"Is that so?" Sean said.

"Yes, it is," Fisher told him.

Sean could feel himself starting to lose it. He hated to be muscled around to begin with, but being muscled around by a fatuous asshole like Alex Fisher was more than he could bear. He was about to ask Fisher how much he was getting paid for doing this when Marvin piped up with, "We're leaving right now, officer."

Fisher nodded towards Marvin. "Now there's a bright boy."

Out of the corner of his eye Sean could see the back of Marvin's neck turn bright red as he turned the ignition key and put the car in reverse.

"I thought I told you not to say anything," Sean said to him once they'd moved a short distance away.

"You did," Marvin stammered. He pushed his glasses back up the bridge of his nose. "And I'm sorry, but Libby would never forgive me if you landed back in jail again."

"I can take care of myself quite nicely, thank you," Sean retorted. He was about to add something to the effect that he'd been doing it for a little over sixty odd years now when he noticed Ditas Raid walking out of the front door of the country club. Maybe he decided the day wasn't going to turn out to be a total loss after all. "Back up a little bit more, and pull in there," he instructed Marvin gesturing to a space in back of him that was flanked by two tall SUVs.

The lot was almost completely filled and Sean was sure that Ditas couldn't see him from where he was standing. Since Fisher's attention was focused on Ditas's approach and the exit path went opposite to where Fisher was standing, Sean didn't think the policeman would catch Marvin's maneuver either. Fisher would just assume he and Marvin had packed up their marbles and gone home like good little boys.

"Why are we doing this?" Marvin asked after he'd done as Sean had requested.

"Because I want to see what Ditas is going to do," Sean explained. He was waiting for Marvin to say something else about Libby not approving at which point he was going to hand him his head, but Marvin surprised him. Pleasantly.

"Cool," he told Sean. "I've always wanted to play detective."

Then Marvin grinned and Sean found himself grinning back. So maybe I was slightly mistaken, Sean found himself thinking. Maybe the guy's not a total loser after all.

The two men watched as Ditas and Fisher talked for a few minutes. Then Fisher got in his police car and took off. Ditas watched him leave before heading for his car.

"What do you think that was about?" Marvin asked.

"I don't know," Sean said. "But it would be fun to ask Ditas." He would have clapped Marvin on the shoulder if he'd trusted his hands not to shake. Instead he said, "Welcome to Beginning Detective Work 101. If you follow my instructions, he'll never know he's being followed."

"My father would die if he knew what I was doing," Marvin commented as both men watched Ditas Raid get into his BMW.

"Then don't tell him," Sean answered as Ditas Raid began

backing his vehicle out of his parking spot. "You're a grown man. He doesn't need to know everything."

Sean could see Marvin thinking over what he'd just said.

"You're right," Marvin finally replied.

Maybe it was his imagination, but it looked as if Marvin was sitting up a little straighter, Sean thought as he coughed and changed the subject. He hadn't meant to get into personal stuff with Marvin.

"The man's got a nice ride," Sean commented as he watched his quarry head for the exit.

"*Car and Driver* rated it in their top five," Marvin said.

"Really?" Sean said. He could feel his pulse start to quicken the way it always had when something was about to go down. He'd forgotten how good the adrenaline rush felt. He hit the dashboard three times. His old signal to move out. "Okay," he said to Marvin. "Here we go."

Sean glanced at Marvin. All things considered the kid was doing way better than he thought he would for his first time out. At least they hadn't crashed into anything yet. Maybe, Sean reflected, he'd just needed to relax a little. Maybe, Sean thought, I was making him nervous before. His daughters kept telling him he scared their boyfriends. He shook his head. He couldn't see it, but maybe they were right.

"Now slow down," he instructed Marvin, "and move over into the other lane. That's right. Always keep at least two car lengths between you and the car you're following when possible. You want to be close enough to see where someone is going but not so close that they notice you."

If Ditas had been looking for a tail, Sean reflected, he would have made them by now, but apparently he wasn't. He was probably too busy listening to his high-end CD player and talking on his cell.

"Where do you think he's going?" Marvin asked Sean.

Sean shook his head. They'd been driving for half an hour now. Fortunately for them Ditas had been using the interstate, which provided them with plenty of cover what with all the vehicles on the road.

"I don't have a clue."

"How much further are we going to go?" Marvin asked. He pointed at the gas gauge. "I'm getting low."

"We're gonna go till we can't go any further," Sean said. He glanced down at his cell which he'd turned off. He probably should give Libby a ring. Then he decided—no. She'll be fine. "You have a problem with that?"

"Not at all, boss," Marvin replied.

"Good." Sean was pleased to see that Marvin's grip on the wheel had relaxed. He leaned over and clicked the CD player back on.

Ten minutes later Ditas Raid went into the exit lane.

"Hang back as long as possible," Sean told Marvin. "Okay. Go now."

"I'm on it," Marvin told him.

Sean could hear Marvin breathing as they followed the BMW down roads that were getting progressively smaller and smaller. The number of cars on the roads got fewer and fewer. Sean sniffed the air. "Cows," he said. A moment later a farm appeared on his left.

"You think he's trying to lose us?" Marvin asked.

Sean shook his head. "He's not driving as if he is."

By now they were bumping down the nearest thing you could get to a dirt road.

"He's got to see us," Marvin said. "We're the only two vehicles on the road."

"You'd think," Sean said.

"Maybe he doesn't care," Marvin said.

Sean nodded absentmindedly as he looked around. The countryside had turned into woods and meadows. He didn't see any houses around, any farms, any signs of human habitation. It was hard to think that this dense country existed just an hour from Longely.

Up in front of them Sean could see wooden fence posts strung with barbed wire. There was a gate. And a sign that read: INWOOD HUNTING PRESERVE. PRIVATE. ENTRANCE PROHIBITED. TRESPASSERS WILL BE PROSECUTED TO THE FULLEST EXTENT OF THE LAW. At least it didn't say trespassers will be shot, Sean thought as he saw the guard shack inside the wire. Some sort of security guard was standing in it.

Cute, Sean thought. Now he knew why Ditas hadn't been paying them any mind. He knew once he got inside the gate there was nothing anyone could do to him.

"Gun it," Sean said to Marvin. They were about fifteen feet away from Ditas's car.

Marvin just looked at him.

"I want to get to him before he gets in there."

"Okey, dokey, boss."

Marvin put his foot down on the gas pedal.

"Not so fast!" Sean yelled as they roared forward at the same time that Ditas stopped.

Marvin applied the brakes. The Outback squealed to a halt. Sean estimated that there was no more than an inch of space left between the two cars, as Ditas got out of the car and came running towards them.

"What the hell do you think you're doing?" Ditas yelled at Marvin.

"He's following my orders," Sean told him as he watched the security guard open the gate and come running towards him as well.

Ditas came around to his side of the car. "Fine. Then what the hell are you doing?"

"I want to talk to you."

"Try making a phone call," Ditas told him as the security guard came up behind him.

Sean noted that he had a holstered 9mm Glock and that his hand was hovering around it. Not that that meant he knew how to use it. Of course you didn't have to at this range. All you had to do was point, release the slide, and pull the trigger.

"Everything all right, Mr. Raid?" he asked.

"Everything is fine."

"You sure?"

Ditas nodded.

"Is the rest of my party here?"

"They came about an hour ago. I'll be here if you need me," the guard said, backing up about a foot or so.

Judging from his stance, the guy's ex-army, Sean thought before redirecting his attention to Ditas.

"Nice ride," Sean said. "How does it do on fuel?"

"Just get on with it," Ditas ordered.

"Okay. I want to talk to you about Leeza Sharp's death," Sean continued.

Ditas gave him a second look. "Now I remember. You're the guy that Fisher arrested at the house, right?"

"Correct."

"The one that the Walker sisters hired to investigate Leeza's death."

"Correct again."

"You're not a delegated officer of the law."

"I used to be."

"But you're not anymore."

"That's true," Sean conceded.

"So that means I don't have to talk to you. You have no legal rights in this matter whatsoever."

"You're correct. I don't," Sean agreed.

"I could call up and have Fisher come down and arrest you."

Sean looked around. "Be a waste of a trip. We're out of West Vale jurisdiction, and I don't think you want to bring the Staties in. It would waste your time."

"And why would I care?"

Sean nodded towards Ditas's car. "Slow your hunting down."

Ditas straightened up. Sean noted that his face was expressionless.

"Get out of here," he told Sean.

"Fine," Sean said. "I was just doing you a favor."

"And what would that be?" Ditas asked.

"I was giving you a chance to talk to me now rather than come to see me in Longely."

"And why would I do that?" Ditas asked.

"Simple," Sean said. "Because you seem to be the only one that gives a damn about Leeza Sharp. When you want to call, my number is in the book," Sean told Ditas. Then he reached down and brought out Libby's bag of cookies. "Cookies," he said. "For you. They're really very good."

Sean noted that Ditas took the bag instead of dropping it on the ground, which he interpreted as a favorable sign.

"Try the ginger bars," Sean advised. Then he tapped Marvin on the hand. "Let's go home," he told him. As Marvin turned around Sean waved at Ditas. "Until later," Sean said. He was interested to see that Ditas kept looking at them till they were practically out of sight.

"What was that all about?" Marvin asked when they were a couple of miles down the road.

Sean stifled a yawn. He felt a nap coming on. God he was getting old.

"Planting seeds," Sean said. "Planting seeds." Then he added, "I hate people like that."

"People like what?" Marvin asked as he turned his eyes away from the road.

"Watch where you going!" Sean yelled.

"Sorry," Marvin said as he righted the wheel, over-corrected, and almost put them in a ditch.

"It's okay," Sean said in his most soothing voice. He wasn't going to have the kid punk out on him now. "I don't like people that hunt," Sean continued once he was sure that Marvin was paying attention again. Fortunately, there was no traffic on the road—if you didn't count the tractor coming towards them. How could the kid be such a bad driver and still be alive? "Correction. People that hunt like that."

"Like what?"

Sean made sure Marvin's eyes were still on the road before replying.

"I'm talking about canned hunting. I'm talking about people who pay big bucks to go in and shoot something down. The people who don't want to get their hands dirty. They might as well just have the animal pose for them and pull the trigger. It demands the same level of skill, which is none.

"I don't know why they don't make these goddamned hunting preserves illegal. They should and they would if the politicians had any guts and weren't getting all their money from people like Jura Raid and his brothers."

"So you're against hunting?" Marvin asked.

"No. I didn't mean to say that," Sean replied. "I have no problem with the guy who goes out in the woods and does what he's supposed to do. I have a problem with people who think they can do anything because they're rich."

Suddenly he felt exhausted. The day had caught up with him. It had been a long while since he'd spent so much time outside. He closed his eyes.

As he drifted off to asleep he couldn't help thinking that the crossbow that had killed Leeza Sharp had probably come from the Raids' hunting preserve. Not that he could get in there to find out.

Chapter 19

"Planting seeds?" Libby said to Marvin. "My dad can't keep a cactus alive."

"I don't think that's what he meant," Marvin suggested.

"I know that," Libby said. Then she looked at the crushed expression on Marvin's face and thought, *I have to be a little less sharp.*

She looked at her watch. Bernie was supposed to have been here twenty minutes ago, but then she'd never known a time when Bernie wasn't late and she wasn't annoyed about it.

"She'll be here soon," Rob said.

He read my mind, Libby thought.

"Nice dinner," he added.

Marvin turned to her. "I don't think you've ever made anything I didn't like."

Libby could feel herself flush. It embarrassed her when people said nice things to her. The picnic had been impromptu but one of the nice things about running *A Taste of Heaven* was that there was always plenty of food around.

She'd simply gathered up some lemon chicken and roasted vegetables, added a potato salad, a green salad, sliced French bread, and several different varieties of fruit tart—all stuff she had on hand at the store—and packed everything in a picnic hamper and that had been that.

And now it was a little after eight o'clock and she, Marvin, and Rob were sitting in the park overlooking the Hudson, waiting for the sun to set. She breathed in the air, which smelled slightly of the river, watched a motorboat making its way downstream, and listened to Rob and Marvin chatting.

Rob, who was sitting across from her, took another sip of his beer. "So how did you get along with the old man?" he asked Marvin.

Marvin pushed his glasses back up the bridge of his nose. "He makes me nervous."

"He makes everyone nervous," Rob said.

"Even you?" Marvin asked.

Rob chuckled. "He would if I were driving him."

Marvin pushed up his glasses. "I nearly had three accidents. In a row."

"I've done worse," Libby confided turning towards him. "Dad used to have this demerit thing when he was teaching me how to drive." She imitated his voice. "That's one demerit. That's two demerits. He made me so nervous that one day I stomped on the accelerator instead of the brake and went right into the front of Mrs. Johnson's store."

"It was years before he'd get in a car with her again," Bernie said as she plopped down next to Rob on the blanket and hugged him. "He told Mom he'd rather bust a crack house than be in a vehicle when Libby was behind the wheel."

"You're making that up," Libby told her.

"Well, maybe a little," Bernie conceded. "Actually I should thank you for doing that. When he taught me how to drive he kept saying, 'Now relax. You're doing fine.' Poor guy. He used to white knuckle it the whole time we were out." Bernie laughed as she took Rob's beer out of his hand and took a sip.

"Hey, drink your own," he protested, taking the bottle back.

"Then get me one," she told Rob. She began playing with

the silver and onyx ring on her finger. "Dad really is a sweetie," she assured Marvin. "He just doesn't want to let anyone know it."

Marvin shook his head. "I don't know."

"You just have to tell him to back off," Bernie said.

Marvin sighed. His shoulders slumped. "That doesn't work with my father," he replied. "It just makes him angrier."

Bernie patted Marvin on the arm. "Well it works with our dad. If you have a good point he'll listen, even if it looks as if he isn't. Anyway, he said he had a good time with you."

Marvin looked dubious. "He did?"

Bernie raised her hand. "I swear. Of course," she reflected, "he also said you were a terrible driver and he'd never get in a car with you again."

Libby interrupted. "Bernie, did Dad tell you what he told Ditas?"

"About coming around to talk to him? Yeah. He told me."

"But why would this guy Ditas do that?" Rob asked as he opened a beer for Bernie and handed it to her. "I know I wouldn't."

"You might. People are strange. They like to talk."

"That certainly covers you," Rob observed.

Bernie whacked him with the flat of her hand and kept on going. "As I was saying, people like to talk, to explain themselves even when it isn't in their best interest to do so. After all, confession is the basis of religion. And psychotherapy. It used to be the basis of most criminal justice systems before they went high tech. Dad was just giving him permission to do something that he wants to do anyway."

Rob smirked. "I like it when you get all intellectual on me."

Bernie snorted. "Everything comes down to one thing with you."

"Which is what you love about me," Rob retorted as Marvin put some more potato salad on his plate.

"It's true Ditas was upset at the cremation," Marvin noted after he swallowed. "But still. Talking to your dad?"

"Ten bucks says he will," Bernie said.

Rob took out his wallet and slapped a ten-dollar bill down on the blanket. "A sawbuck says he won't." He looked at Marvin. "Are you in or are you out?"

"In. I guess."

"Sucker," Bernie crowed as she held out her hand for Marvin's money. "Libby will hold it, won't you?" she asked her.

"That's me. Reliable," Libby said.

Bernie patted her knee. "There, there. I didn't mean to insult you."

"I boosted two lipsticks in tenth grade," Libby confessed.

"I'd forgotten about your criminal career," Bernie said at the same time Marvin said, "You did?"

Libby nodded. "They called my dad and he came and got me. It was awful."

"What did he do?" Marvin asked.

"Nothing," Libby replied. "He just took me home. He said nothing he could do to me was as bad as what I could do to myself. It would have been better if he had hit me."

Marvin lowered his voice. "I stole my dad's BMW."

"You're kidding," Bernie said.

"No. I did. I wanted to go to a concert in New Paltz and he wouldn't let me."

"Did he find out?" Rob asked.

"Oh yeah," Marvin said.

Rob snorted. "Mine gave me a real good whack when he found out I'd taken his truck."

"Mine didn't talk to me for two months."

"I think I'd rather be hit," Rob said.

"I would have, too," Marvin said.

Poor guy. How awful to have someone like that for a father, Libby thought as she watched Marvin shovel another spoonful of potato salad into his mouth. Now would be a good time to change the subject she decided.

"It would be nice if Ditas did come in and talk."

"He will." Bernie took a piece of the lemon chicken Libby had made and bit into it.

"Because," Libby continued, "we haven't turned up much, and the sisters called to tell Dad they're coming in the day after tomorrow to talk to him."

"Boy, I bet that's going to make him happy."

"I think he'd be happier if he had something to tell them."

"I think he'd be happier if he were having a root canal. But he does have things to tell them," Bernie countered.

"Like what?" Libby asked.

"Motives. We got lots and lots of motives." Bernie touched the chicken leg to each finger as she enumerated each item. "We know that the brothers are having business problems. We know that Esmeralda is in love with Jura. We can surmise from what Marvin said about Ditas's conduct at the funeral that he felt something for Leeza. We don't know what that something is yet. But hopefully we will.

"I think we can also surmise from Jura's decisions concerning the funeral that he was really pissed at his bride-to-be—unless the way he treated her body is some kind of weird Estonian ritual, which I'm pretty sure it isn't because I went on the net and checked."

"I don't know," Libby said dubiously.

"When are Eunice and Gertrude arriving on Sunday?" Bernie asked.

"Around four. Why?"

"Good. That leaves us plenty of time."

"To do what?" Libby asked even though she really didn't want to know. She'd sleep better that way.

Bernie smiled. "We're going to the estate tomorrow and try and talk to the household staff and see what else we can dig up."

"It's Saturday," Libby protested. "Everyone will be home. Jura won't let us in."

"You're quite right he won't—if he's there. No one is going to be at home. Everyone is at the hunting lodge for the weekend using big guns to shoot poor innocent furry creatures."

"One of the things I like about you," Rob said giving Bernie's arm a squeeze, "is that you're always so hesitant about giving your opinion."

"And one of the things I like about you," Bernie cooed, "is that you're never sarcastic."

Libby coughed and Bernie and Rob turned to face her.

"But how do you know that?" Libby asked.

"The cook told me." Bernie finished the rest of her chicken and started on another piece. "I called up the house and told the cook I wanted to stop by this Saturday to drop off a thank you present for allowing us to use her kitchen and we got to chatting and she said that everyone was off hunting."

"Then wouldn't the staff be gone too?" Marvin asked.

Bernie nibbled the last scrap of flesh off the chicken leg with her front teeth, deposited the leg in the container reserved for bones, and wiped her hands on a napkin before replying.

"No," she said when she was done. "They get every other Saturday off. Which is good for us."

"But if no one is there," Rob said. "What's the point?"

Bernie reached for a fruit tart. "Someone I was going with once had a job—and I'm not making this up—on this big estate in Montana. The only thing he had to do was drive the owner's Bentley around the property for exactly one mile at eight-fifteen in the morning. Then he brought it back to the door, kept the motor running, and waited for the owner to come out. Not bad, huh?"

"But why?" Rob asked.

Libby picked the slice of kiwi fruit off the top of the mini fruit tart and popped it into her mouth before replying.

"Because that's what the owner wanted," she said after she'd swallowed. "Something about breaking the engine in. The point is: If you're rich no one questions you."

Chapter 20

"You worry too much," Bernie told Libby as the guard buzzed them through the gates of the Raid Estate. "I told you we'd get in."

"They didn't even bother to check and see if we're expected."

Bernie turned the windshield wipers on again. "Why would they? We're caterers. No one gives people like us a second glance. For all practical purposes, we're invisible," Bernie said.

Libby picked off a speck of chocolate icing that she'd somehow managed to get on her white T-shirt.

"Not completely," Libby said, thinking of the guard's reaction to Bernie. He'd spent all the time Bernie had been talking to him staring at her boobs, not that Bernie seemed to care. In fact, she seemed to enjoy it.

"What do you mean?" Bernie asked.

"Nothing," Libby replied as Bernie continued down the road that led to the rear end of the house. "I just thought Jura would have left instructions to keep us out. That's all."

"Why should he?" Bernie asked her sister again. "He didn't know we were coming."

Libby grunted. Bernie looked at her. She was staring out the window.

"Every time we come here it rains," her sister complained.

"Seems to be the case," Bernie agreed.

Again Bernie noted that the farther away from the front they got, the worse the road became. As she parked the van next to the entrance to the kitchen she reflected it was always interesting to see the non-public face of households. It was a little like peeking into someone's bedroom. You got to find out what really went on. In the back of the Raid Estate the grass was overrun with weeds and there were no flowerbeds or specimen plantings. A line of five garbage cans stood up against the outside wall.

"Do you know," Bernie said, "that in Estonia the groom's friends try to kidnap the bride during the bridal procession and the groom has to defend her. How emblematic is that?"

"Emblematic?" Libby asked.

"The word originally meant a raised ornament on a vessel, but now it means . . ."

"I know what it means," Libby snapped.

Instead of asking her why she'd asked then, Bernie opened her door. Over the years she'd noticed that her sister always got snarky when she was nervous.

"Shall we go?"

Libby began working at a cuticle with her teeth. "Dad said we should talk to the shopkeepers."

"That was because we all decided we couldn't get in the estate. And don't worry," Bernie assured her. "We'll talk to the shopkeepers later."

"I still think we should have discussed this with Dad," Libby said. "He's going to be upset when he finds out."

"We're not ten and he'll get over it. Tell me something," Bernie asked Libby. "Why did you come along with me if you feel this way?"

Libby sighed. "Honestly?"

"Yes. Honestly."

"Because I didn't think they'd let us in the gate."

Bernie shook her head in mock dismay. "Oh ye of little faith. Well they did let us. And here we are."

Libby studied the house for a moment before replying. "I still don't think they're going to talk to us. Why should they? They'd lose their jobs."

Bernie pointed to the package of chocolate-chip cookies she'd taken from the store. "That's why we have these along."

"I think you're giving them too much credit."

"Well, cash would be better," Bernie allowed. "Unfortunately I'm short of that commodity these days."

"Fine. But you'd didn't have to take the ones with the macadamia nuts," Libby grumbled. "Macadamias are expensive."

"I'll buy you a jar," Bernie told her.

Libby grunted again.

"Two jars."

"Better."

"That's extortion," Bernie complained.

"Take it or leave it."

"Obviously I have to take it," Bernie told her as she pulled up the strap of her camisole.

Instead of replying Libby opened the car door and got out. The girls walked to the back door. A moment later a young woman answered the door.

The woman was wearing jeans and a T-shirt and her bleached blonde hair was buzzed. As Bernie introduced herself and Libby she wondered how she'd do in a hair cut like that? It was a definite look for sure. Rob would probably hate it though.

When the woman began to speak she had a heavy accent that Bernie couldn't place.

"Estonian?" she asked, hazarding a guess.

I must be right, Bernie told herself as the woman's face lit up and she started babbling away. Bernie was getting one word out of ten when Joe Raid glided up behind them. *Great,* Bernie thought as she ignored Libby's I-told-you-so expression. *Okay. So maybe Dad was right. So much for interviewing the household staff.*

But then Bernie thought: No. Joe Raid showing up like this might not be such a bad thing after all. In fact, it was a good thing. Neither she, her sister, nor her dad had spoken to him yet. This would be a good opportunity to find out a little more about him. Karma at work again. Maybe she should increase her meditation time.

"Yes?" he said.

Bernie pointed to the falcon perched on the leather gauntlet Joe was wearing on his arm.

"Nice peregine," she said.

"That's Maghid." He scratched the back of her neck with his free hand. "I'm beginning her training. So you know something about these birds?"

"I've done a little reading. What made you become interested in falconry?" Bernie asked. "Not many people are."

"I've always been interested in raptors. The idea of joining your spirit with something like this . . . to partake of a pastime that goes back three thousand years." Joe shrugged as a man dressed in a T-shirt and jeans appeared next to him.

"Take her back to her cage," Joe told him. He gave the bird another scratch. "Good-bye, my sweet. I will see you soon."

He stripped the glove off as the man carried Maghid away. "They sense things you know. They sense things that people don't. Now, may I help you?" he asked.

"Yes. We're here to get our pots from the cook."

"Ah."

Bernie watched as Joe took a pack of cigarettes out of the pocket of his shirt, extracted one, lit it, and took a puff. His movements were methodical. The cigarettes were Camels, the lighter was gold. Probably Tiffany, Bernie decided.

As she watched him put his lighter back in his pocket Bernie had the feeling she could strip down naked and he wouldn't care. So either he was gay or unlike his brother Ditas he wasn't, in her mother's phrase, susceptible to female blandishments. Bernie knew that there were some men like that—fortunately she hadn't met too many of them.

Joe blew a cloud of smoke out into the air. "She did not tell me this."

Bernie held out the box of cookies. "We've also come to give the cook a present for storing our stuff."

Joe held out the hand without the cigarette. Bernie noticed that his nails were manicured.

"I will take them and give them to her."

Bernie turned up her smile another couple of watts. "So how is Jura doing?" she asked. She'd always found that when you didn't get the response you want, ignore it and try again.

"Jura?" Joe asked.

"Well all of you really. That was so terrible. On Leeza's wedding day too," she gushed.

"Yes, it was terrible," Joe agreed. "The worst thing imaginable."

But he doesn't sound as if he means it, Bernie thought. *He doesn't sound that way at all. He could be talking about getting a parking ticket.*

"And now with all your business problems."

Joe interrupted. "What business problems?"

She'd definitely struck a chord Bernie thought as she tried to appear reluctant to bring the subject up. "The ones you're having with quality control."

"We have no problems." Joe declared.

"But the store I was at . . ." Bernie put her hand to her mouth and feigned dismay.

"Which store?" Joe demanded.

Bernie gave him the name.

Joe threw his cigarette on the floor and stomped it out with his foot. "Those people are idiots. They know nothing."

"I'm sorry," Bernie said. "I just thought that with Leeza involved in product control . . ."

"You are mistaken," Joe said.

Bernie opened her eyes even wider. Later Libby told her she looked like a grouper.

"She wasn't involved in product control?"

Joe made a *pfsst* noise with his mouth. "That one thought chicken nuggets were good food. She had no palate. The only thing she was good at was spending money."

"Family businesses are always tricky," Bernie chirped, ignoring the puzzled look she was getting from Libby. "I know in our case my uncle and my father were going to buy into their third Arby's franchise together. They had the deal all set and everything and then my uncle's new wife went out and spent the money they were going to close the deal with. They didn't speak for years after that."

"That would never happen in this family," Joe protested in a tone that made Bernie think it already had. "Leeza had nothing to do with the business. Nothing."

"Oh. I thought she was your brother's personal assistant."

"She answered his phone and made his appointments. That was all."

"That's good. Because on my mother's side, my great uncle married his secretary. She was thirty years younger than he was and she convinced him to sign over a big portion of the shares in the business to her and his brothers got so angry. . . . well. Maybe you read about the killing."

Joe shook his head.

"It was years ago. One of them got life. It was terrible."

"I'm sure it was," Joe said, looking bored as he lit another cigarette.

"Maybe we should go and see the cook," Bernie said tentatively as he stood there smoking. "We don't want to take up more of your time."

"I do not know where she is," Joe said.

Bernie showed him the box of cookies again. "Perhaps we could leave these for her in on the kitchen counter."

"You do not trust me to give them to her?" Joe asked.

"No. No," Bernie countered. "It's not that."

"Then what is it?" Joe demanded.

"We need our pots," Bernie said.

"Yes," Libby chimed in. "We're making Swedish meatballs in them for another catering job. In fact, I promised I'd give the cook the recipe for your brother Jura."

Meatballs? Bernie thought. *Where the hell did Libby come up with Swedish meatballs? Especially in the summer. Actually, who ate them at all? Like Jell-O molds, they were strictly a fifties artifact.*

Joe must have thought the same, Bernie decided, as she watched him raise his eyebrows.

"Jura likes Swedish meatballs?" he asked

Libby nodded. "He likes mine. They're really quite wonderful. The meatballs are made of veal, pork, and beef and are flavored with small pieces of lemon peel, black pepper, and a dash of cinnamon, then rolled in flour and very gently sautéed in butter and simmered in a cream sauce."

"It sounds like a recipe for a heart attack to me." Joe flicked his second cigarette onto the floor and crushed it with the heel of his shoe. "Not that it matters since as I have already told you, I do not know where she is."

"Perhaps we can just go in the kitchen and get our pots then?" Bernie asked. "I'm pretty sure I know where they are. It'll just take a second," she added.

Joe was just about to answer when the man Bernie had met in the hall three weeks ago came rushing toward them. Only that time he had a uniform on. Now he was wearing jeans and a T-shirt. The T-shirt made his chest look even bigger. The scowl on his face had grown too. He didn't look like a happy man.

He had introduced himself as Jura's personal assistant, Bernie remembered. What the hell was his name? It was Russian. Bernie clicked her tongue against the roof of her mouth as she tried to remember. Then it came to her. It was Vladmir. Vladmir Myers. Or was it Meyers?

Bernie noticed he stopped short for a second when he saw them before continuing on. Then he came over and whispered something in Joe's ear. Joe nodded and turned back towards them.

"I must ask you to go now," he told Bernie and Libby.

And then before Bernie could think of anything else to say, Joe Raid was shooing them out the door.

"At least it stopped raining," Libby said when they were outside. "But it's sticky as hell. I hate it when it gets this humid."

Bernie grunted and moved her ring up and down her finger. Unlike her sister, she believed in ignoring the weather. Short of a major blizzard she never dressed for it. That, she believed, would be giving in.

"I guess Joe didn't think a whole lot of Leeza," she observed.

"Except for Ditas no one seems to have." Libby started back to the van. "Not even Jura," she added.

"Sex and money," Bernie mused. "Sounds like the making of a classic short marriage to me."

"Well, at least Jura saved on a divorce lawyer," Libby observed.

"Not to mention saving on the funeral," Bernie said thinking of what Marvin had told her. She opened the box of cookies she was carrying, took one out, and then offered the box to Libby. "Did you add coffee flavoring to these?" Bernie asked after she'd taken a bite of the chocolate-chip macadamia-nut cookie.

"Do you like it?" Libby asked.

"It definitely works." Bernie finished the first one and reached for a second. "These are addictive."

Libby grinned.

"You think people will pay five cents more a cookie for them? Otherwise they're not worth making because of the macadamia nuts."

"I would." Bernie broke the new cookie in two and ate it. "What kind of chocolate did you use?"

"Lindt."

Bernie nodded her approval at her sister's choice. "Did you know," she said suddenly, "that chocolate has a melting temperature of between 86 and 97 degrees Fahrenheit? That's why chocolate has such good mouth feel. It really is a miraculous substance," she added as she took another cookie out of the box and ate it. "No wonder the Mayans worshipped it."

Bernie brushed the cookie crumbs off her hands and turned and considered the Raid Estate. "This really is a large place, isn't it?"

Libby nodded.

"Three brothers living in the same house and working in the same business and then this woman walks in the door trailing trouble behind her and everything goes to hell in a hand basket, as Mom liked to say," Bernie mused.

"You're making this sound like one of those old black-and-white movies Dad is always watching on TV," Libby observed.

"When you come down to it, I'm not so sure it isn't." Bernie crossed her arms over her chest and continued to stare at the house. "I wonder who would know if Leeza Sharp was getting part of the business when she and Jura married," she mused.

Libby moved a pebble with the toe of her sneaker. "Maybe Esmeralda. She seems to know all of Jura's business."

Bernie rested her chin on the back of her hand. "I bet Leeza's getting a piece of the action didn't make her happy either."

"Personally, I think it was Leeza getting a part of Jura that made Esmeralda unhappy. I don't think money had anything to do with it."

Bernie tapped her ring against her front teeth. "You may be right," she said.

Libby clutched her chest. "Ohmygod. I'm having a heart attack from the shock."

"Very funny, Libby. Very funny."

Chapter 21

As Libby drove towards the gate, she decided that she was glad to be getting out of this place. The Raid Estate made her uneasy. Bernie would say the place had bad karma, but you could pretty much say that about any place where someone was murdered.

The question was which came first: Was a person killed because the place had bad karma, or did the killing create the karma? Libby was trying to decide when Bernie pointed towards the vee in the road they were coming up on and asked her to bear left.

"I want to take another look at the murder scene," Bernie explained. "As long as we're here it seems silly not to."

"Not to me. Anyway there isn't going to be anything to see," Libby protested. "The police will have swept the place clean."

"I know. I want to see it anyway to make sure I have everything straight in my mind. It'll just take a few minutes."

Libby thought about her to do list. They were already running behind. "If you want to talk to the shopkeepers we need to do that now so I can get back to the store. I have three fruit tarts I have to deliver to Bree Nottingham's house by 7:30."

Bernie looked at her watch. "We have plenty of time."

"No, we don't," Libby countered.

"If you're that concerned about the fruit tarts call Amber and tell her to make them," Bernie suggested.

"She can't do crusts."

"Then have her buy some ready-made ones."

Libby gasped and slammed on the brakes. That was like suggesting she use instant mashed potatoes. "Are you insane?" she cried.

Bernie rolled her eyes. "Sorry. I forgot I was talking to the domestic goddess incarnate for a moment."

"How would you feel if I told you to get your shoes at K-Mart?"

"All right," Bernie said. "You've made your point."

"On top of everything else," Libby added. "I don't think we should just go looking for trouble. Joe Raid won't like us driving around his estate."

"He's not going to know." Bernie indicated the road up ahead. "Once we swing to the right, we're out of sight of the house."

Libby still wasn't convinced. "But what if he's phoned ahead to the gate and they're waiting for us to leave and we don't turn up?"

"So they'll come and find us and we'll leave. Big deal. Anyway, it's not as if we're going to be there that long." Bernie touched Libby's arm. "Please."

Maybe it was the "please" that did it but Libby could feel herself weakening. "Just a couple of minutes?" she found herself saying.

Bernie nodded.

"And you promise you'll help me with the pie crusts?"

Bernie raised her hand. "I gave my word, didn't I?"

Libby sighed as she veered to the right. Bernie reached over and gave her a hug.

"You're the nicest big sister ever," she told Libby.

Libby grunted. She just hoped Bernie was right about Joe Raid not being able to see them.

"Swedish meatballs?" Bernie said as Libby slowed down to go around a pothole.

"Arby's?" Libby replied. "Murder?"

Both girls started giggling.

"Tell me," Bernie asked. "If you were going to pick one of the brothers to go to bed with, which one would it be?"

"None of them," Libby said. "I think they're all creepy in their own unique ways. How about you?"

"Hmmm. Maybe Joe. No. He's really cold although he might be good in bed. There's really something very intense about him. No. I'd have to go with none too."

Libby turned her eyes back to the road. She could tell they were getting nearer the creek from the look of the vegetation.

"Do you remember where the tent was?" she asked Bernie. It all seemed the same to her.

"Not exactly, but Leeza had all those white roses planted around the tent so it shouldn't be hard to find."

"I forgot about those," Libby allowed.

"Maybe we should walk," Bernie said as Libby maneuvered the van around yet another pothole. "I hate to think of getting stuck here now."

Much as she didn't want to admit it Libby decided her sister was right, though walking was the last thing she wanted to do. It was hot and humid. Her T-shirt was sticking to her back. She just knew she was going to get poison ivy or get eaten alive by mosquitoes or catch Lyme disease. She pulled off the road and parked the van under a nearby group of trees. Why did she let Bernie talk her into this kind of stuff she wondered as she killed the ignition. She should know better by now.

Of course she was attacked by bugs the moment she got out of the car. "Can we do this fast?" she asked her sister as she swatted at a gnat.

"Just waiting for you," Bernie told her as she began walking.

Libby could hear the creek off to the left and the call of some birds but other than that everything was quiet. Almost too quiet, Libby decided. She never thought of herself as a city girl, but the quiet out here bothered her, but maybe that was because of the circumstances.

"How far do you think?" she asked her sister, swatting at another flying thing.

"Not very."

As Libby followed Bernie she couldn't help but admire the way her sister managed to pick her way over the roots and loose rocks in her espadrilles. She was tripping over them and she was wearing sneakers. She was such a klutz. Then the next thing she knew Bernie was striding down to the creek bed.

"What are you doing?" she hissed at her.

"Cooling off." And Bernie took off her shoes and walked into the water.

"Stop that," Libby told her.

"Oh, come on," Bernie motioned for her to come down. "It feels great."

"No." Libby felt an overwhelming surge of anxiety mingling with resentment towards her sister. She hadn't wanted to be here anyway and now that she was, she wanted to do what they had to do and get out.

"You really don't know how to loosen up, do you?" Bernie asked her after she'd gotten her shoes back on. "You have to be in control all the time."

"There's nothing wrong with that," Libby shot back.

"Yes, there is."

"What?" Libby demanded.

Bernie opened her mouth and closed it again without answering. Then she turned and marched up the path. For the next couple of minutes neither of them spoke. Which was okay with Libby. Then Bernie turned her head towards her.

"I think the tent is up there."

She took two more steps and stopped. Her shoulders went rigid.

Uh oh, Libby thought as she came and stood beside her sister. It took a moment for her to process what she was seeing.

"It's like someone took a backhoe to the area," she whispered.

"I think some one did," Bernie replied.

Libby looked at the scene in front of her. The path to the house was now partially obliterated. Small mounds of dirt stood here and there. Most of the white rose bushes that Leeza had had planted for the wedding were gone. Some were lying on their sides. Others were buried under piles of dirt. Broken branches and petals were scattered all over the ground. Like wounded soldiers, Libby thought.

Bernie shook her head.

"There must have been twenty rose bushes," Libby observed.

"Well now there are three," Bernie said. She clicked her tongue against the roof of her mouth.

Libby turned towards Bernie. "Why would someone do this?" she asked.

Bernie nodded towards the three pallets full of slate that Libby had somehow missed. "It looks as if they're building a patio."

Libby bit at her cuticle. "Remember when you had that pet guinea pig . . ."

"Gerda," Bernie said.

"And she died when we were away at school and when we got home Mom had thrown out the guinea pig and the cage and the food and everything and you were so angry."

"And then I couldn't stop crying. It was like she'd never existed," Bernie said. "And Dad went to the dump and somehow or other he found her and the cage and brought them back and you and I and Dad buried Gerda in the backyard."

"Mom never liked that guinea pig," Libby said.

"She hated her. She always called her a rat," Bernie recalled.

"I think that's the way whoever's done this feels about Leeza," Libby said.

"Hating something is bad. But it's something. It's better then obliterating it," Bernie said softly.

Libby nodded. Suddenly she felt very cold.

"Are you okay?" Bernie asked her.

"I'm fine," Libby said.

But she wasn't. She could feel her heart starting to beat rapidly. She was having trouble breathing. *I'm having a heart attack*, Libby told herself. Then she thought, *No. I'm having an anxiety attack.*

"Do you want to leave?" Bernie asked her.

Libby shook her head. God, how she hated these things. Why did she let everything get to her? Why wasn't she more like Bernie or her dad?

Bernie put a hand on her shoulder and gave it a squeeze. "Why don't you wait over there," she said, indicating a large maple tree. "I'll be done in a few minutes.

Libby nodded and started towards it. Her head was swimming. But once she had her back against the tree she felt better. Somehow the bark against her skin was soothing. She kept her eyes focused away from where the rosebushes had been, away from where the tent had stood. For a moment she watched as Bernie searched the branches for any evidence that Leeza's killer had left behind.

"Nothing there," Bernie said as she got down and began studying the ground.

Two squirrels captured Libby's attention. One was gray and the other was black. They seemed to be playing tag with one another. *Probably teenagers,* Libby thought. They were chasing each other up and down the trees and around the woodland floor. Then they went up a maple tree, down the other side and disappeared from sight almost in front of her.

Libby wondered where they'd gone. She couldn't see them. It was very puzzling. She started walking over there.

"Where are you going?" Bernie called after her.

"Nowhere." She kept going. Maybe she had rapid onset glaucoma. Maybe that's why she couldn't see the squirrels.

A moment later Bernie joined her.

"Find anything?" she asked her.

Bernie frowned and brushed a tendril of hair off her face.

"No. You were right. It was a dumb idea," Bernie told her. "Especially considering. If there was anything of any interest there that the police didn't find it's not there anymore. What are you doing?"

"There were some squirrels I was watching," Libby stopped. She felt stupid. "I just wanted to see where they went off to." She started to turn. "Let's go."

"No." Bernie was gripping her arm and she had that expression on her face that Libby knew only too well. "Show me where the squirrels disappeared."

Libby walked another ten paces or so. "Here. But why do you care?"

Bernie walked over to where Libby had been pointing. Libby watched her standing there moving her ring back and forth on her finger and muttering to herself.

"I don't know," Libby could hear her saying to herself. "I just don't know. Maybe. It is possible."

Libby joined her. "What are you talking about?"

"It's such a long shot," Bernie said.

"What?" Libby demanded. "What's a long shot?" she asked as the two squirrels she'd been watching seemed to reappear from nowhere in front of them.

Bernie turned and hugged her.

"I love you and your anxiety attack," she said. "And the squirrels."

And with that Libby watched as her sister squatted down and slowly brushed some dirt away with the edge of her palm. Then she stopped, rocked back on her heels, and stared at the spot.

"What are you doing?" Libby asked.

Instead of answering Bernie leaned forward, made a fist, and rapped on the earth.

"It's sounds like you're knocking on a door," Libby said.

Bernie looked up at her. She had a big grin on her face. "It does, doesn't it? Damn, I'm good," she said as she went back to sweeping the dirt away with the flat of her hand.

Libby looked again. She couldn't figure out why her sister was doing what she was. She didn't see anything. And then as she kept staring she realized that the ground did look a little bit different. More solid? Maybe. And the texture was different from dirt. So was the color. Somehow it was more uniform.

Then Bernie was fumbling around.

"Where did that come from?" she asked as she watched Bernie grab hold of something and pull it up.

It was a ring. The ring was brown like the dirt. Libby reflected she could have tripped over it and she never would have seen it. She'd just have assumed she'd stumbled over a tree root.

Bernie moved a little ways back. And pulled. Suddenly the earth began to move.

"Oh my God!" Libby yelled. Then she clapped her hands over her mouth. She couldn't believe she'd just yelled like that.

"Look at that," Bernie said, pointing at the hole in the ground that had suddenly appeared.

"What is it?" Libby whispered.

Bernie chewed on the inside of her cheek for a moment before replying.

"If I'm not mistaken," she said, "and I don't think I am, this is a passageway to the Raid Estate."

Libby took a step forward. The whole thing seemed surreal.

"I bet that's how Leeza's killer got out of the house without being seen," she said. "He just stepped out, called Leeza, then waited for her to arrive."

Bernie stood up and brushed the dirt from her hands and her skirt. "And then he closed the entrance and brushed the dirt over it. Leeza would never have noticed."

"And it was raining," Libby said. "So any footprints would have been washed away."

Chapter 22

"You can stay out here," Bernie told Libby as she moved the cover a little over to the left. "You don't have to go in if you don't want to."

"No. I want to," Libby said.

She could feel Bernie's eyes appraising her.

"Really?' she said.

"Really," Libby replied.

"Because it'll probably be cramped," Bernie warned.

"I'll be fine," Libby told her.

At least she hoped she would be. Even though she was scared to death she had to go. She realized she was tired of being afraid. Anyway, what would she say to her dad if anything happened to Bernie? That she hated the dark? That she didn't like closed in places? She peered down the steps. They seemed really, really steep.

"How did you know about this?" she asked Bernie. "I never would have made the connection."

Bernie was drumming her fingers on her thighs. "Remember right after Leeza's death, Bree Notthingham was in the store and she told us that the Raid house was an exact copy of the estate built in England for Lord . . ." Bernie stopped. She couldn't believe she'd forgotten his name. "Well, you know who I mean."

"Of course," Libby replied. Actually she didn't have the slightest idea.

Bernie snapped her fingers. "Lord Chesterton-Wilkes. Anyway, I knew when Bree was talking about the place that there was something, but I couldn't remember exactly what it was.

"I should have though. It's a well-known fact that lots of those old estates had escape passages built into them. It wasn't an uncommon thing at all. And when you said that thing about the squirrels—I don't know—suddenly everything clicked and I remembered that this was one of the houses that did."

"Is there anything you don't know?" Libby asked her.

"Hmm." Bernie thought. "How to balance my checkbook. How to tell north from south. Stuff like that. Actually," Bernie confided, "the only reason I know is because this guy I was going out with for a while told me about it. Chad was a set designer and he was doing lots of research on secret passages in old castles and manors for a project he was working on. That was the one that slept with his nine-foot Burmese python in his bed by the way."

"I don't think you told me about that one. I would have remembered about the snake," Libby murmured as she considered the stairs. They seemed to disappear into nothingness.

"Anyway, this was one of the houses he was researching. I actually saw blue prints. He'd gotten a copy faxed to him from some library in England. The perks of working in the movies. You could be a secretary for someone at Miramax and everyone bows down and kisses your toes."

"Must be nice." Libby could feel her mouth drying up. She knew that if she could just keep focused on other things she'd be fine. "So where does the passage lead?" she asked Bernie.

"I think into a study on the first floor. But I'm not exactly sure. Reading blue prints is another thing I can't do." Then she added, "Maybe we shouldn't do this now. Maybe we should just go back to the store and tell Dad."

Libby knew Bernie wanted to go down there, that she was saying that because of her. "Just get the flashlight in my backpack," Libby told her.

What did her father say about fear anywhere is fear everywhere. If she didn't start expanding her horizons now, she never would.

"I can get Rob and sneak back in."

"No," Libby said. "I want to."

"Are you sure?"

"I'm not a friggin' basket case," Libby snapped.

Bernie held up her hands. Like she'd said. Snarky. "Okay." And she started for the van.

"And bring back some cookies too," Libby called after her. Something told her she was going to need them.

There were five steps going down. Not as many as Libby thought there would be. But they were slippery and steep. In a way, Libby decided later they were the worst part because you didn't know what to expect. Once she was in the tunnel it was a little easier. First of all there were lights overhead that gave off a very low level of illumination. You still needed the flashlights, but still it was better then none at all. At least if the batteries gave out, you wouldn't be left alone in total darkness.

Just breathe, Libby kept telling herself as she followed behind Bernie. God, was she glad she'd had two flashlights in her backpack. The tunnel was very narrow. If Libby moved her arms away from her sides her fingers touched the walls. The material they were made out of felt cold and a little damp which made Libby think about being underground and about a horror movie she'd seen when she was little about being buried alive.

She could feel her heart start to beat very fast. *No, no,* she told herself. *Think of a field. Think of sunlight.*

She felt Bernie squeeze her hand. "Some of these tunnels go on for miles," she told her. "A lot of them went under moats so when the castle was under siege, the lord and his people could slip out and get away."

For once Libby was glad to hear Bernie chattering away. "Pretty remarkable when you think about the engineering that must have been involved. In fact I heard of one tunnel in a pub somewhere in Wiltshire that connects to a boy's school close by. I bet the guys loved that."

Libby managed to get the words, "I bet they did," out of her throat.

"You and Marvin looked pretty cozy at the picnic." Bernie poked her in the ribs. "He really, really likes you, you know."

"I know," Libby heard herself saying.

"And you're beginning to like him a little too. Come on, admit it," Bernie said when Libby didn't reply. "Well?"

"Okay. Just a little," Libby admitted.

"Told ya you would if you gave him a chance," Bernie said.

"Dad doesn't like him," Libby said suddenly.

"Dad won't like anyone you go out with," Bernie told her.

"Why?"

Libby could hear Bernie laugh.

"Because you remind him of Mom of course.

"He makes Marvin nervous."

"He makes everyone nervous."

Libby cleared her throat. "Marvin doesn't try and kiss me or anything," she found herself saying to Bernie. For once she was glad it was dark. That way Bernie couldn't see her flushing.

"He's just very shy. Maybe you have to make the first move."

"But what if he says no," Libby demanded.

"He won't," Bernie said.

"I would die if he did," Libby replied.

"He's not going to. I'll bet you a facial on it," Bernie said as she played her flashlight ahead of them. "Why would he? He's liked you since you were twelve."

Then all thoughts of Marvin fled as Libby saw a wall.

They were coming to the end of the tunnel. Her heart started beating rapidly again. She began feeling dizzy. "Maybe we should go back," she said.

Bernie patted her on the arm. "It'll be fine," she said. "You'll see."

"But what happens if someone is in there?" Libby whispered.

"I'll open the door very slowly."

"But . . ." Libby began.

"No. We came this far. Let's finish the job."

Libby wasn't sure whether she said the word okay or just thought it but the next thing she knew Bernie was telling her to hold her flashlight higher. Libby watched as she pushed on a door. It made a very loud creak. Libby held her breath. Bernie pushed a little bit more. A ray of light flooded into the tunnel.

Libby closed her eyes. *Please don't anyone be there*, she prayed. If there isn't I'll bring two batches of cookies to the homeless shelter this week. She could hear Bernie opening the door a little bit more.

Then she heard Bernie say, "It's all right."

Libby opened her eyes. Bernie was standing in the opening of the passageway. Then she stepped out into the room. A moment later Libby followed.

"I don't think we've been in here," she said looking around.

The room was much smaller than some of the ones they'd seen and definitely less grand. In fact, it looked like what it was. An office. It looked like a place where people actually did some work, Libby decided.

The walls were painted an off-white and there was light green carpet on the floor. A large rosewood desk and black leather office chair sat in the middle of the room. On it sat a laptop and a printer. There was a phone off to the left and a coffee mug filled with pens and pencils next to that as well as a stack of yellows pads.

On either side of the desk were two wooden file drawers. From what Libby could see, the walls were covered with framed articles about Raid Enterprises. A bookshelf stacked with copies of newspapers and magazines flanked the left-hand wall. Three chairs were placed near it.

Bernie tapped her fingers against her thighs as she looked around the room.

"I wonder if this is Jura's office?"

"Who cares?" Libby replied. "I think we should go. I think we should go right now."

The fact the windows to the right offered a view of the front of the house added to her unease. After all, she reasoned, if she could see out, anyone passing by could see in. Which in this case would be less than desirable. Even Bernie wouldn't be able to talk her way out of that situation.

But instead of heading back to the tunnel Libby was appalled to see Bernie walking over to the desk and sitting down in the chair behind the desk.

"What are you doing?" Libby demanded.

Bernie indicated the filing cabinet. "I thought I'd just take a quick peek through the files."

"You're nuts," Libby hissed.

Bernie scowled at her.

"You're the one that's always talking about efficiency."

"So?"

"So it seems a pity to have gone through everything we did and turn around and leave."

"All we did was walk through a tunnel," Libby was surprised to hear herself saying. "And I was talking about baking three kinds of cookies from the same dough when I was talking about efficiency. I wasn't talking about breaking and entering. Are you going to answer me?" she demanded as Bernie opened one of the file drawers and started going through the files.

"This would go faster if you would take the other drawer," she told Libby without lifting her head. "But you can suit yourself."

Libby tightened her fists. Now, she told herself, was not

the time to lose her temper. She could do that later. At length. Back at the store.

"What do you want me to look for?" she asked between clenched teeth. If she didn't help Bernie they'd be here even longer.

Bernie kept thumbing through the files as she talked. "Anything interesting."

"Interesting meaning what specifically?"

"Meaning anything that seems germane to Leeza or the brothers of course."

"Of course," Libby repeated. She was about to say something else but then she realized that the quicker she got this done, the faster they'd get out of here.

She went and pulled a chair over and began glancing through the files. They seemed to be mostly contracts of one sort or another.

"There's nothing here that I can see," she told Bernie as she opened a folder marked insurance.

Bernie nodded. "I can't find anything either, but keep looking."

Libby did. Everything that she was coming across had to do with household expenses. Everything was itemized down to the last roll of toilet paper. And Bernie thought she was bad about that kind of stuff. But at least he paid his staff a living wage, even if it was on the low end of the spectrum.

Libby had finished the first drawer and was almost at the end of the second one when she heard Bernie say, "I found something."

But before she could ask what she heard footsteps in the hallway outside.

"Damn," Bernie cried.

Libby watched as her sister took the folder out of the bottom file cabinet drawer, and then shoved it closed with the flat of her hand. The drawer slammed shut. Surely the people in the hall had to have heard it, Libby decided about the same time she realized Bernie was speaking to her.

"Come on," her sister was saying. "We've got to get out of here."

Yes, they did, Libby thought.

And she wanted to do what Bernie was telling her. But for some reason her legs didn't seem to be working. Bernie grabbed her arm and yanked. Libby felt her legs begin to move. But she couldn't take her eyes off the door. The voices on the other side of it seemed to be getting louder.

"Now," her sister said to her. "We've got to get out of here now."

"I can't."

"Yes, you can. We have to make Bree's fruit tarts."

Suddenly Libby could feel something in her release. The next thing she knew she was running like hell. Now all they had to do was get off the estate.

Chapter 23

Sean had expected Ditas to show up, but he hadn't expected him to show up so soon. Whatever was bothering him must really be eating him up, Sean thought. It had been what? A little over two days since he'd given him his card. He'd expected him to come by next week. Or the week after.

As Ditas sat down, Sean found himself wishing that the girls were here. He'd like them to see this guy. Get their opinion. They'd gone out to canvass the shopkeepers in West Vale over two hours ago. Allowing for travel to and from the town they should be back by now. Unless they'd run into a chatty Cathy.

For a few seconds he toyed with the idea of calling Bernie on her cell, but decided against it. If something bad happened she'd call him. Anyway, Libby was with her. Which was good. At least Libby had some common sense. And with that thought, Sean focused all his attention on Ditas Raid.

"So," Ditas said to Sean as he watched Amber put a pitcher of fresh-squeezed lemonade and a plate of Hungarian nut cookies out on the table in front of him, "I never thought I'd come see you."

"Really?" Sean said as Amber poured him a glass of lemonade. "That's odd because I was positive you would."

"Why is that?" Ditas asked as Amber poured him a glass of lemonade as well and left the room.

Sean smiled while he considered the approach he was going to take. The thing to remember, he reminded himself, was that this guy wanted to talk. The only thing he had to do was make it possible for him to do it.

Finally Sean said, "Because I have good instincts." Which was a nice general non-threatening statement. Ditas must have thought so too, Sean decided because he took another sip of his lemonade.

"This is really wonderful stuff," he said.

"It is, isn't it?" Sean observed. "My daughter makes it fresh every day."

Ditas nodded and took another sip.

"Ditas, Jura, and Joe," Sean said when he'd put his glass down. "Odd combination of names."

"Well, the first two are Estonian, but when Joe was born my grandmother had died so my parents felt they no longer had to please them. Lucky guy. You can imagine what it was like going to school with names like Ditas and Jura. Me and my brother used to get into fights at least once, maybe twice a week." Ditas leaned over, snagged a cookie, and conveyed it to his mouth. "These are also excellent," he observed.

"Everything my two daughters do is excellent," Sean replied as he studied Ditas's face. He looked tired, Sean decided. "After all, that is why your brother's bride-to-be hired them."

Ditas didn't say anything.

"So why have you come?" Sean asked.

Ditas lowered his eyes and stared at his hands.

"Take all the time you want," Sean told him. "After all, I'm not going anywhere."

While he was waiting for Ditas to speak he snuck a glance at this watch. If Bernie hadn't checked in with him by the time Ditas left, he'd break down and call her.

Finally Ditas lifted his head up.

"I guess you're going to hear this sooner or later," he told Sean.

"And what would that be?"

Ditas fell silent again. Sean waited. He could hear people chatting outside on the pavement. A little girl was asking if she could get a cookie at *A Taste of Heaven.*

"You know," Ditas began, "how sometimes you see something in someone that no one else does? That there's an instant connection between you."

Sean nodded encouragingly.

"Well, that's what it was like with me and Leeza. We just connected." Ditas took another sip of his lemonade. "We started talking. It turned out she and I both had the same taste in music and we liked the same movies. We both thought that *The Wizard of Oz* was the best movie ever made. We both liked Westerns. We both loved cartoons. We both watched the cartoon channel. Jura never goes to the movies. Or a show. Or even reads a book. He's too busy working. Leeza was sweet. Jura didn't see that, really. Most people didn't, but she was."

"Did she like Jura?" Sean asked.

"She liked me better," Ditas replied.

"It must have been an awkward situation," Sean observed neutrally.

Ditas nodded his head vigorously. "It was. It really was."

"But she was going to go ahead and marry your brother despite all of this."

"Yes," Ditas's voice dropped.

"And have this big wedding."

"It was what she wanted," Ditas answered. "She told me she had been planning her wedding since she was twelve. It was very important to her."

"And now she'd found a man that could pay for it," Sean murmured.

Ditas didn't say anything.

"Tell me," Sean asked him. "Did you ask her not to?"

"Not to what?"

"To marry him. Did you ask her to call off the wedding. If she liked you better . . ."

Ditas focused his eyes on a spot above Sean's head. "Not exactly . . ."

"Why not?"

Now Ditas directed his gaze at the floor.

"Why?" Sean repeated thinking that he wasn't going to find the answers he was looking for there.

"It wasn't my place."

"But surely . . . if you cared for her. . . ."

"My brother is blood," Ditas told him. "No matter what, family always comes first."

"I heard that you and your younger brother aren't talking," Sean threw out. "It must make for nice family dinner conversations."

Ditas shifted in his chair. "Family is family."

"And business is business." Sean studied Ditas's face for a moment. Then he said, "Jura could have kicked you out of the business, couldn't he?"

"No. But he could make it hard for me," Ditas admitted. "He is the senior partner."

"I see," Sean said. He took a sip of lemonade after which he reached over and broke one of Libby's cookies in half and ate it. He brushed the crumbs off his hands and his legs. "Tell me," he said suddenly. "Did Jura know you were having an affair with his bride?"

Ditas startled. "I never said I was sleeping with her, never."

"Not in so many words, but, hey . . ." Sean let his voice drift off. "Leeza was an attractive woman. I mean it stands to reason. Unless you have a problem in that area . . ."

"No. No." Ditas hit the arm of the chair he was sitting in with his fist. "Never."

As Sean watched Ditas' face flush, he reflected vanity was a wonderful thing. A man would rather confess to cheating on his brother than admitting that he couldn't get it up.

"So then you did?" Sean asked him.

Ditas didn't say anything.

"What were you going to do after the wedding?" Sean persisted. "Continue?"

Ditas licked his lips.

"At least tell me why you're here," Sean urged.

"I'm here," Ditas said. "Because no one is doing anything about Leeza's death."

"And what would you like me to do?"

"Find the person that killed Leeza and have him arrested."

"And you want to tell me who that is?"

Ditas shook his head. "I don't know."

"I don't believe you."

Ditas licked his lips again. "I've given you all the help I can." And he stood up, turned around, and headed out the door.

As Sean listened to him going down the stairs he pondered the reasons he'd come. After several minutes of doing that he reached for the phone and called Libby. He had a question about Ditas he wanted to ask her, as well as make sure she and Bernie were okay.

They'd been gone a while now and with that van you never knew. It had sounded as if something was misfiring when they'd taken off. He wished they'd get a new vehicle. But once Libby got attached to something, it was hell getting her to get rid of it and get something new, Sean thought as he waited for Libby to answer.

"Is everything all right?" he asked her once she finally did.

"Of course," his eldest daughter replied.

"Because you're late. I was afraid you'd broken down."

"We're fine, Dad. Really."

"Did the shopkeepers have anything interesting to say?"

Sean could hear the slight hesitation in his daughter's voice before she answered, "Absolutely."

Sean frowned. "Like what?"

He wasn't happy when Libby began to hem and haw on the other end. It meant she was lying. "All right," he said. "What are you two up to?"

"Nothing, Dad. Really."

"Tell me," he demanded.

"There's nothing to tell."

"I mean it."

At which point Libby spilled the beans, as his dear departed wife Rose would have said.

Unfortunately.

The older he got Sean reflected, the more he realized that there were certain things he really didn't want to know. Sometimes he wished his oldest daughter were a better liar. It would be easier on his nerves.

Chapter 24

Bernie sighed as she rang the bell to Bree Nottingham's house. The woman had the perfect house, the perfect husband, the perfect life. If Bree ever had a child, Bernie was positive it would be the perfect infant and would poop only perfectly shaped little turds into her perfect diaper. Just thinking about Bree made Bernie want to watch an extreme wrestling match while she chowed down on Twinkies.

Looking at the red roses climbing up the trellis, the ivy covering the trunk of the maple tree, and the antique wicker chair on the porch, Bernie reflected that the whole lot of them looked as if they could have come from the prop department of an Merchant-Ivory film.

Actually, she was surprised that Bree hadn't grown her own organic fruit for the tarts and delivered it to the store in little straw-filled, hand-woven cane baskets. There was, Bernie decided as she juggled the three tarts to keep them from falling, a lot to be said for bad taste.

"You're late," Bree Nottingham informed her when she finally answered the door.

Bernie could tell from the flare of her nostrils that she was annoyed. "I know," she began but before Bernie could tell her why she was, Bree was motioning her into her house.

"Some of my guests have already arrived."

Bernie could see three people sipping margaritas and chatting as she went by the living room. I could use one of those right about now Bernie thought as she followed Bree into the kitchen.

"When I called the store Libby said you were on the way," Bree informed her. "It only takes five minutes from the store to here. You've taken fifteen."

"Thirteen actually." Bernie nodded at her watch with her chin. "I had to get gas," she explained as she put the fruit tarts down on the kitchen table. Formica, of course. Leave it to Bree to be into the whole fifties thing.

"I always fill up my tank when it gets to be half full. That way I don't inconvenience people."

Good for you Bernie thought as she watched Bree reposition one of the pins that were holding up her French twist, a gesture that made Bernie painfully aware of just how messy her hair was.

No matter what she did with it, it always looked bad in the summer. Slick it down with product and it looked greasy, leave it to its own devices and it stuck out all over the place. At least she'd showered Bernie thought, as she looked at Bree immaculate in her linen shift dress. For a little while she'd been thinking she wouldn't even have a chance to do that.

By the time she and Libby had talked their way back out through the gate at the Raid Estate—they'd had to explain that Libby had been overcome with a desire to pay her last respects to the site of Leeza's death—gotten home, listened to her father's ranting about their lack of common sense, and helped Libby with the fruit tarts, not to mention done a stint behind the counter, she'd barely had time to jump in the shower let alone reapply her mascara and eyeliner.

Bernie thought about her father again. He'd been all over them when they'd walked in the door. Apoplectic was the word she'd choose to describe his state of mind if asked. Granted, he'd been worried. But there was no need for him to carry on like that.

They weren't two and four anymore. They were more than capable of handling themselves. Besides, she and Libby had never been in any danger. No one had seen them in the study. They'd managed to get through the door and close it before anyone had come in.

Bernie put the fruit tarts on the table. Hopefully by the time she got back to the store her dad would be in a better mood. Self-righteousness was so unproductive, Bernie decided as she watched Bree inspect the strawberry tart.

"Is everything all right?" she asked Bree, knowing that it wouldn't be.

Because it never was.

Bree was a person for whom no detail was too small to obsess about. In fact, Bernie realized maybe the trick to dealing with someone like Bree was to give them something obvious to criticize right off the bat. That way it would be over and done with.

"I was wondering where the strawberries came from?" Bree asked, interrupting Bernie's train of thought.

"The Stevens' farm."

Bree pursed her lips. "They're adequate, but I think Owens's produce is better, don't you? And the next time it might be interesting if Libby scattered some finely chopped, toasted filberts across the top. For contrast."

The thing that made Bree's suggestions so annoying, Bernie realized as she watched her pat yet another stray lock of hair back into place, was that they were always right. Owens's produce was better and the nuts would add a pleasing crunch.

"Not that it's my place to say this," Bree added. "But I'm a little concerned that Libby will get too involved with your dad's new hobby. I would hate to see the store suffer. You know how she gets."

"Don't worry," Bernie said through gritted teeth.

Bree patted her arm. "One of the things I love about you is the way you always spring to your sister's defense."

One of these days I'm going to tell her what I think of her,

Bernie promised herself as Bree asked, "So has he found anything out?"

"Lots," Bernie lied.

Bree leaned forward. "Tell me."

"I'd love to but I can't talk about it yet. Early stages," Bernie found herself taking a perverse pleasure in saying.

"Poo. How disappointing." Bree flicked an invisible piece of dust off the table top. "But I did hear that you and Esmeralda had a little chat." She smiled at Bernie's expression. "I sold her sister her new house."

"I didn't know she had a sister."

"She has two." Bree pointed to a woman coming into the kitchen. "There's one of them now. I sold her the Kleinman place. It's a perfect match."

Bernie nodded as Bree introduced Jo Ann to her. She and Esmeralda do look alike around the eyes, Bernie thought as Jo Ann took a sip of her margarita. Strawberry from the looks of it, Bernie decided. Only Jo Ann is the prettier one.

"So where do you know Esmeralda from?" Jo Ann asked her.

Bernie was just about to answer but Bree got there first. *As per usual*, Bernie thought.

"She and her sister were the ones that were supposed to have catered Leeza's wedding."

"Ah, yes. Such a tragedy," Jo Ann said.

"Did you know her?" Bernie asked.

"Leeza? I met her a few times when I dropped something off at the office for Esmeralda." Jo Ann tapped the band of her ring against her glass.

And she doesn't look as if she liked her one bit, Bernie observed. It might be interesting to hear what she has to say about her.

"I can't imagine what it was like working in an office with her," Bernie said.

"Well . . ." Jo Ann sighed. "I don't mean to speak ill of the dead but she was a difficult person."

"I'll say," Bernie agreed, remembering Leeza's unending list of demands.

"It was very hard for my sister to see someone waltz in and take over, especially after working so hard for all those years. Men can be so stupid, don't you think?"

"Totally blind," Bernie said, thinking of some of her old boyfriends.

Jo Ann frowned. "Especially when it comes to young women."

"I'll drink to that," Bree put in.

Jo Ann raised her glass. "Me, too." Then she took a hefty gulp. "And that dress Leeza was making Esmeralda wear. . . ." Jo Ann shook her head at the memory.

"It was pretty bad, wasn't it?" Bernie agreed.

"Hideous," Jo Ann said. "Not to mention absolutely unflattering."

"So why did she agree to wear it?"

"How could she say no?" Jo Ann said.

Bernie thought for a moment. "You're right. She couldn't. I remember being in a wedding party and for some reason the bride made us all wear lime-green chiffon dresses that pouffed out in back. My ass looked like a Mack truck. So did everyone else's. It was not a pretty sight. And they were incredibly expensive on top of everything else."

Jo Ann laughed. "So was Esmeralda's."

"Come to think of it," Bernie said. "How come she was Leeza's maid of honor in the first place? It doesn't sound as if either woman was the other's biggest fan."

"No. Esmeralda really didn't like her at all." Jo Ann rang a finger around the rim of her glass. "I can't tell you how tired I got about hearing her complain about Leeza did this and Leeza did that."

"Then why did she agree to do it?"

"Because she's nice."

"Hey, I'm nice, but I'm not that nice," Bernie pointed out. "Wearing a bad dress for someone I don't like. I don't know. It would take a lot to make me do that."

"Actually," Jo Ann lowered her voice, "Jura begged her to do it. Otherwise she wouldn't have."

"She likes him a lot doesn't she?"

"Way too much."

"Women can be pretty dense, too," Bree observed. "Allowing themselves to be strung along. I say time is short. If you're not getting what you want, move on. Exchange that one-bedroom for a loft."

Jo Ann took another sip of her margarita then put her glass down on the table.

"I tried to get her to change jobs once Leeza came along, but she wouldn't. She didn't want to leave Jura, not that she'd ever admit it. Her behavior is so obsessional. I can't even guess at what she sees in him. I mean I know you can't control where your heart takes you, but it's not as if we're talking about Romeo and Juliet here. She's not fourteen." Jo Ann shrugged. "At least she finally got a raise. And, of course, there's the hunting."

"She hunts?" Bernie couldn't control a shudder.

Jo Ann laughed. "I feel exactly the same way. It's barbaric. But my sister is a competitive shooter. Has been for years. She claims it relaxes her. Don't ask me how. Me, I'd take a massage any day. In fact, she met Jura on the rifle range. Worst thing that ever happened to her in my opinion. But then what do I know, right? I'm only her flesh and blood.

"Last year, Jura took her along on the family's annual safari to Kenya or somewhere like that. She was in heaven. Rifle and crossbow. And she insisted on showing me the video. Come to think of it, maybe seeing Leeza with an arrow stuck through her heart wouldn't have bothered her." Jo Ann put her hand to her mouth. "I shouldn't have said that, should I?"

"It's fine," Bernie assured her.

Jo Ann picked up her glass. "I think this should be my last margarita."

"You should stop by our store," Bernie told her.

"Love to." Jo Ann turned to go, then stopped, and shook her head. "Bree, I almost forgot to tell you what I came in here for. Lucy called to tell me to tell you she's on her way." And with that she walked out of the kitchen.

Bernie watched her leave as Bree took the tarts out of their carriers and put them on plates.

"Nice lady," Bernie said.

"Good job, too. She sells annuities. She must make half a mil a year, although I think she could cut back on the booze a little." Bree took another look at the fruit tarts. "Libby's really done an excellent job. Although I'm not sure I agree with the combination of kiwi and blueberries. Visually speaking, peaches and blueberries might have been a better bet."

"The peaches were mealy." Bernie began playing with her ring.

"So what did you think about Esmeralda's boob job?" Bree asked suddenly. Bernie frowned. "Why?"

"Because I recommended the doctor. Do you think they're a little large?"

"Maybe a tad," Bernie allowed.

A slight frown creased Bree's forehead. "I just wish she'd consulted me about the size, but if that's what it takes to raise her self-esteem then so be it."

"Which doctor?"

Not cheap Bernie thought when Bree mentioned one that was in all the fashion magazines.

"Now if I could just get her out of that nasty little apartment in Avalon and into something decent, I'm sure she'd feel so much better. I don't think people realize how much their surroundings affect them. I tell you Esmeralda is almost as cheap as Jura and his brothers."

"I'd hardly call Jura cheap," Bernie objected. "Look at what he was spending on the wedding."

Bree shook her head. "I thought you were savvier."

"How do you mean?"

"First of all," Bree explained, "the wedding was for show.

Jura doesn't like spending money on anything that doesn't impress. And it was probably paid for out of corporate funds."

Bernie thought about how the checks for the wedding dinner had been written.

"I'm right, aren't I?" Bree said.

"Yes," Bernie said. "I think you are."

"Exactly." Bree placed an antique silver pie knife on each plate. "Like the house they live in. Almost all of their out-of-pocket expenses are paid for by their corporation, which includes the house and the staff."

"Isn't that unusual?" Bernie asked as Bree stepped back to admire her handiwork.

Bree moved one of the knives a millimeter to the right. "Not really. You'd be surprised how often it's done. And speaking of moving . . . what about you? The daughter of a friend of mine is leaving for L.A. and she has the cutest little apartment out on Milbrook.

"It's one of those grandmother apartments. A converted garage. It's got the most cunning second floor. It would be perfect for you. You should think about it."

Bernie nodded. "I will," she promised but what she was really thinking about was the fact that Esmeralda liked to hunt.

Chapter 25

Sean studied his daughters. On his insistence they'd come up to his room as soon as they'd finished closing the store, and they didn't look happy about it. He knew that the last thing they wanted to do at this moment was talk about what had happened this afternoon at the Raid Estate. But that was too bad. He'd waited long enough.

Libby was sitting in the armchair while Bernie was perched on the edge of his bed. He took a deep breath. They were his flesh and blood but sometimes he didn't understand them.

He didn't understand them at all. He'd never had this sort of trouble with his men. Ever. He'd always managed to communicate with them. So what was the problem here? What should he be saying that he wasn't?

"Are you calm enough so that we can talk now?" Bernie asked him.

Sean wheeled his chair forward then wheeled it back to where it was.

"I'm always calm."

"You weren't earlier," Bernie pointed out.

"Given the circumstances I thought I was admirably restrained. You two were supposed to talk to the shopkeepers that service the Raid Estate," he told them. "You weren't supposed to commit a felony."

"Was what we did a felony?" Libby replied.

"What else would you call breaking and entering and stealing property?" Sean asked her.

"How about being enterprising," Bernie said.

"Ha. Ha. I'm sure that the judge would allow that as a defense at your trial. That is if you didn't get shot first."

"Hey, we didn't know we were going to discover a secret entrance into the house," Bernie said. "Which turned out to be a good thing. Even you have to admit that. Plus you've always told us to talk to the main players first. We were going to talk to the shopkeepers next. Right, Libby?"

"Right," Libby echoed.

"Don't throw my words back at me," Sean snapped. In spite of being right why did he feel as if he was on the losing end of this discussion? "What if you'd gotten caught? You're already in trouble in West Vale."

"But we didn't get caught," Bernie pointed out. "No one knows what we did."

"That was only pure dumb luck," Sean pointed out.

"It was skill," Bernie insisted.

"No, it wasn't," Sean replied.

"Come on, Dad." Bernie went over and rubbed his shoulders. "Admit it. We did great. For one thing we know now how whoever killed Leeza got out of the house to set off the remote control device without being seen."

"I'm not admitting anything." But Sean could feel himself begin to thaw. That was the problem right there. He could never stay mad at his girls long enough.

"You would have done the same thing in our position," Bernie told him.

"I most emphatically would not."

Bernie leaned over his shoulder. Her hair touched his cheek. "Did you look at the folder we got?"

"Stole."

"Okay. Stole," Bernie allowed.

"Yes," Sean said grudgingly. Originally he'd been going to throw the papers out in the trash as an object lesson to his daughters on the results of their folly, but given the circumstances he didn't have that luxury.

"And?" Bernie said.

Sean didn't say anything.

"They were interesting, weren't they?"

"Mildly," Sean admitted.

"Oh come on," Bernie said.

Even though he didn't want to, Sean had to admit that Bernie was correct. Perhaps he couldn't interpret the fine points of what he was reading, but he could understand enough to get the general gist of the thing. According to what he'd read, upon his marriage Jura was deeding over almost a quarter of his portion of the company to Leeza. As his friend Paul had once said to him, there's nothing stupider than a middle-aged man who falls in love for the first time with a younger woman.

"All right. It's interesting in the light of what Ditas told me while he was here," Sean allowed.

"Well, that's a definite motive," Libby said when her father was finished relating the conversation he'd had with Ditas.

"Yeah," Bernie said. "Jura is giving Leeza all this money because he's gaga over her and then he finds out she's screwing around with his brother. It would piss me off."

Sean made a face.

"What's the matter?" Bernie asked him. "You don't agree?"

"I don't know. It's too neat."

"You like things neat. Remember you always say simple is better."

"Yeah." Sean bit his lip. "But . . ."

"But what?" Libby asked.

"Suppose Ditas is lying to me."

"About having an affair?" Libby asked.

Sean nodded.

"But he was the one that was upset at the funeral." Bernie

pointed out. "He was the one that was upset after Leeza died."

Sean bit the inside of his cheek. "But suppose that's all an act."

"Why do it?" asked Libby.

"Well, if you really don't like your brother, if you hate him, it's as good a way as any to get him in trouble."

Bernie stood up and turned on the window fan. A picture of Ditas glaring at Jura flashed through her mind. But still. . . . "That's a fairly elaborate con."

"I know it is. I'm just exploring all the options."

"It argues a real cold person. Almost pathologically cold."

"Agreed."

"So what makes you believe that about Ditas?" she asked her dad when she'd sat back down.

"I don't know. A feeling in my gut," Sean said slowly. "It's probably nothing but it strikes me that Ditas gave it up too easy. Here's this guy and he comes right up and he tells me with very little prompting on my part that he's having an affair with his brother's girlfriend. I mean that kind of thing makes you look really bad. He doesn't have to tell me squat. Nada. So why do something like that?"

"To make himself feel better?" Libby asked. "You always used to say that confession is good for the soul."

"And you always fell for it," Bernie said to her sister.

"Very amusing," Libby retorted.

Sean ignored his daughters. He drummed his fingers on the arm of his wheelchair. "No. The more I think about it, the more I don't like this whole set up."

"And let's not forget about Esmeralda," Bernie said. "She's apparently in love with Jura, she working for him for all these years, and then Leeza waltzes in and takes over.

"And to add insult to injury, Leeza makes her serve as her maid of honor. Talk about rubbing salt in the wound. Then Leeza dies and she has Jura again, not to mention a raise."

"How do you know about the raise?" Sean asked.

"Bree told me."

"So it's safe to say Esmeralda has benefited from Leeza's death."

"It certainly is."

Sean watched a seagull perch on his neighbor's roof. The damn things were everywhere now. They were the new pigeons. "You don't happen to know if Esmeralda knows how to use a crossbow?"

"Funny thing you should ask," Bernie replied. And she related what Esmeralda's sister had told her in Bree's kitchen.

Sean rubbed his forehead. Instead of getting clearer things were becoming muddier. He needed to clarify.

"Okay," he began. "What do we have? All our suspects have a familiarity with all sorts of weapons. All of our suspects had access to a crossbow. All of our suspects had access to the scene of the crime and all of our suspects had a motive for murdering Leeza Sharp.

"Jura's is jealousy. Or rage at being made a fool of. Ditas could also have been jealous because Leeza was marrying his brother. Esmeralda could have been jealous of Leeza because she wanted to marry Jura. And Joe . . . maybe Joe wants control of the business."

"And don't forget both brothers benefit financially from Leeza not marrying Jura, not to mention the fact that someone is ripping off the business by selling inferior caviar," Libby reminded Sean.

"No. I haven't forgotten. I think we have to narrow things down a little." Sean studied the seagull. The thing had a beak like a razorblade. "For one thing I think it would be helpful if we could get a peek at everyone's bank accounts."

"See if anyone unusual shows up," Bernie said.

"Exactly," said Sean.

"And how are we going to do that?" Libby asked.

Bernie turned to Libby. Sean didn't like the smug expression on her face.

"Easy," Bernie told her. "One of Dad's law enforcement buddies will take a look-see, right Daddy?"

Sean didn't reply. Why had he said anything?

Bernie jumped off the bed. "And you're saying what we did was illegal."

"It's not the same thing."

"Yes, it is. So when *you* do it, it's okay. When we do it, it isn't?"

"Hey," Sean protested, "this is a gray area here." But even to Sean's ears that sounded lame.

"I call that a double standard, don't you Libby?" Bernie said.

"Absolutely," Libby agreed.

"But what I'm doing isn't dangerous," Sean objected as Bernie folded her arms across her chest and stared at her father.

He stared back and was mortified when he turned away first. That never would have happened five years ago. Five years ago he could have stared down anyone on his force.

"I tell you what," Bernie said. "How about we compromise? We'll be a little more careful and you'll be a little less protective?"

"Seems fair," Sean finally said although he wondered about how Bernie would define the concept of more careful. But this did not seem the time to engage in that discussion.

Bernie and Libby were both hugging him when he heard the side door open downstairs. A "hello" floated up the stairs.

Sean looked at his daughters and they looked back at him.

"Oh no," he whispered. "It's the Walker sisters."

Chapter 26

As Bernie watched Eunice and Gertrude settle themselves in the armchairs across from her father she thought that this time, in her humble opinion, they'd gone too far with the color thing. The two of them were sporting flaming orange hair tipped with yellow, purple dresses, and red Converse high top sneakers. It was not a pretty sight.

Maybe, Bernie thought, the English kings and queens knew what they were doing with their sumptuary laws. Maybe commoners shouldn't wear purple. Maybe they shouldn't have access to too many bright colors at once. Just looking at Eunice and Gertrude was causing her visual distress.

"So," Gertrude said as she helped herself to one of the chocolate chip cookies Libby had brought up from downstairs. "I hope you don't mind us dropping by like this."

"Not at all," Bernie lied to cover for her father who couldn't seem to get those words out of his mouth.

"We were in the neighborhood," Gertrude said.

Eunice reached for a chocolate chip cookie. "Which is why we decided to pop up. It seemed silly not to. Especially since we have an appointment down in the city tomorrow. These are wonderful my dear," she said after she'd taken a bite.

"Indeed they are," Gertrude said. "You're almost as good a baker as your mother."

"She's better," Sean said.

Bernie watched Libby give their dad a grateful smile.

Eunice dabbed the corners of her mouth with a napkin. "I suppose you know best, although no one will ever equal Rose's lemon meringue pie. That was a work of art."

Gertrude leaned forward. "But we haven't come to discuss Libby's baking."

"Indeed not," Eunice said. "We've come to find out how the case is proceeding."

"Yes, we're most interested," Gertrude said.

Both sisters looked at Sean expectantly. Like birds looking at a big, fat, juicy worm, Bernie decided.

"Well," her father began, "we are turning up some interesting potential leads. We've found that . . ."

Gertrude lifted up her hand palm out. "What we want to know is: Have you found Leeza's murderer or haven't you?"

Bernie jumped in. "If you let my dad finish, he was just trying to explain—"

Eunice cut Bernie off. "Because we have."

"You have?" Sean, Bernie, and Libby chorused.

"Yes," both Eunice and Gertrude said together. "We believe it is Vladimir Meyers."

"Jura's assistant?" Bernie asked.

Eunice and Gertrude nodded their heads vigorously.

"That's the one," Gertrude said.

"But why suspect him?" Sean asked.

"He's not on our list," Bernie said.

"Well he should be." Eunice punctuated her remark with a bite of her cookie. "It has come to our attention that he had . . . ah . . . relations with Leeza after which he became consumed with jealousy."

"Gee, whatever happened to casual sex," Bernie interjected as her father shot her a warning glance.

"Casual sex as presently constituted is nothing more than the commodification of the female species," Eunice snapped.

"Really?" Bernie said.

"Yes, really," Eunice asserted. "If you read your Marx you would know this."

"And how do you know about Meyers?" Sean asked the sisters before Bernie could reply.

"The cook's daughter told us."

"How do you know the cook's daughter?" Sean asked.

Eunice drew herself up. "I told you we know everyone. She goes to school with one of our nieces. At the University of Pennsylvania."

"No," Gertrude corrected. "Pennsylvania State University."

"I always get those confused," Eunice said.

"Have you spoken to the cook directly?" Sean asked the sisters trying to get the conversation back on track.

They looked at each other.

"We haven't had the time," Gertrude said. "We've been too busy learning how to make sculptures with a chainsaw."

"Chainsaws?" Sean couldn't believe what he'd just heard. "You're using chainsaws?"

"They're smaller now," Eunice said. "Much easier to control."

"I know what they are," Sean replied.

"Good," Eunice went on. "I'm glad you do, but rather than concerning yourself with our artistic endeavors you need to find proof that Vladimir Meyers murdered Leeza."

"I thought you hired me to find out who killed Leeza."

"We just told you who did," Eunice snapped.

"Have you considered the fact that he might not have done it?"

"No. He did," Gertrude said. "We're positive. And we want him brought to justice."

"Because," Eunice said, "if you don't get him, we will."

"Meaning?" Bernie asked.

"Obviously meaning we will take care of the problem ourselves," Gertrude told her.

"But you can't," Bernie protested.

"Of course we can. In other circumstances we would invoke the justice system, but since the justice system in this country is controlled by the capitalist cabals . . ."

"Don't you mean cabal as in singular," Bernie interjected.

Gertrude ignored her and continued on. "To wit, we as the proletariat have the right and the duty to perform this function."

"And how would you do that?" Bernie asked feeling both horrified and fascinated at the same time.

"By any means necessary," Eunice said.

She stood. Gertrude followed.

"We are leaving for Tanzania at the end of the week," Gertrude announced. "So we expect this matter to be resolved by then. If it isn't, we'll want our money back."

"We will expect to hear from you," Eunice said.

Bernie watched as the two women turned and marched down the stairs. "Tell me they're not thinking about doing what I think they're thinking about when they said they'd take care of the problem themselves?" she said to her father after she'd heard the door shut.

"That was quite a sentence," Sean replied. "But yes, I think they might have been talking about killing him."

"No they weren't," Libby objected.

"Then what were they saying?" Sean demanded.

"That they'd take care of the problem."

"And exactly how are they going to do that?" Sean asked when Libby didn't reply.

"Don't be silly," Bernie protested. "Eunice and Gertrude couldn't hurt anyone."

"Maybe," Sean said. "But remember when they thought their neighbor had killed their cat and they rigged the door handle of his car so that he got a shock when he touched it? Or when they were going to make a bomb in their basement and blow up the bank to protest their loan policies towards minorities."

Libby went over and got a cookie. "That was a long time ago," she protested. "They were a little more . . . intense . . . then."

"People don't change," Sean replied.

He massaged his forehead. He should have known better than to have anything to do with the sisters. They were like Mary and her lamb, only wherever they went chaos followed.

Bernie got up and started pacing. "But the bomb didn't go off, and they shorted out the car."

Sean looked up at his daughter. He wished she'd sit back down. Watching her was making his head worse.

"Okay," he said. "So maybe this time they won't get fancy. They'll get real simple and decide to shoot this guy instead. They've won trophies for skeet shooting in case you've forgotten."

"Shooting at a clay pigeon is different than shooting at a person," Bernie retorted.

"With them you never know," Sean said.

"You're just saying that because you don't like them," Bernie protested.

"No," Sean said. "I'm saying that because they're crazy, and you never know what a crazy person is going to do. That's what makes them dangerous."

"Maybe he's right, Bernie," Libby chimed in. "I mean what if they did do something awful."

"They're not going to."

"But what if they do?" Libby insisted.

Bernie moved her ring up and down her finger. "I suppose it wouldn't hurt to cover our bases," she conceded. "What would you suggest?" she asked her dad.

Sean motioned for the phone. "I think it's time to call Clyde."

Libby ate the rest of her cookie. "Why?"

"Hopefully," Sean said, "he's going to make sure that Eunice and Gertrude don't hurt anyone or get hurt themselves." Because calling the cops was out of the question. His dear, departed wife would never forgive him if he did.

* * *

Sean watched Clyde tuck into a piece of Libby's blueberry pie.

"You didn't have to come over," he told his old friend. "We could have talked on the phone."

"And miss the pie?" He patted his stomach. "After all I can't let this shrink down. That'd make my doctor too happy. So, Libby," he gestured towards his plate. "What kind of thickener do you use in your pie?"

"Just a teaspoon of tapicoa. Otherwise the filling gets too gummy."

"Couldn't agree more," Clyde said as he took another bite. "My dear wife puts in five or six tablespoons of flour. Way too much."

Sean took a taste. There was no denying it. The pie was stellar. In his opinion it was the pinch of cinnamon that made it.

"So?" he asked Clyde as he decided that Clyde ate faster than anyone else he knew. "What do you think?"

"About the sisters?"

"Well, I know what you think about the pie."

Clyde put his fork down and dabbed the sides of his mouth with his napkin before speaking.

"Okay," he began. "From what you tell me their comments could be interpreted as a threat. Is it a credible threat? It might be, but then in my experience lots of people make threats and most of them don't carry them out. And Eunice and Gertrude are always running off at the mouth about something or other. Of course they do have those rifles and they are good shots."

"Very good shots," Sean reiterated. "I think it's better to err on the side of caution in this case."

Clyde drummed his fingers on the arm of his chair. "We're talking about covering the sisters for five days at the most, right?"

"That is correct," Sean said.

"And then they'll be out of the country," Bernie interjected, "so we don't have to worry about them anymore."

Clyde nodded. "The problem as I see it is manpower. I can put in a couple of hours trailing around after them and so can a couple of my friends, but they're gonna be times when I can't get anyone on them. Although we are talking about two senior citizens here. They can't be doing too much."

"You'd be surprised what they can do if they put their mind to it," Sean noted.

What had Rose once called them in a moment of absolute exasperation? It had been something like havoc and woe, hadn't it?

"What about using Marvin as a fill-in," Bernie suggested. "Unless we have something like a typhoid epidemic he usually has some spare time on his hands."

The last time he was in a car with Marvin flashed through Sean's mind.

"Why don't we hold him in reserve," he suggested.

Libby's mouth turned down. "Why? He's a good driver."

"No, he's not. We almost got into four accidents in less than an hour."

"You were yelling at him. You made him nervous."

"Okay. Okay." Sean put his hand up to stop Libby from talking. "Marvin can help. If it's okay with Clyde."

Clyde nodded. "It's fine with me."

After all, Sean thought how hard was it going to be to keep tabs on Eunice and Gertrude? Even Marvin should be able to manage that.

Chapter 27

Libby was studying the bunches of zinnias for sale at one of the stands in the West Vale Green Market when her cell phone rang. It was Bernie.

"What do you mean Clyde lost them?" she demanded. Then she lowered her voice as the man in front of her shot her a nasty look and said something to the effect of people talking on cells should be shot. "How could Eunice and Gertrude disappear? It's not as if they're exactly inconspicuous."

"Clyde said he was following them in the mall and they went into the ladies room and they never came out. Or rather, to be precise, he didn't see them when they did. After twenty minutes, he asked a woman to go in and check and they weren't there."

Libby thought for a moment. "I bet they put on wigs."

"I bet you're right," Bernie agreed. "If they had regular brown hair no one would notice them. And maybe they changed their clothes to something a little drabber than usual."

"Which meant they knew Clyde was following them," Libby concluded, glad that it wasn't Marvin that had screwed up.

"And they're not at their residence here," Bernie added. "Clyde already checked. Then he and Dad drove down to the city and schmoozed up the doorman at Eunice's and Gertrude's apartment building. They haven't come back there either. Dad said Clyde is really pissed."

"I'm sure he is," Libby said.

"Serves him right for being overconfident," Bernie said.

"Agreed," Libby said. "So what now?"

"Well, Clyde is going to keep a watch on the Stanford Place in case they come back there and he asked Marvin to keep an eye on Eunice's and Gertrude's apartment building down in the city. I mean they have to turn up sometime, right?"

"Right," Libby said as she dodged around a woman with a stroller. "Although . . ." She hesitated.

"What?" Bernie said.

"Well, they've obviously picked up on Clyde. Maybe they've checked into a hotel."

"That wouldn't be good," Bernie said.

"No it wouldn't, would it?" Libby agreed. "Not good at all."

"Well, let's not think about that at the moment. How are things coming on your end?"

"I'm just about to make contact now," Libby told her.

"And you remember what you're going to say?"

"Every word," Libby told her and she clicked off, dropped her cell in her bag, and plunged into the greenmarket.

Although now that she was actually here, the plan she and Bernie had worked out last night over a pitcher of fresh-squeezed lemonade and about a pound of ginger cookies seemed disingenuous at best. What if the cook didn't come up with the answers she wanted? Then what? How she was going to move the conversation from food to Leeza Sharp?

Of course it had been her idea to try to run into the cook here. She was positive she'd show up at the greenmarket. Why go to the supermarket when you could get wonderful and interesting produce for less? She figured the cook would be here around eleven after the vendors set up because that's when the best stuff was available. After twenty minutes or so of waiting, sure enough there she was, a canvas shopping bag dangling from her wrist, sipping from her cup of coffee.

Libby watched her study the piles of carrots in one of the booths. Her attention was totally focused on the vegetables as she picked up first one bunch of carrots, put it down and reached for the next one.

She looked the way she had the last time Libby had seen her, small and nondescript. Only this time she was dressed in a denim skirt, T-shirt, and sneakers. A baseball cap was perched on top of her head. As Libby moved towards her she noted that her hands and shoulders were out of proportion for her size which made Libby wonder if hers were too from all that chopping and lifting and stirring she did.

"What do you think of these carrots?" Libby pointed towards a small bunch of carrots that were dark red. "Have you tried them? I understand they're sweeter."

The cook looked up and shook her head. "Jura and his brothers are very unadventurous when it comes to food. They'd never eat carrots that color."

"It must make your life boring," Libby said.

The cook shrugged. "A little, but working there beats working in a restaurant any day of the week. So what are you doing here?"

"I wanted to try the goat cheese from Albemare Farms. I hear it's quite good."

The cook pointed to her left. "They're over in the third aisle towards the back. Their feta isn't bad, though it's a little too tangy for my taste."

"So how are things back at the estate?" Libby asked.

The cook sighed. "Pretty much back to normal, except now we have all this construction since Jura decided to build a large outdoor entertaining center down by the creek where the tent was. Silly waste of money if you ask me.

"And the falcons don't like the commotion one bit. Joe said something about moving them to the hunting preserve for the duration. It couldn't happen soon enough to suit me. Beady-eyed little buggers give me the creeps."

Libby picked up a bunch of red carrots and indicated to the seller that she'd take them.

"The Walker sisters said everyone is still very upset. Must make it difficult for you. I've always found people are crabbier when they're emotionally overwrought."

The cook harrumphed. "I don't know why they're saying that."

"They said your niece told them that."

Libby was interested to see the cook's face darkening at the mention of her niece's name.

"You know what college kids are like. They think they know everything."

"Even when they don't," Libby said.

"Exactly," the cook agreed.

"It must be nice to have a niece," Libby continued. "I don't think my sister will ever get married."

"I'll give this one to you," the cook said. "She's a real piece of work."

"She's young."

"Not so young she doesn't know what she's doing."

The cook looked up and motioned for someone to come over. Libby followed her gaze. It was Vladimir. *Damn, what's he doing here*, Libby thought as the cook nodded in his direction.

"She even tried to go after *him.* And then she got mad when nothing happened. And then she got even madder when I laughed. I probably shouldn't have done that, but when I explained why I was laughing she called me . . . well she called me something I don't want to repeat . . . and walked out leaving me to finish prepping for a dinner for twenty people."

"I don't understand," Libby said.

The cook made a derisive sound. "Can't you tell?" she said.

"Tell what?"

"Vladimir is gay."

"No, he's not."

The cook pointed to the man standing near Vladimir. "There's his boyfriend right there. Not that Jura knows about him," she added. "Vladimir would be out on his ass if he did. He doesn't like men that are light in the loafers, if you get my drift."

"Definitely," Libby said as Vladimir came over.

He, his friend, the cook, and Libby chatted for a few moments. Then Libby said goodbye and moved on. She still had to talk to the shopkeepers about the Raid brothers. After all, someone had to do it and Libby had decided it might as well be her. Besides, one of the stores carried the type of almond paste she needed for tomorrow's pear and almond tart.

"Light in the loafers, huh? I haven't heard that expression before," Bernie mused as she watched Libby unpacking the loot she'd scored at the farmer's market. "I wonder where it comes from?"

"Don't know, don't care," Libby said as she regarded the bunches of emerald green arugula she'd just purchased.

Maybe she'd make a salad with the greens, a handful of chopped walnuts, and a sprinkling of parmesan cheese. The arugula looked so perfect she wanted to do something that would highlight the greens' innate spiciness.

Bernie peeled away the broken tip of one of her fingernails. "If what the cook said is true, why do you think the niece said what she did to the sisters?"

Libby wrenched her gaze away from the arugula. "Haven't the foggiest. Maybe Vladimir is bi and he did sleep with Leeza. But then if he is bi he wouldn't be crazed with jealousy when Leeza went off with someone else, would he?"

"No, he wouldn't be," Bernie agreed. "Maybe the cook was lying about his being gay."

Libby considered the possibility for a moment. "I didn't get that feeling," she replied. "Anyway, why would the cook lie about something like that?"

"I don't know," Bernie allowed.

"Sometimes you make things too complicated," Libby observed.

"Maybe I do." Bernie conceded. Her dad always said that simplest is best. She looked at the bunches of stubby, red carrots Libby had just taken out of her shopping bag. "What are you going to do with those?"

"I thought I'd make them into a carrot salad, Moroccan style."

Bernie picked up the bunch and weighed it in her hand. "It's interesting because the first carrots showed up somewhere between the eighth or tenth century in Asia and they were a reddish purple. And here we are going back to the beginning again."

"Indeed." Libby took the carrots out of Bernie's hand broke off the tops and started washing them.

"Did you talk to the shopkeepers?" Bernie asked her.

"Yes. Nothing of interest. The consensus seems to be: The Raids have standing orders placed; they pay their bills regularly; there is very little contact with the staff because the orders are delivered; and they don't tip. Has Dad made any progress so far with the financial stuff?"

"Nothing of any interest. Bree was right. All of the Raid brothers' living expenses are paid out of corporate funds and Raid Enterprises isn't doing so well. Business is down around 30 percent, but then everyone's is down. Except for security firms that is."

"We're not down," Libby pointed out.

"No. We're not, are we?"

"You know what interests me," Libby said as she took a large saucepan, filled it with water, and placed it on top of one of the burners, "is that despite the dip in revenues, Jura spent all this money on the wedding. I would never do something like that. Talk about divisive."

Bernie flicked a speck of dirt from one of the carrots off the counter. "Isn't it though. For all practical purposes, the money for the wedding came directly out of Joe and Ditas's pockets. I mean imagine what you'd feel like if I took all of the money out of our joint savings account—if we had one—and spent it on something for me."

"I'd want to kill you."

"Exactly my point," Bernie said. "And then, on top of everything else, Leeza was an outsider."

Libby gave Bernie a quizzical glance. "Outsider?"

"A non-Estonian. Not one of them."

"So what?"

"Estonians are tight."

"How do you know that?"

"Because it stands to reason. Small groups tend to stick together."

Libby dropped the carrots into the pot and turned on the flame. "I wonder if Leeza's murder was an economic crime instead of a crime of passion?"

"Can't it be both? Money breeds passion," Bernie was saying when her cell rang.

"That was Marvin," she told Libby after she'd clicked off. "He said Eunice and Gertrude still haven't shown up at their apartment and that he's hot, and he's catching the next train out of Grand Central. He also said to ask you if you want to go out later tonight."

Libby could feel herself flushing.

Bernie laughed and hoisted herself up on the counter. "I've said it before and I'll say it again. You're getting to like him."

"No, I'm not."

"You know you are. You're blushing. And if you didn't like him you wouldn't have stuck up for him in front of Dad. Come on. Admit it."

Libby ducked her head. "Okay. You're right. Satisfied?"

"Yes, I am." Bernie began drumming her heels against the wooden cabinets. "Tell me," she said to her sister. "Do you think Esmeralda and Jura were sleeping together before Leeza came on the scene or do you think Esmeralda just had a full on crush on him?"

Libby began slicing up the carrots. "It would be interesting to know."

"Wouldn't it though," Bernie agreed. She jumped off the

counter and went to look for the phone book. "I wonder if Esmeralda's neighbors could provide any info."

Libby kept slicing. "I guess it depends on how nosy they are."

Chapter 28

Libby cruised down Miles Street looking for Esmeralda's address. The last time she'd been here, she reflected, the town had pretty much been Irish and Italian. Now judging from the signs it looked as if it was mostly Latino.

If she had time Libby decided maybe she could stop at a few of the bodegas on the way back and see if they had anything interesting in the way of food. She loved doing stuff like that because you never knew what you were going to find. Like some genuine queso blanco. That would be nice. There was a Sonoran chicken recipe she'd been dying to try, but she needed the cheese to make it work.

As she drove by the houses, she couldn't help reflecting that they looked as if they'd all been cloned. She'd hate to have to come home drunk. They were all four-story brick affairs with concrete stairs with black iron railings affixed to them. Maybe the builder's brother-in-law had owned a brick factory, Libby reflected as she looked for Four Hundred and Thirteen.

According to Bernie, Avalon had been built as a company town to house the workers from the pharmaceutical plant. But then the plant had left for the South and the town had stayed.

Libby glanced at her watch. It was a little after three and

she had to be back at the store in an hour and a half to start work on the dinner party she was catering for Mrs. Burns. That left her not very much time to do what she was going to, especially not if she wanted to do a little food shopping as well.

This was probably going to be a waste anyway, she decided as she scrutinized the numbers on the houses. Most of the people would probably be at work, but when she'd said that her father had pointed out that most investigative work was a waste of time.

You just asked questions, he'd told her and hoped that eventually you got answers that led to something else. Most of the time you didn't. Which was all very nice and everything. Her dad could afford to be philosophical. He wasn't running a business like she was.

Finally Libby spotted the number she was looking for and parked the van almost in front of it. At least there wasn't a parking problem here she thought as she unstuck her blouse from her back. Then she reached into her backpack and brought out a sugar cookie. And this time, thank heavens, she wasn't going into a tunnel.

She didn't know if she could do something like that again. Walking through that passageway had been the totally scariest thing she'd done in a long time. As she ate her cookie, Libby studied the house Esmeralda lived in. The place looked like all the others. The only thing that distinguished it was that someone had chained a dirt bike to the stairs.

Come to think of it, what happened to her bike? It had disappeared from the hallway when she'd been in eighth grade. Probably Bernie had taken it and lost it like she'd lost her charm bracelet, Libby thought as she grabbed her stack of *A Taste of Heaven* menus and her bag of sample muffins.

The faster she got this done, the faster she could get back to what she really needed to do which was wash the sand out of the basil so she could start making pesto for the dinner. She slowly mounted the outside stairs. There was so much humidity in the air it felt soupy. Then she opened the outside door, and stepped into the vestibule.

According to the names on the buzzers, Esmeralda lived on the top floor in apartment one. There were six flats altogether. If this were a movie, Libby reflected, right about now she would be jimmying the door open, going upstairs to Esmeralda's apartment, picking that lock too, and going inside. As it was, she started ringing bells. No one was home. Or if they were they weren't answering. So much for Bernie's brilliant idea.

She turned and weighed her options as she started down the stairs. Go to the van? Try the buildings on either side? Definitely the buildings she decided after a moment. Canvassing them would only take another ten minutes, at the most. Then she could honestly tell her dad and Bernie she'd done as much as she could.

She'd just finished ringing the bells to the building on the left and had started walking towards the building on the right when someone tapped her on the shoulder. Libby spun around.

A youngish girl, complete with multiple piercings and spiked, dyed coal-black hair was staring at her.

"If you're looking for Laci, she's not home," she said.

"I'm not looking for Laci," Libby told her.

"You're not her aunt?"

"I'm not even her relative."

"Then what are you doing?"

"Distributing flyers for my restaurant."

"Really?" The girl took the gum she'd been chewing out of her mouth and dropped it in the street. "Then how come you didn't leave any just now?"

Good question, Libby thought. Now if she could just think of a good answer.

"Are you the social worker?" the girl asked.

"Do I look like a social worker to you?"

The girl looked her up and down. "Yeah, you do. Especially the shoes."

"Well, I'm not." She hated to admit it but maybe Bernie was right about her getting rid of her sandals Libby thought as she opened up her bag of muffins. Perhaps it was time she started wearing heels. "Here. Have one."

"What kind are they?" the girl asked warily.

"All kinds. Blueberry. Chocolate chip."

"I like Dunkin' Donuts blueberry muffins."

"Mine are better. Really," Libby told her.

The girl hesitated. Finally she said, "I'll try the chocolate chip."

"Here." Libby handed her one.

"So what are you really doing here?" the girl asked after she'd taken a bite.

Libby sighed. She was so bad at this stuff. Which was why she usually told the truth. It was easier.

"I'm trying to find out something about a woman."

"Who?"

"No one you know."

"How do you know who I know?"

The girl was right. "Okay it's Esmeralda Quinn."

The girl took another bite of her muffin. "Sure I know her. She's always complaining that Laci plays her music too loud and getting her into trouble. I mean she was bad before, but now with that weirdo guy she was seeing back again, man she's impossible. I mean according to her, Laci should just curl up and die. Who goes to bed at eight-thirty at night? She acts as if she's two hundred years old."

Libby could feel her heart start beating faster.

"What weirdo guy?"

"I don't know. He had a funny name."

"Jura?"

"Yeah." The girl grinned. "Or something like that."

"Does he stay over?"

"Yeah. Is he going to get in trouble, if he did?"

"No," Libby asked. "Why?"

"Too bad. I'd like him to. The guy is a jerk. My mom says people like that get what they deserve anyway, but then she believes in alien abductions too. Can I have another muffin?" the girl asked.

"You can have the bag," Libby told her.

Bernie had just finished waiting on a customer when her cell rang. "So was I right or was I right?" she said to Libby after she'd finished talking.

"Okay. Okay," her sister told her.

"Admit it. I won," Bernie replied.

"You are beyond competitive," Libby shot back.

"Like you're not," Bernie was on the verge of telling her when Jo Ann Quinn marched into the store. "Libby, I gotta go," she told her sister and hung up.

As Jo Ann approached the counter Bernie reflected that she looked slightly hung over from Bree's party last night.

"Hi," Jo Ann said. "I thought I'd take you up on your offer and try your takeout. What do you recommend?"

"The ginger chicken," Bernie said promptly. She could probably eat it every day of the week.

"I'll take a pound." Then she pointed to the string bean salad. "Also half a pound of that if you don't mind."

Bernie reached for one of the take-out boxes as Jo Ann leaned in towards the counter.

"About last night," she said.

"Yes?" Bernie replied as she slipped on her disposable vinyl gloves and looked around for the scoop. Where had Amber put the dratted thing?

"I had a few too many margaritas."

"Don't we all at some time or another," Bernie said.

"When I drink I talk too much."

Bernie measured out the ginger chicken. "So do I."

"I never should have said what I did about Esmeralda, especially to you."

Bernie folded the flaps together and started on the string beans.

"You didn't say anything."

Jo Ann bit her lip. "I shouldn't have talked to you at all. If I'd known what you were doing, I wouldn't have."

"Why not?"

"For the same reason you wouldn't talk about your sister to me if our positions were reversed. I just thought I ought to tell you."

Man, does she have a guilty conscience, or does she have a guilty conscience, Bernie thought after Jo Ann had left.

Sean looked at Libby while she readjusted the fan. At nine o'clock at night it was still seventy degrees outside—way too warm for him. "Did you get the girl's name?" he asked her.

Libby hunched her shoulders up which Sean knew meant no. He hated that gesture. It was like wearing a kick me sign.

"I should have, shouldn't I?" she told him.

He started to say, *damned right you should have,* but changed it to, "It doesn't matter anyway."

Which wasn't exactly true. It did matter. When you wrote up a report having a name to put in it was a necessary thing—in fact, it was the first requirement—but he had to remember he was dealing with civilians. Anyway if he said that to Libby she'd just go all soppy on him and he'd have to spend twenty minutes picking her up and dusting her off.

How he'd raised a daughter as thin-skinned as Libby was a mystery to him. Look at her the wrong way and she turned to mush. But she was better than she used to be, he reminded himself. At least now she didn't begin to sob every time you told her she'd done something wrong.

"I'm sorry," Libby repeated. "I just—"

Sean cut her off. "It's fine. Let's go over what we do know."

Libby's shoulder's came down a notch.

"You start," Sean told her.

"Well, we know that Esmeralda was sleeping with Jura before Leeza came along."

Sean nodded approvingly.

"And we know that Leeza took her place," Bernie said as she came in and handed her father a Cosmopolitan.

Sean took a sip. He'd rather have a beer but, hey, he wasn't going to look a gift horse in the mouth as it were.

"And we know that Esmeralda got a raise when Leeza died." Libby added.

"And we pretty much know from what the girl Libby talked to said that Jura's back in Esmeralda's bed again," Bernie said.

"Maybe he's just sleeping there," Sean suggested.

Bernie rolled her eyes. "Yeah. No doubt because Esmeralda's apartment is so nice that he prefers staying there than in his, what, million-dollar home? Of course he went back to her—she's there."

"It's true. Men always go back to the familiar when they can," Sean conceded.

"Conservation of effort," Bernie said.

"Isn't that a law of physics?"

Bernie laughed while Sean tapped his fingers on the armrest of his wheelchair. "In any case I think it's safe to say that for Esmeralda nothing but good comes out of Leeza's death."

Bernie twirled a lock of hair around her finger.

"And everything bad comes out of Leeza being alive."

"Sounds like a strong motive to me," Sean said.

"Me, too," Libby agreed.

"I wonder if she's involved in that caviar scam?" Bernie mused. "It would be interesting to find out."

"But doing that would be hurting Jura, wouldn't it?" Libby exclaimed.

"Exactly," Bernie said. "How does the song go? You always hurt the one you love."

Sean took another sip of his drink, even though it was a little sweet for his taste. "I've changed my mind. I'm beginning to like Esmeralda for Leeza's murder. I'm beginning to like her a lot."

Chapter 29

Bernie pushed a strand of hair off her cheek as she looked at the store she was about to enter. She just hoped Ernie was correct about this place because her feet were killing her. She didn't know what she was thinking of wearing her three-inch pink wedges when she was going to be pounding the pavements in New York. Whoever thought that detective work was glamorous or fun obviously hadn't done any.

But at least this time she'd had enough sense to check the temperature before she'd caught the train down into the city. The forecast had said it was going to be in the nineties so she'd put on her light beige silk-slip dress, which was the closest she could get to not wearing anything without getting herself arrested.

The store was located directly off of Canal Street, a little way out of Chinatown. "Ernie, please be right," Bernie whispered out loud. Ernie who was one of her ex-boyfriends, now made a living as a professional poker player and moved in the demimonde as the French liked to say. According to him this place sold, what he so euphemistically called "recycled luxury goods" and other people called stolen merchandise.

The store certainly didn't call attention to itself, Bernie reflected. In fact, the place looked as if it were abandoned. The windows were half-covered with newspaper and the glass that was showing was so dirty Bernie had to squint to make out the words *Novelty Items* written in gold lettering on the window.

Unopened cardboard cartons were piled next to the door. The door itself had no name or number on it. Unless you knew where you were going you'd never find the place. She just hoped that this scheme would work.

Okay, here we go, she said to herself as she straightened her shoulders and pushed the door open. Hopefully she'd find out who was selling caviar off the books. Her dad hadn't come up with anything yet. Maybe she could. Anyway, she figured it was worth a shot.

A blast of frigid air greeted her as she stepped inside. The place felt like a meat locker. She didn't need a sweater she needed a parka she reflected as she rubbed her shoulders to keep them warm. And a flashlight wouldn't hurt either.

The guy must have a 10-watt fluorescent bulb in the overhead fixture Bernie decided as she threaded her way through stacks of shipping cartons with Chinese characters on them and around buckets designed to catch drips from the ceiling.

She wondered how much the owner of the place was paying off the building inspectors to keep this place open, as she approached the man standing behind the counter. Tall and gaunt, he was wearing a black turtleneck sweater. Very appropriate for a ninety degree New York summer day. But it wasn't the sweater that got to Bernie, it was the mutton chop whiskers. She was hoping this wasn't a new guy facial hair style; goatees were bad enough. He lit a cigarette and took a puff.

"Yes," he said.

"I'm looking for something," she said. "Maybe you can help me."

"Everyone is looking for something," he replied.

Cute. This guy's seen way too many French movies, Bernie thought as she watched him take another puff of his cigarette. Then he stubbed it out in a large ashtray that was overflowing with other slightly smoked cigarettes. Piles of what Bernie took to be invoices were stacked up beside it.

"I'm trying to quit," he explained as he followed her glance.

Bernie watched as he shuffled the papers together and put them under the counter.

"I take two puffs and put it out," he continued.

"Is it working?" Bernie asked.

"Not very well," the man admitted. "Now what are you looking for?"

"I'm catering a party next week."

The man inclined his head. "Mazel tov."

"And I'm looking to buy some caviar for it."

"Caviar is always good."

"And I was told you sell some here."

"Who told you this?"

"Ernie."

The man eyed her up and down. "You don't look like someone Ernie would know."

"I used to go out with him."

The man nodded and lit another cigarette. "I guess he hasn't exactly come up in the world since then."

"I guess he hasn't. He said to call him if you want to check."

The man waved his hand in the air. "Not necessary. Why come here?"

"I understand your prices are very good."

"Best in town," the man allowed.

"I'm interested in five pounds of Caspian beluga from Imperial Enterprises."

The man inclined his head. "Your people have good taste."

"Yes they do. But what I really want," Bernie continued, "is to set up a regular account here."

She watched as the man nodded. His head looks as if it's on a spring Bernie thought as he said, "Very nice."

"Because my associate and I are thinking of offering it as a regular item on our menu and we do volume." Bernie took out the onc of the cards she'd had made up and gave it to him, although she had a little trouble doing that because her fingers were getting numb.

The man held it up to the light and read it out loud. *"Sophie Castle. DJM Enterprises. Classic Elegance for Your Event. Able to Handle Parties from 20 to 2,000. Competitive Rates. Call 212-472-3838.* So Sophie why haven't I heard of you before," he said as he put the card down on the counter.

"I don't know." Bernie put on her best imperious stare. "We were mentioned in *Vogue* last month."

The man lit another cigarette and took a puff. "I don't read *Vogue*."

Bernie leaned forward. "I don't care what you read. We're moving into this market and what I want to know is can you supply me on a regular basis?"

"I don't see any problem."

"Like I said, I'm talking large volume. Beluga. Caspian. From Imperial."

The man grimaced. "Specifying companies makes it trickier."

"That's your problem, not mine."

"I'm not sure I can do that."

Bernie shrugged. "Fine. Then I can go somewhere else. I have two other places on my list."

The man looked at her. "I have to make a call."

"And while you do that I'd like to see the cooler you store the caviar in."

"Why do you want to do that?"

"To make sure the product is properly stored. I don't want to pay for something we can't use."

"I don't have a cooler," the man said.

"Then how do you guarantee quality? This product has a very short shelf life."

"I know what it has. I get it directly from the distributor and then I send the shipment directly to you in specially prepared coolers."

Bernie silently thanked Ernie for his information—never mind that it had cost her two hundred bucks—while she shook her head. "That's not good enough."

"Then what do you want?"

This is it Bernie thought. She took a deep breath and let it out.

"I want to meet with the person you're getting it from and ascertain your delivery method."

"That's not the way he works."

Bernie shrugged. "Well that's the way I work."

The man thought for a moment. Then he said, "What if I have him call you?"

Bernie managed to suppress her smile.

"That might be sufficient."

"Good." The man tapped the card Bernie had given him. "This number?" he asked.

Bernie nodded. Ernie had supplied the phone as well. She hadn't asked where it came from and he hadn't told her. "And then we'll discuss price."

"You've had a busy day, Miss Ace Private Detective, what with going down to the city and sleuthing around and all," Rob was saying to Bernie as she took a long lick of her chocolate-chip-mint ice cream cone.

"That's Ms. Ace Private Detective to you," Bernie told him.

They were sitting on a bench over by the Arctic Freeze eating ice cream. It was a little after nine and Bernie was watching a mother and father lead two ice cream gobbling pajama clad little kids back to their SUV and remembering how her parents used to do the same thing when she and Libby were young.

"Did you know that ice cream cones made their debut at the 1904 St. Louis World Fair?" Bernie asked Rob.

"Doesn't everyone know that?" Rob asked tucking into his vanilla. "So you think this guy is going to call you?"

"Absolutely." Bernie nibbled on a piece of the chocolate. Chocolate and mint were, she decided, an inspired combination.

"How can you be sure?"

"Why wouldn't he? He wants to do business. Tell me, why do you always get vanilla?"

"When I find something I like I stick with it," Rob explained.

Bernie cocked her head. "Is that true with everything?"

Rob grinned. "Talk about leading questions."

Bernie was about to reply but just then the cell Ernie had supplied Bernie with went off.

"See," she said to Rob as she fished it out of her bag. "Like I said. No one can resist me."

But evidently they could because when she answered the person on the other end clicked off.

"Damn," Bernie said, "I think whoever was calling recognized my voice."

Rob took another lick of vanilla. "That's not a good thing."

"It doesn't matter." And she pressed the menu button until she got to Calls Received. "See." She handed the phone to Rob. "I have the number right here."

"But you can't trace it," he told her.

"That's true." She licked a dribble of ice cream off the side of her palm. "I can't. But my dad can."

Chapter 30

As Libby darted a glance back at the large bulge under the red and white-checkered tablecloth in the back of the van a drop of sweat made its way down her nose. If she felt this hot she could only imagine what Bernie and Rob were feeling curled up underneath thc tablecloth, a plastic tablecloth at that.

Where the hell was the cold front the weatherman had promised would arrive this morning? she wanted to know. It was already a little after two o'clock in the afternoon for heaven's sake, and it was just as hot as it had been yesterday. No. It was hotter.

"We're almost at the gate," Libby told Bernie and Rob.

Bernie popped her head out from the tablecloth. "Thank God. I feel like a steamed clam."

"What if the guard won't let us in?" Libby asked her sister.

"That's why we have the bolt cutters. Keep your eyes front," Bernie instructed.

"Right." *Don't blow this*, Libby told herself as she refocused her attention on the road. "I hope Marvin's all right," she whispered.

"He'd better be," Bernie said. "Otherwise I won't be able

to kill him. Or you. Now stop talking. Remember you're supposed to be the only one in the van."

"I remember," Libby replied.

It had to say something about the Raid family that both of their residences were guarded, Libby decided as she approached the checkpoint that signaled the entrance to the hunting preserve. Then she went back to contemplating Marvin. Or rather his phone call. She glanced at her watch. It had only been an hour ago, but it seemed like a lot longer.

What the hell had he been thinking of she asked herself for the tenth time since she'd answered the phone. That he'd found Eunice and Gertrude was good. But what had ever possessed him to hide himself inside the trunk of Gertrude and Eunice's car? She'd really like to hear his explanation, but she was going to have to wait until she found him since his cell was apparently out of commission. Or he was. But Libby decided not to think about that possibility.

"I'm here at the Raids' hunting lodge," he'd whispered like he was some newscaster on CNN giving a live update. "I've just gotten out of the trunk of the Walker sisters' car and from what I can see everyone is here."

"What are you talking about?" Libby had asked.

"Jura, Vladimir, Joe, Ditas, and Esmeralda are here. They and Eunice and Gertrude are going target shooting. I'm going to see if I can get closer and hear what they're saying."

Then the line had gone dead and that had been that. She'd always thought of Marvin as being super cautious and now he was turning into 007. It was bad enough her sister was crazy, Libby thought bitterly. She didn't need Marvin acting like a lunatic, too.

And she didn't even want to think about what Gertrude and Eunice were doing here. A spot of skeet shooting? A spot of Vladimir shooting? And while she was on the subject, why hadn't Clyde's men picked up the Walker sisters, for heaven's sake? They were supposed to have been watching them.

"You're getting overemotional. He didn't say he needs

help," Bernie had pointed out when Libby had gone running into the kitchen to tell her about Marvin's call.

"Just because you don't ask for something doesn't mean you don't need it," Libby had retorted. "We got him into this mess, we should help get him out."

"We don't know he's in a mess," Bernie had argued. Miss logic.

Libby had slammed the ladle she'd been holding down on the cutting board. "Let's see. He's trespassing. He's in a place with armed guards and lots of guns. The Walker sisters are there. So are four people who could or could not be responsible for another human being's death. Am I missing something?" She'd held up her finger. "Oh, yes. I forgot. The Walker sisters might be there to shoot Vladimir Meyers."

"Then let's call the police," Bernie had suggested.

"And say what? That there's a trespasser on the grounds of the Raid hunting compound?"

"Exactly."

Libby could feel herself getting angrier and angrier. "Wonderful choice. Marvin calls for help and I get him arrested. He'll probably never speak to me again."

Bernie grinned.

Libby wanted to slap her. "This has to do with fairness."

"If you say so."

"I do. Oh never mind. Don't help me. I'll do this myself."

Bernie held up her hand. "No you won't."

Libby contemplated her sister. "You don't think I can, do you?"

Bernie put her hands on her hips. "I don't think anyone can do this by themselves. And I'm doing this for the same reason you went through that tunnel with me—even though you thought it was a bad idea."

"Are you sure?" Libby had asked her.

"I'm positive." Bernie reached in and took a handful of blueberries from the colander in the sink. "I'll find the article with the floor plan of the estate and call Rob, while you get Amber and Googie in here. And for God's sake, don't tell Dad."

"Believe me, I won't," Libby had told her.

So now she, Bernie, and Rob were riding off to rescue someone who was, according to Bernie, probably fine. And if everyone died, Libby thought, it was all going to be her fault. Okay. They wouldn't die. They'd get arrested. But Bernie had come up with a plan. Libby had to give her that.

"It'll work," Bernie had said. "After all, if it worked for the Trojans it should work for us. In times of trouble always consult the Greeks."

"Right," Libby had said. "Doesn't everyone?"

So there they were. Libby, dressed in one of Bernie's camisoles and a mini skirt, was going to drive the van loaded with muffins and sandwiches and cookies to the guard post and claim that Eunice and Gertrude had called her and asked her to deliver the order.

Hopefully, the guard would let her in at which point she'd go inside the hunting lodge to talk to the sisters while Rob and Bernie, who'd been hiding in the van, would slip out and start looking for Marvin. As she stopped the van in front of the guard post, she hoped that Bernie's luck rubbed off on her instead of the other way around.

Remember to smile, Libby told herself as she watched the guard approach. She took a deep breath and said to the guard with as much assurance as she could muster, "Eunice and Gertrude Walker asked me to come by."

The guard looked down at his clipboard and told her she wasn't on the list.

"What do you mean?" Libby cried indignantly. Channel Bree Nottingham when you do that Bernie had told her. "I came all the way out here. I have to be on the list."

"Well ma'am, you're not."

"Check again," Libby ordered. "Eunice and Gertrude Walker told me they had taken care of it."

"They didn't," the guard declared.

Even though it felt ridiculous Libby made her lips go into a pout per her sister's instructions. "I can't believe they forgot."

"Well, they did," the guard told her. "I'm going to have to call it in."

"Go ahead," Libby told him. She smiled despite the fact her heart was beating so loudly that she was sure he could hear it. "But this was supposed to be a surprise lunch for Jura and the rest of his party." She opened up the box containing the chicken salad sandwiches she'd made to show him. "And I don't think the sisters are going to be too happy having their surprise ruined. You know what they're like when they don't get their way."

The guard wrinkled his nose. "Do I ever."

Libby turned the voltage up another notch. "Please," she entreated.

The guard bit his lip. "I don't know."

"Look at me," Libby commanded. "Do I look dangerous to you?"

The guard grinned. "Not in that kind of way. Go on."

Libby felt absurdly pleased with herself as she drove through. Maybe Bernie is right, Libby decided. Maybe you never should underestimatc the power of a tight top and a short skirt.

Bernie threw the tablecloth cover off of her and Rob's heads and wiped her forehead with the back of her hand. She felt as if she'd just come out of a sauna. She didn't want to think about what her hair looked like. She could probably do a passable imitation of Medusa right now.

"You did great," she told Libby as they drove towards the hunting lodge. "Just great."

"I did, didn't I," Libby replied.

Even though Bernie couldn't see Libby's face, she could tell from the tone of her voice that she was smiling. "Now just keep everyone talking for the next three-quarters of an hour while Rob and I search the house. When we're ready to go we'll call you."

Libby nodded. "We've already gone over this."

"You have your cell set on vibrate?" Bernie asked as she whacked Rob for snickering. "Two rings when we're ready, one ring if we have a problem. You know," Bernie added, "Marvin is probably hitchhiking back to town."

"Then we would have seen him," Libby shot back. "There's only one road in or out."

"Maybe he already got a lift," Bernie countered.

"Then why hasn't he called?"

"Because his cell is dead."

Libby just grunted.

Because she doesn't have a good reply, Bernie thought as the van jounced along. Five minutes later the van rattled to a stop. Libby turned and gave the thumbs up sign as she gathered up supplies. Bernie watched her open the driver's side door. A moment later she heard two raps on the side of the van, the agreed upon all clear signal.

Bernie opened the rear door and she and Rob jumped down and ran along to the side of the building. "God, this place is big," she whispered as she spotted the side door.

Somehow when someone said log cabin, Bernie always pictured a *Little House on the Prairie* type of deal. But this lodge was big. Not Rockefeller big, but large enough.

When they got to the side door, Bernie took a deep breath, put her hand on the door knob and pulled. It gave.

"I hope it's not alarmed," Rob said.

"Me too," Bernie replied. She didn't want to say it never occurred to her that it would be. After all, why should it be, really? Not with guards patrolling the place. That would indicate full on paranoia. Then she thought about Jura and decided maybe the door had been alarmed after all.

Well, she'd find out soon enough. She stepped inside. Rob came after her. The place was air-conditioned. Which was good. If she were going to get shot at least it should happen in comfort.

"Tell me again what we're going to say if we run into anyone?" Rob asked.

"We're going to say we came in with Libby, and that my dad called and wanted to talk to Eunice and Gertrude, and that we went looking for them."

"And you expect people to believe that?" Rob asked. "What about the guard?"

"The guard must have missed us and yes I do expect to be believed. People always believe me."

"Why?"

"Because I'm so cute." And Bernie motioned for him to come on.

Her father always said that you had to have Plan A, Plan B, and Plan C. *Well,* Bernie thought, *what I have is really half of Plan A.* She just hoped they ran into Marvin soon because she had no idea what they were going to do if they didn't find him.

She closed her eyes and tried to visualize the layout of the lodge as pictured in the magazine article in *Design*. The top floor contained bedrooms, while the bottom floor was made up of—if Bernie remembered correctly—the coatroom, the living room, dining room, den, music room, weight room, sewing room, as well as the kitchen, pantry, laundry room, and heaven knows what else.

And of course there was the greenhouse, not to mention the indoor/outdoor area where Joe's falcons were kept when they were in residence here, and last but not least the gun room, which according to the article Bernie had read had equipment for everyone from eight to eighty. Eight-year-olds hunting? Now there, Bernie decided, was a truly scary thought.

The question was: Where the hell was Marvin in all of this? Even a small hint would have been helpful. But since that wasn't going to happen Bernie decided to try another tack. She closed her eyes, took three deep cleansing breaths—

why was it always three she wondered?—and tried to visualize Marvin in all his rotund splendor.

"What are you doing standing there like that?" Rob hissed at her.

Bernie opened her eyes. "Trying to feel Marvin's energy."

Rob slapped his forehead with the palm of his hand. "Why didn't I think of that? Hey, maybe what you're doing can replace a GPS system."

"Hey. Just give me half a minute."

And Bernie closed her eyes again. Her teacher had always told her that the way to find something is not to look for it. Which sounded really helpful until you got into a situation like this. Bernie took another deep breath and tried visualizing the hunting lodge, but for some reason she kept on seeing sheep. Maybe she should start doing her prostrations again she thought as she opened her eyes.

"Okay," she said. "Let's go to the left."

"That's where Marvin is?"

"Yes," she lied. "That's where Marvin is." What the hell. There was a fifty percent chance she was right.

Fifteen minutes later Rob was saying to Bernie, "Admit it, you don't have a clue where Marvin is," as they were walking down the hallway on their way to the media room.

"I admit it," Bernie said. So far they'd been in the den, the weight room, the sewing room, the library, and two bathrooms, and if Marvin was there, he was invisible. Further, there was no sign that he had been in any of the places they'd been through—that of course being too much to ask. "This is ridiculous," Bernie added. The size of the lodge combined with the quiet was giving her the heebie-jeebies. "For all we know, he could be eating lunch with the Jura, Ditas, Joe, and the Walker sisters in the gazebo at this very minute."

Rob frowned. "Gazebo? Why a gazebo?"

"Why not a gazebo? They have them on English estates."

"How could I have forgotten?" Rob tucked his sunglasses

back in the front of his T-shirt. "He could also be a prisoner, you know."

"Yeah, *Design* just forgot to include the plans for the dungeon in their floor plan. I understand they're all the rage these days."

"I'm serious."

"So am I." Bernie held up her hand. Were those voices she was hearing? "Do you hear anything?"

"Oh yes," Rob said.

Bernie watched him look around for somewhere to hide. "The closet," he said.

But when he opened the door, it was full.

"We're not going to fit in there," Bernie mouthed. *Think. Think*, she told herself. And suddenly she remembered. The room where the falcons were kept was a couple of feet away. She hesitated for a moment, but then she decided the birds couldn't be that bad—it wasn't like she was going into a cage of man-eating lions.

She motioned for Rob to follow her. The voices were getting closer. Jura and Vladimir from the sound of them. *Well on the bright side, at least we know Vladimir is still alive,* Bernie thought as she reached the door. Without pausing, she flung it open and stepped inside with Rob following on her heels.

The falcons all turned their heads. *They're looking at us like we're lunch,* Bernie thought. Maybe this hadn't been the best choice she decided as one of the scenes from Hitchcock's *The Birds* flashed through her mind.

This is not good she told herself. Always maintain an optimistic attitude when possible. Maybe they just didn't look friendly because of the way their beaks curved. If she recalled correctly their name was derived from *faix* which in Latin which meant sickle, a word choice no doubt having to do with the shape and sharpness of their beaks. Not very comforting when you thought about it.

"Did you know that only the females hunt," Bernie whispered to Rob. "The males are called tercels."

"No, I didn't know and I don't care," he whispered back.

As Bernie looked at Rob it struck her that although both she and he were backed up against the far wall the front side of the cage, which was composed of wire, was facing the outside. Anyone walking around the left side of the building could see them.

"We have to get out of here," Rob mouthed pointing to the outside.

"I know," Bernie mouthed back.

But there was nowhere to go. From the sound of their voices Jura and Vladimir were getting closer. She looked at the falcons again. They were clicking their beaks. That didn't seem like a good sign either, not that she knew much about avian habits.

"Good birdies," she cooed. She did like them in theory. She just liked them better when someone else was holding them.

The clicking became louder. Suddenly she heard Jura saying something about Joe complaining that someone was feeding the falcons when they weren't supposed to and Vladimir replying that he'd look into it as one of the falcons flew over and landed on Bernie's shoulder. She could feel talons digging through her T-shirt into her skin. It felt worse than the time Brandon had put his pet iguana on her shoulder. She gritted her teeth. *Don't scream*, she told herself. Jura and Vladimir are right outside the door.

She reached up and tried to remove the falcon, but the bird seemed perfectly happy on her new perch and responded to Bernie's efforts by digging its claws in a little deeper and clicking her beak in Bernie's ear. *Not a good thing*, Bernie thought as she tried not to visualize the falcon biting off a piece of her earlobe. Why had she worn her big hoop earrings? she thought as she could feel the bird tug on it. Then it must have gotten bored because it flew back to its perch.

Bernie sighed with relief as she brushed off a couple of the falcon's feathers that had landed on the front of her T-shirt. One stuck to her hand and she picked it off.

And that's when it struck her. She put her hand up to her mouth. All this time it had been right in front of her and she hadn't seen it.

Unfrigginbelievable.

Chapter 31

Libby was not happy. Things were definitely not going the way she and Bernie had planned. At all. For openers—and for closers too for that matter—Ditas was proving to be less hospitable than the Greeks had been to the Trojans. Well actually Libby didn't know that, having pretty much slept through her literature class. She just assumed it.

She'd gotten as far as the lodge's kitchen before Ditas had swooped down on her. She'd been thinking that she'd expected to see a barebones kind of setup like at the West Vale mansion instead of something that looked as if it had come out of a shelter magazine when Ditas had stormed through the door.

"How the hell did you get in here?" he demanded not giving her a chance to tell him the story she and Bernie had concocted.

Libby didn't even get the word "guard" out of her mouth when Ditas started in again.

"They shouldn't have let you in without calling the main house and informing someone," he growled. "They know better than that. This is a hunting preserve, not a nursery school. You could have gotten shot wandering around."

"It wasn't their fault," Libby told him. "I . . ."

"I don't care whose fault it is," Ditas shouted. "I'll sort

that out later. What I want to know is what are you doing here?"

Libby lifted the large picnic hamper she was carrying. "Eunice and Gertrude asked me to bring this by. They . . ."

Ditas grimaced. "I should have known this had something to do with them. Fine. I'll give it to them." And with that he yanked the hamper out of Libby's hand.

"But . . ." she objected.

"Anything else?"

"Well . . . Do you have lions here?" Libby blurted out. *Dumb*, she thought. *Really dumb*.

Ditas looked at her as if she were demented.

"What in heavens name made you ask something like that?"

Libby knew she should say something else, anything else, to keep the conversation going, but she couldn't think of what. Her mind had gone blank. If Bernie were here, she'd come up with something to say Libby thought. But Bernie wasn't here. She was. And the words weren't coming.

"Fine," Ditas said.

Libby felt powerless as he put his hand around her arm and propelled her out the front door. Then he accompanied her to the van, waited while she started it, and stood there as she pulled out of the driveway. She could see him until she went around the bend in the road. What was she going to do? Bubbles of panic began percolating through her chest.

"I am such a pathetic loser," she wailed.

"No, you're not," Libby heard someone say.

She slammed on the brakes. Now she was going crazy as well.

"Hey, be careful," the voice said as Libby whipped her head around.

"Marvin? Is that you?" she asked at the identical time that he pulled the same red and white-checkered tablecloth that Rob and Bernie had hidden under off his head.

"Who did you expect? Big Bird?"

"Oh my god." Libby put her hand up to her mouth. She

wanted to hug him and hit him at the same time. "What are you doing here? Rob and Bernie are still in the lodge looking for you."

"They are?" Marvin said as he made his way towards the front of the van.

"Of course."

Marvin wiggled into the front seat. "Oh dear," he said settling himself down.

"'Oh dear' is right," Libby said. Now that he was closer she could see he had a small grease stain on his cheek, his glasses were askew, and his hair was matted down. He looked so bedraggled all of her anger melted away.

"You could have suffocated in that trunk," she said as she reached into her backpack, took out a bottle of Evian, removed the cap, and handed the water to him.

"Believe me at one point I thought I was going to," Marvin told her after he'd finished it.

"What if you couldn't have gotten the top opened?"

"I wedged a little piece of paper in the lock so it couldn't close all the way." He wiped his hand across his mouth.

Libby took the bottle back and handed Marvin a peach. "What were you thinking, doing something like that?"

"I guess I wasn't," Marvin confessed as he took a bite.

"But it was very brave of you to do it," Libby told him while she thought: *Did I just say brave instead of stupid? I'm beginning to sound like Bernie.* "So tell me what happened."

Marvin readjusted his glasses. "Well, my dad didn't need me today so I decided to take the train down to the city and check out the garage in the apartment where Eunice and Gertrude live, you know, just for the hell of it.

"When I got there I asked the doorman if Eunice and Gertrude Walker were in and he said they'd come in but he hadn't seen them come out. Did I want him to buzz them? And I said no—I mean what would I say to them—and the guy gave me this funny glance and I decided I'd better leave before I blew everything.

"I was going to call your dad, but then I thought what if they're using their car and they've already left. The doorman wouldn't have seen them go so I went around the corner to the building's garage and asked the parking attendant if they'd left and he told me they'd called for their car twenty minutes ago."

"I'm surprised he told you that."

"I paid him fifty bucks. For another fifty he showed me where the car was. I wanted to be sure it was the right one before I called your dad. And there it was: their big old Oldsmobile brougham. So then I tried to call your dad or Clyde but my cell wasn't getting a signal in there and then as I was trying to figure things out Eunice and Gertrude came down and put a couple of things in their trunk—they didn't see me because I was back behind one of the support columns.

"Then they went to talk to the parking attendant and the trunk popped back open. I guess they hadn't closed it all the way. Well, I didn't know what to do. I didn't want to lose them. It wasn't like I had a car to follow them with."

Marvin readjusted his glasses. "I don't know what came over me. I think I've been watching too many action movies lately, but before I knew it I'd crawled inside and closed the door after me. It was awful. The trunk smelled of gasoline and it was so hot I thought I was going to pass out at which point I decided this wasn't such a good idea after all. But it was too late. Before I could do anything, Eunice and Gertrude had come back and we'd taken off.

"I tried to call you when I was in the trunk but I couldn't get my cell phone out of my pants pocket. By the way, this peach is very good," Marvin said as he took another bite.

"It's from Pennsylvania," Libby said automatically while she handed Marvin a napkin.

He wiped his hands. "So I called you when we got here. Then my cell died. I'm sorry. I didn't mean for you to come and get me."

"And you would have gotten back how?"

"Hitchhiked?" Marvin made a face. "All I can think about

is how your father is never going to talk to me again after something like this."

"He's not going to know," Libby told Marvin as she punched Bernie's number into her cell. "At least not if I can help it. We're going to pick up Bernie and Rob and get out of here."

But that wasn't the way it worked out, because as Libby bitterly reflected, with Bernie things never went according to plan.

"We'll meet you at the side door in ten more minutes," her sister told her after Libby had explained the situation. Then she'd clicked off.

Libby tried calling Bernie back, but she'd shut off her phone.

"Great," Libby said to Marvin. "Simply great. You don't suppose Ditas will shoot us if he sees that we're still on his property? I mean, respectable businessmen don't do things like that, right? That would be excessive, don't you think?"

"In my view it certainly would be," Marvin replied as he straightened his glasses again. "Unfortunately, I can't vouch for Ditas's thoughts on the matter."

"Well, at least Libby found Marvin," Bernie told Rob. "That's a good thing."

He nodded. "I don't think I've ever seen so many weapons in my life."

"Amazing, isn't it?" Bernie answered as she looked around the gunroom. And she'd thought the gunroom at the West Vale house had been full. This one was crammed to the gills. "They could take over a small country with the amount of stuff they have in here."

As far as she could see, the only thing missing was a small nuclear device and actually it wouldn't surprise her if there was one hidden away somewhere, she thought, as she looked around the room trying to spot where the crossbows were.

She could understand the rifles. She could even, if pressed, understand the 9mm Glock—although as far as she knew they were not used for target practice or hunting. But the semi-automatics? The missile launcher? Please. Were they arming themselves for the end of civilization as we know it? Then Bernie spotted what she was looking for.

"Here we go," she said as she headed over to the far corner of the room.

She estimated there had to be somewhere between twenty and thirty crossbows, compound bows, and long bows hung on the wall. Nearby there were two shelves on which were arranged boxes of arrows, as well as boxes with different tips for hunting and target practice.

Bernie slipped her ring up and down her finger. What she was looking for had to be here somewhere. She started going through the arrows. There were arrows with two green feathers and one white one, arrows with two red feathers and one white one, arrows with two white feathers and one red one, arrows with two yellow feathers and one white one.

Damn. She straightened up and massaged the small of her back. She'd gone through the two boxes and what she was looking for apparently wasn't here. She couldn't be wrong. She just couldn't be. She glanced at her watch. She'd told Libby she'd meet her at the door in ten minutes, and it was almost past that now.

All right, she told herself. *Calm down. What you're looking for is here. You're just not seeing it.* Bernie closed her eyes, took a deep breath, and made her mind go blank. After a few moments she opened her eyes and scanned the area. A little ways down, half hidden behind an umbrella stand made out of an elephant foot she spotted a long leather box lying on the shelf. This is it, she said to herself as she moved towards it. She didn't know how she knew, but she did.

She grabbed the box and took the top off. Ten arrows lay nestled inside the velvet lining. They were all fletched with feathers from Joe's falcons. Here it was. The proof she'd been looking for.

"I can't believe I didn't spot this sooner," she said to Rob. Something about the arrow in Leeza's heart had bothered her from the first. She just hadn't known what it was until now.

"And look at this." Rob lifted up a glass-enclosed box full of displayed butterflies. "Didn't you say Leeza was buried with a butterfly pin? Suggestive don't you think?"

"Only to someone with an overactive imagination," Bernie heard someone say.

She spun around. Joe was standing in the room along with Vladimir and Jura and Ditas. How could she and Rob have not heard them? As she looked at the three men she was once again struck by the family resemblance. They all had the same cleft chin, the same thin mouth. Jura was the biggest, followed by Ditas, and Joe. It was like the three bears.

"Now put my specimen collection down," Joe told Rob. "It's worth a great deal of money."

"Don't you think it's more than coincidence that Leeza was buried with a butterfly pin? Did you give one to her?" Bernie asked.

Joe laughed and shook his head. "I bet you got high marks in creative writing when you were in school."

"No. I got high marks for finding the truth." At which point Bernie turned to Jura and raised the arrow she was holding. "It looks as if your brother's arrow killed your bride," she told him.

Jura didn't say anything. Neither did Ditas. *I could be talking about the weather for all the reaction they're showing,* Bernie decided. *What's wrong with them?* she wondered as Ditas told Jura, "We have to get a new security team. I'm not paying hundreds of thousands of dollars each year for this." And he gestured towards Bernie and Rob.

"Didn't you hear what I just said?" Bernie asked him.

"Of course he heard," Eunice said as she stepped in the doorway flanked by Esmeralda on one side and Gertrude on the other. "He already knows. So does Ditas. They knew from the moment they saw that arrow."

Bernie did a double take. For a moment she almost didn't recognize the sisters. Their hair was brown flecked with gray. They were both wearing short sleeve polo shirts and khaki pants and sneakers. She realized why Clyde had lost them in the mall. With their hair a normal color they blended into the landscape—just two old ladies no one would give a second glance to.

And then she thought about what they were saying and realize Eunice was right. Ditas and Jura knew about Joe. Given the circumstances, they had to have.

"When I'm wrong, I'm wrong," Eunice said to Bernie.

"It wasn't Vladimir after all," Gertrude agreed.

Vladimir did a double take. "Me? What do I have to do with anything?"

"Eunice and Gertrude thought you murdered Leeza," Bernie explained. "They were going to have you killed."

"I never said any such thing," Gertrude huffed.

"You intimated it," Bernie told her.

"Me?" Vladimir pointed to his chest. "You were going to kill me?"

"You sound like a parrot," Eunice snapped. "And we weren't going to have you killed," Eunice said.

"No. We were going to do it ourselves," Gertrude chimed in. "I've found over the years that it never pays to trust hired help with important tasks."

Eunice nodded. "But don't worry about it," she continued. "Now we have Joe in our sights."

Bernie was amused to see that Joe took a step back.

"Are you threatening me?" Joe demanded.

"Oh dear me. Perish the thought," Gertrude told him. "What could two little old ladies like us do?" She held up her hand. "Especially since I'm getting some arthritis in my trigger finger. Just a touch really. Isn't that right, Eunice?"

"Yes," Eunice replied. "But it really hasn't seemed to affected your aim a whole lot."

"No it hasn't, has it?" Gertrude said. She smiled complacently.

"You're nuts!" Joe cried.

"So we've been told," Eunice agreed. And she walked over and looked at the arrow Bernie was holding. Then she went over to Joe. "You always were the greediest of the three," she told him.

"I don't know what you're talking about," he told her.

"Of course you do. To be honest," Eunice continued, "I didn't like Leeza very much. She underwhelmed me. Her values were just as bad as yours are and if Eunice and I didn't know her mother, I wouldn't have cared what happened to her. But we did and Gertrude and I never shirk our responsibility."

Gertrude gestured to the three brothers. "In my mind you're all guilty," she told them. " Joe, you killed her, and Jura and Ditas, you knew and did nothing about it which amounts to the same thing."

"It doesn't matter what you think," Joe said. "It matters what holds up in court. Right, Jura?"

Jura bit his lip.

"Right?" Joe repeated.

Bernie looked at Jura's face. "You cared for her, didn't you?" she blurted out.

"He didn't care for her," Joe told Bernie. "Leeza was using him. All she wanted was his money."

"That doesn't mean he didn't love her anyway," Bernie said as she watched Jura walk over to the window.

"Lady," Joe said, "you must be seeing something there that I don't. That's all I can say."

Bernie was about to reply, when she heard something. Then she noticed that everyone was listening, so they must have heard it too.

"What is that racket?" Gertrude asked.

"It's the fire engines," Libby cried as she and Marvin came bounding through the door.

"Fire engines?" Jura cried. "Is there a fire somewhere?"

"You mean there isn't?" Libby told him. Then she turned to Bernie and Rob. "Marvin suggested it. I'm sorry. It was the only thing we could think of to do when you guys didn't show up."

Chapter 32

"See the headline in the *New York Post?*" Libby said as she placed her father's breakfast tray on the table in front of his wheelchair.

Her dad put on his reading glasses and picked the paper off of the tray. ONE ROTTEN EGG GIVES UP THE OTHER. He opened to the story and scanned it, while Bernie entered the room.

"I guess brotherly love doesn't trump everything," Bernie said as she sat down on the foot of his bed.

Sean took a sip of his coffee. "My guess is the D.A. leaned on Jura and Ditas pretty hard."

"Or more likely he told Jura that his brother was stealing from him," Bernie said.

"From what you said about Jura that would do it," Sean observed. He put the paper down and started eating his breakfast.

Libby watched as he bit into his scrambled eggs. "What do you think?" she asked.

He nodded. "Nice."

"I added some curry powder. I thought it would make a pleasant change."

"Very good," her dad mumbled with his mouth full.

Libby leaned forward and planted her elbows on her knees.

"So tell me," she asked, "Why do you think Joe used one of his arrows to kill Leeza with when he could have used a dozen others and no one would have known."

Sean swallowed and put his fork down.

"That was the whole point. He wanted Jura to know he had done it. From what the article says, he was furious at Jura for allowing this interloper to come into the business and spend tons of money on herself. Leeza was creating total havoc in the family. Sleeping with Ditas, stringing Jura along. The business was going to hell. Joe killed her to restore order and the fact that he used a signature arrow was to show everyone what he'd done and maybe . . ." Sean paused.

Libby leaned forward. "Maybe what?"

"Maybe . . . I'm just speculating here . . . but maybe he had another motive as well."

"Which was?"

"Perhaps Leeza was blackmailing him. Perhaps she'd found out that he was selling caviar on the side and she was demanding her cut. Otherwise she'd go tell Jura."

Libby nodded. Everything her dad said made sense to her, but there was something else that was bothering her. "Wasn't Joe afraid of the police? Wasn't he afraid that they'd catch on when they saw that arrow?"

Sean snorted. "You've seen what's in West Vale. One of the Raids says jump and the police there say: How high? No. I don't think he was one bit concerned. Anyway, none of the police hunted with the Raids. They didn't know that Joe fletched his own arrows. And the arrows were gone by the time they got there. Look how long it took for Bernie and you to make the connection between the falcons and the feathers on the arrows."

"I should have figured it out sooner," Bernie told her dad as Eunice, Gertrude, and Marvin entered the room. "They came to say hello," Bernie explained.

"Actually we came to settle up," Eunice said.

Gertrude nodded her agreement.

Libby was interested to see that they'd dyed their hair

turquoise and were wearing matching Grateful Dead T-shirts and jeans. She was glad. Somehow she liked them better this way.

"We decided not to ask for our money back after all," Gertrude told her father. "After all, you did solve the murder."

"We would just like a strict accounting of your expenses."

Sean put his fork down. "You know for a couple of communists you're awfully cheap."

"The word is frugal and just because we believe in equality doesn't mean that we believe in waste. We believe that everyone should work according to their capacity. So when you send us your expense sheet we will reimburse you."

"Here." Eunice handed Libby a piece of paper. "I've written down our address so you can e-mail it to us."

"But I thought you were going to Tanzania," Libby said.

"We are," Eunice replied. "Haven't you heard of the term global village?"

Sean took the piece of paper out of Libby's hand and put it on the tray.

"I have some questions," he said.

"Like what?" Bernie asked.

"Like how come all of you were out at the hunting lodge in the first place. When I asked the first time everyone pretended they couldn't hear what I was saying."

Libby looked at Bernie who looked at the sisters who looked at Marvin.

"Well," Marvin stuttered when Eunice cut him off.

"This brave young man came to our rescue. Joe had invited Gertrude and me to the lodge for a good-bye party. Well, the more we thought about it the more nervous we became so when we were almost there we called Libby and Bernie to join us—which they did."

"They didn't tell me that," Sean said.

"Of course not," Eunice replied. "I specifically told them not to. I didn't want to worry you. Plus, I must confess that I was angry that you were having us followed. I knew the girls would never do anything like that. However, the guard wouldn't let your daughters in and they had to resort to—let us say illegal means—to gain entry.

"Fortunately for all of us, they also asked Marvin to keep an eye on us on the principle that six eyes are better than four. He beat Bernie and Libby into the compound by climbing over the north wall." Eunice turned to Marvin. "Isn't that right, dear?"

"Yes," Marvin stammered.

Eunice nodded approvingly. "Then that clever boy found us in the compound and managed to keep an eye on us without anyone being the wiser. He would make an excellent spy. So when Joe and Ditas and Jura found us in the arms room, Marvin saw what was happening and did the only thing possible. He called the fire department. And that's the whole story." Eunice went over and patted him on the shoulder. "He really is a hero, you know."

Libby watched her father looking at Eunice. He was speechless.

Finally he managed to say, "Eunice, you expect me to believe that?"

"Yes, Sean. I do."

"We're not liars," Gertrude added. Then she turned to Libby and said. "Dear, would you mind going down and getting Eunice and me a pot of tea. Oolong would be nice. We're parched."

As Libby departed she decided that her father looked as if he didn't know what to believe. She was measuring the tea into the pot when Gertrude appeared next to her.

"Marvin really is a very sweet boy, and it really was very brave of him to hide himself away in our trunk."

"It was, wasn't it," Libby agreed.

"No it wasn't. I was just being polite. Actually it was moronic, but that isn't the point I wish to make," Gertrude continued. "It would be a shame if your father decided never to speak to him again because of some silly notion that he had endangered your lives."

"He wouldn't do that."

Gertrude snorted. "You know what he's like. He has many admirable qualities but you'll agree that he does have a nasty habit of holding a grudge and that his baby girls are the most precious thing in the world to him."

Libby bit her nail. "Do you think Dad believed what you told him up there?"

Gertrude reached over and took a ginger muffin. "He's going to have to, isn't he?"

"I don't know," Libby said.

"It has been my experience," Gertrude said as she peeled the paper off the muffin's sides, "that if you repeat something enough it becomes true."

"So why are you doing this?" Libby asked her. "You don't have to."

"Your mother would have wanted me to. So I am. Even if the object of your affection is from the petite bourgeoisie."

"You are a snob," Libby said.

Gertrude grinned. "Indeed I am."

Recipes

Grilled Marinated Quail

Six quail, split

For marinade

½ cup dry red wine
¼ cup olive oil
3 or 4 juniper berries
a sprig of thyme
a sprig of parsley
2 bay leaves
1 crushed clove of garlic
a pinch of nutmeg
1 tsp salt
1 tsp sugar
a dash of hot pepper sauce

Place quail in glass pan. Mix all ingredients together. Pour marinade over quail. Marinate for at lease two hours. Dry and grill over hot coals for 12–20 minutes, turning frequently. Serve on a bed of mixed greens with a dab of cranberry chutney. This marinade also works well on chicken.

The following two recipes are from a friend of minc, Linda Nielsen, who is an avid cook and collector of recipes and cook books.

Triple Citrus Cheesecake

Filling

4 (8 oz.) packages of softened cream cheese
1 cup sugar
2 tbsp flour
1 tsp vanilla
1 tbsp each fresh lemon, lime, and orange juice
1 tsp each grated lemon peel, lime peel, orange peel
4 eggs

Crust

1 cup graham cracker crumbs
⅓ cup brown sugar
¼ cup melted butter

Mix together, press into the bottom of a 9" springform pan, and bake at 325°F for ten minutes.

Mix all ingredients for filling together until they are combined. Pour into crust. Bake at 325°F for 60–65 minutes until the center is set. Cool. Then remove rim from pan and refrigerate 4 hours or overnight. 12 servings.

Frosted Pumpkin Bars

2 cups flour
1 tsp baking soda
2 tsp baking powder
½ tsp salt
2 tsp cinnamon
½ tsp powdered ginger
½ tsp ground cloves
½ tsp ground nutmeg
4 eggs
1 cup vegetable oil
2 cups sugar
15 oz. can solid-packed pumpkin

Preheat oven to 350°F. Sift together all dry ingredients. Mix oil, eggs, sugar, and pumpkin. Add dry ingredients to wet and mix well. Pour the batter into an ungreased jelly roll pan (17x21x1) or a 9x13 cake pan. If using larger pan, bake 15–20 minutes, if using cake pan, bake 25–30 minutes. Cool in pan and frost with cream cheese frosting. Cut into 3x2-inch bars.

Cream Cheese Frosting

8 oz. softened cream cheese
½ cup softened butter
1 tsp vanilla
4 cups powdered sugar

Combine butter, cream cheese, and vanilla together, then add sugar, and mix until smooth.

My neighbor Sarah Saulson is both a gifted weaver and cook. This is her recipe.

Zucchini Stuffed with Herbed Goat Cheeses

4 oz. aged hard goat cheese
4 oz. soft goat cheese
2 egg whites
6 zucchini, 3–5 inches long
Bread crumbs
A solid handful of mixed fresh herbs, such as chives, parsley, oregano, rosemary, basil

Using grating attachment of food processor, grate hard goat cheese.

Switch to mixing attachment, add soft goat cheese, egg whites, herbs, salt and pepper. Process until smooth.

Slice stems off zucchini. Cut in half lengthwise. Use a spoon to remove seeds. Trim bottoms if necessary so each sits firmly on baking sheet. Fill zucchini with cheese mixture. Sprinkle lightly with bread crumbs. Place on a baking sheet sprayed with olive oil. Bake at 350°F for 30–40 minutes. Serve warm or at room temperature.

Sarah brought this recipe back from Baton Rouge. The stock makes the dish.

Shrimp and Corn Soup

2 lbs fresh shrimp in shells
1 cup fresh crabmeat
1 medium onion, diced
1 medium green pepper, cored and diced
2 stalks of celery, diced
2 large tomatoes, peeled and chopped coarsely
4 cups of fresh or frozen corn kernels
¼ cup of scallions, diced
salt, black and hot red pepper to taste.

Peel shrimp, setting aside the shells.

Fill medium stock pot halfway with water, add salt to taste and bring to a boil. Add shrimp shells, one bay leaf and Tony Cachere's seasoning. Turn down to medium heat and simmer for one hour. Then strain stock and return to pot.

In a separate skillet, sauté celery, onions and green pepper in hot olive oil for about 3 minutes, then add to the stock, along with tomatoes and corn. Simmer for ten minutes, then add shrimp and crabmeat, season with salt and pepper to taste. Simmer another 5 minutes, then remove from heat. Serve in small soup bowls and sprinkle with diced scallions as garnish.

Roasted Potatoes, Chicken and Rosemary

3 boneless chicken breasts, cut into strips
20 little red potatoes, quartered
1 dozen cloves of garlic, peeled
juice of one lemon
1 tsp garlic powder
handful of fresh rosemary, plus more for garnish
salt, pepper
¾ cup olive oil

Marinade:

Combine lemon juice, ½ cup olive oil, salt, pepper, garlic powder, lots of rosemary. Marinate chicken strips overnight.

Preheat oven to 350°F.

In a large roasting pan, lay chicken in one half. Pour marinade over them. Toss potatoes and garlic cloves with salt, pepper, olive oil, and rosemary in a separate bowl. Put in other half of pan.

Roast chicken for 45 minutes. Remove. Stir remaining liquid into potatoes. Continue to roast until done, another 30 minutes.

Garnish with more fresh rosemary. Serve at room temperature.

As picturesque Longley, New York, gets ready to ring in the holiday season, caterers Bernadette and Libby Simmons are coping with their busiest time of year. If that's not enough to make them run around like crazed elves, they're recruited for a cooking show contest that pits celebrity chefs against each other—and gives rise to murder . . .

Visions of sugar plums are most decidedly *not* dancing in Libby's head, especially since she and her sister are set to appear on *The Hortense Calabash Cooking Show*. The premise is to give six professional caterers random ingredients and have them whip up a holiday meal. Libby knows that cooking under pressure is not her forte—plus, the camera adds ten pounds! She'll look like a stuffed Christmas goose.

The icing on the fruitcake is that Hortense Calabash is a grinch of year-round proportions. And the other contestants are some of the most demanding—and difficult—chefs in the business. But, as Bernie points out: the show will be great (and, more importantly, free) publicity for their store, *A Taste of Heaven*.

Bernie and Libby are thrown into the mix as arguments and accusations simmer on the set. Holiday spirit has left the building—and leaves a body—when Hortense, all dressed up as Santa Claus for the opening sequence, is killed by an exploding oven. It's soon clear that Hortense's demise was far from accidental.

Now as Bernie and Libby stir up the past, they open up a king-sized can of motives. Each contestant had a previous run-in with the horrible Hortense, who engaged in blackmail, rumor-mongering, and illicit affairs at every turn . . . but which chef couldn't stand the heat? With the holiday rush in full swing and a killer still on the loose, the caterers of Christmas present have no choice but to wrap up the mystery before their geese are well and fully cooked . . .

Please turn the page for an exciting sneak peek of
A Catered Christmas
coming next month in hardcover!

Libby looked around the TV studio. She just knew she was going to hate being on TV, she was going to hate being on the Hortense Calabash show, and she was going to hate being in this stupid contest, but most of all she was going to hate being away from the store at Christmas time.

"I think I'm going to throw up," she blurted.

Bernie considered the remark for a second, then she pointed to her pink suede wedges. "Well, don't do it on these. I just got them."

"You're a veritable fountain of compassion," Libby told her sister as she gestured toward one of the TV cameras on the set.

"You'll be fine," Bernie said. "Just think of these as your friends."

"They may be your friends," Libby retorted, "but they're certainly not mine."

"Getting a little snappish, are we?"

Libby began biting her cuticle, realized what she was doing, and stopped herself. "Anyway, I have nothing to wear."

"What's wrong with the tweed skirt and fitted, pale-blue blouse we bought down in the city last week?" her sister asked.

Another mistake, Libby reflected. Now she'd have to tell

Bernie she'd returned them. She took a deep breath and let it out. "I took them back. They were too tight." She took another deep breath while she watched her sister roll her eyes. "Well, they were," Libby said in what she realized was a defensive tone of voice as she looked at Bernie standing there in her burgundy leather pants and hot pink vee-neck sweater. It wasn't Bernie's fault she didn't understand, Libby reminded herself. She'd always been the thin one.

"They made me feel like a sausage."

"No, what you're wearing makes you look like a sausage. I keep telling you, loose clothes make people look fatter, not thinner. And anyway, you're not that fat."

"That fat?" Libby squeaked. "That's a little bit like saying I'm not that ugly."

"I'm not doing this."

"What's this?"

Bernie ignored her and gestured to the black pants and shirt Libby was wearing. "At least don't wear black on camera."

"I'm not going to," Libby said even though she had been. She felt more comfortable in it; it made her feel invisible. "I'm wearing my brown pants and yellow shirt." When Bernie didn't say anything she added, "I'm sorry. I just think that spending two-hundred dollars on a blouse is a little much."

"Two-hundred-and-ten dollars to be exact," Bernie said absentmindedly as Libby watched her look around the studio. "And it was a Krista Larson for heaven's sake."

"So what?"

"It made you look great, that's what."

Libby watched Bernie walk over to one of the sinks and turn on the faucet. Nothing came out. She walked over to the second sink and tried that faucet. Water poured into the sink, but it didn't go down; it was clogged.

"Good," Libby said.

Maybe they wouldn't have to tape after all. Maybe she and Bernie could go back to the store and she could finish the batch of Christmas cookies she was in the middle of decorating. After all, they couldn't cook if things in the kitchen didn't work.

She was sighing with relief when Bernie put her hands on her shoulders and said, "Look, let's forget about the clothes. Let's forget about everything. Let's just concentrate on winning."

Libby took a step back. "We're not going to win."

Bernie dropped her hands to her sides. "Why shouldn't we win?" she countered. "We have as good a shot at it as anyone else."

And that interchange, Libby decided, pretty much defined the difference between herself and her sister.

"I think I need a cookie," Libby said.

"Or a stiff drink," Bernie observed.

"A cookie." And Libby started rummaging around in her backpack for one of the chocolate-chip, ginger cookies she'd made earlier in the day. Given the circumstances, what was another pound or two? She took a bite. The cookie was good, but not good enough. Usually chocolate did it for her, but it didn't seem to be working today. Maybe Bernie was right; maybe she needed a drink. Something like a Long Island Iced Tea. Or a large bottle of Pinot Noir. Or a tranq.

Libby took another bite of her cookie anyway as she contemplated what was in store for her and Bernie this evening. It was no big deal. Why should she be nervous? There'd just be thousands of people out there watching her cook. What was the problem with that? Just because she probably wouldn't be able to get any words past her vocal cords because they would be constricted in terror.

And so what if she dropped say . . . a chicken . . . on the floor, or burned it, or it didn't cook all the way through? What then? The great Julia had done things like that all the time on her television show. But, Libby told herself, she wasn't Julia Child. And Julia didn't have The Heavenly Housewife, a.k.a. Hortense Calabash of *The Hortense Calabash Cooking Show* critiquing her food.

Not that Julia would have stood for Hortense's nonsense.

Julia would have bashed Hortcnse over the head with a frozen leg of lamb, or a Christmas goose, if she ever pulled any of her stunts on her. Just the thought of that made Libby smile. But Libby knew she'd never raise a strand of spaghetti to Hortense, let alone a blunt instrument. Ever.

Libby took a third bite of her cookie. As she swallowed she could almost see the slight flare of Hortense's thin nostrils, the minuscule lifting of one of her eyebrows when she didn't like something. What had she said to Rudolfo, the chef from *Mesmerize,* after she'd tasted the pate he'd made? Wasn't it something along the lines of "My, what an interesting group of ingredients you've chosen to use. This tastes rather like a mix between raw eggplant and liver I once sampled in Uzbekistan."

Libby had never seen a man turn white with anger before; he'd spluttered, but no sounds had come out. Needless to say, *Mesmerize* had gone out of business two weeks later. A week after that Libby had heard through the caterer's grapevine that the pate had actually been fine. Hortense had just needed a little something to boost her ratings that week. No wonder Rudolfo had sent her a chocolate cake filled with a mixture of ganache and pureed hog intestines as a thank you for being on her show.

Or how about the time there'd been that woman on the show demonstrating one of the recipes form her new cookbook on how to use a pressure cooker, and Hortense had taken a bite of the stew she'd prepared and said, "My this is tasty," then came the dramatic pause—never a good sign—"if you're partial to the kind of stew they sell in the supermarket in cans." And another career had bit the dust.

Libby shuddered as she finished her cookie. What if Hortense said something like that to her about something she and Bernie made. And while it was true that her store, *A Taste of Heaven,* had a loyal and devoted clientele, people were fickle. They tended to believe what they heard on TV.

"What do you think she's going to give us?" Libby asked Bernie.

The surprise ingredient thing was probably the worst part of the whole contest deal as far as Libby was concerned. She spent hours and hours planning out her menus and here she and Bernie were being asked to cook a whole Christmas dinner with some strange ingredient that Hortense was going to give them in an hour. Then if they won the first round, they'd have to do it again and again.

"A boar's head," Bernie replied. "She's going to give us a boar's head."

"Be serious," Libby said.

"I am. Boar's heads were the most popular item associated with medieval Christmas feats." Bernie paused for a moment. "Although they didn't have Christmas foods the way we think of them. Well, that's not entirely true. They did have plum pudding and mincemeat pies."

Libby sighed. Her sister was full of more information then you'd ever want to know.

"I wish there was a way we could find out," she mused.

"You and everyone else on the show."

Of which there were seven; actually, five if you didn't count she and Bernie. Five caterers. Libby rubbed her forehead. She never watched reality shows on TV as a matter of principle and now she was going to be on one!

"Of course we could always sneak into the cooler and take a look," Bernie said. "I bet they have the ingredients stored in there."

Libby ignored her. It was bad enough they were in the studio.

"This sucks," she said instead. "At least Bree could have given us three or four months notice instead of letting us know at the last minute she'd booked us on here."

"Back to the weight thing, are we?" Bernie asked.

"Not at all," Libby retorted even though she was. If she had had even two months notice she would have gone to Weight

Watchers or Atkins—or booked a cruise to Antarctica. Or Siberia.

Libby shut her eyes. She could picture Bree Nottingham, real estate agent extraordinaire, breezing into her store the day she'd made her announcement. Even though it had been cold and gray she'd been dressed in pink, the color of the moment according to Bernie: pink tweed Chanel suit, pink sling-back heels, pink Chanel purse.

"You're so lucky to have this opportunity," Bree had trilled after she'd explained to Libby what she'd done. "I had to fight to get you on the show, but I said, 'Hortense, we have to use some of our local talent. It's only fair.'"

Lucky was not the word Libby would have used. "Maybe I could come down with typhoid or bubonic plague."

Bernie tucked a strand of hair behind her ear. "It would probably be bad for business."

"Worse then me on television?"

Bernie shook her head. "Get a grip."

"But I'm not a competitive person," Libby moaned.

"You are now," her sister said.

"You sound like Dad."

"I am like Dad."

"I know."

Libby reflected that her dad was extremely excited that she was going t be on the show. So was her boyfriend, Marvin, for that matter. In fact, that's all her father or Marvin had been talking about for the last three days.

"The whole world will be watching," Marvin had told Libby, a comment that had sent her straight to the freezer for some homemade, coconut ice cream.

As Libby looked around the set again, she wondered who the hell had a television studio built on to the back of their house anyway? Hortense Calabash, doyenne of the cooking channel, queen of sauces, and resident of Longely, that's who. Libby couldn't even use the excuse that she and Bernie were too busy in the store this time of year to take the time out to do this.

"Hortense's house is only fifteen minutes away," Libby remembered Bree Nottingham telling her.

Like she was some kind of moron. Of course Libby knew how far away Hortense's mansion was. They lived in the same town for heaven's sake, not that she ever saw her. They didn't exactly move in the same social set, which was fine with Libby. But then everyone in the world knew where Hortense's house was. Okay, they had known a couple of years ago. According to the latest polls, her popularity was being eclipsed by a show on cooking caveman style. But it was still pretty popular.

"We've been friends since camp," Bree had chirped.

Good for you, Libby had wanted to say to Bree. That woman had been the bane of her existence since the fourth grade.

"I should kill her," Libby observed. "I'd be doing the universe a favor."

Bernie raised an eyebrow. A well-manicured one, Libby couldn't help noticing. Maybe she should get her done too—before tonight—but the thought of putting hot wax on her eyebrows and then ripping the hair out made Libby shudder.

"Hortense?" Bernie asked as Libby was contemplating what the wax thing would feel like on other parts of her anatomy. "What would her legion of crazed fans do? How would they know what to cook or how to serve it?"

Libby frowned. "No," she said, "I meant I want to kill Bree Nottingham for making us do this."

"She didn't make you," Bernie pointed out in her most reasonable—albeit irritating—tone of voice.

"Not in the literal sense, no," Libby conceded. But when the social arbiter of Longely tells you to jump, and you're in the catering business, you ask what hoop she has in mind.

"Well then, there you go," Bernie said. "Anyway," she continued, "this will be good exposure for the store."

"*A Taste of Heaven* doesn't need any more exposure," Libby replied. "We've got more customers then we can handle as it is."

"Not if you hired on more staff," Bernie pointed out.

"We don't have the room."

"We could expand," Bernie replied.

"That would mean moving," Libby said.

"And we're fine where we are," Bernie finished for her.

"Well, we are," Libby retorted as she watched Bernie saunter over to the sink.

She and her sister had had the "moving discussion" at least once a week for the past year, but Libby was holding fast to her convictions. She knew too many other places that had been doing well until they expanded. What Bernie didn't seem able to grasp was the amount of planning that the kind of expansion Bernie was talking about would involve.

But then her sister had always been like that. Diving headlong into something seemed to work for her, Libby remarked to herself. She didn't know how, but it did. It was like Bernie's shoes. How she could walk, let alone work in them was something that Libby had never been able to fathom.

As Libby watched her sister pass by the mini Christmas tree sitting on the end counter, she reflected that it felt strange being on the set. It wasn't as if she was a big fan of Hortense, because she wasn't; in fact, she hated her, hated everything she stood for. But still. She'd watched Hortense's program on TV from time to time with her dad.

She'd seen those cabinets with the red door pulls and the signature gleaming dark red Viking range while sitting in her living room, and here she was on the set looking at them for real. Somehow they seemed smaller in real life then they did on the screen. It made her feel odd in a way she couldn't explain.

"I'm not sure we should be in here," Libby repeated. She knew she'd said it before, but she couldn't help herself. After all, the doors to the studio had been closed and a sign posted had the words NO ENTRANCE clearly written in big, back letters. "We should be in the green room."

"We will be there—eventually," Bernie said. "That's one of the advantages of living nearby. We get to come early."

"But the sign. . . ."

Bernie gave her the look. "I didn't see it. Did you?"

"Not after you hid it behind the table."

"I didn't hide anything," Bernie protested. "Is it my fault if the thing slipped?"

"But. . . ." Libby started to protest.

Bernie cut her off before she could say anything else. "I just wanted to take a look around before everyone else comes on the set." She pointed to a door over to the right. "According to Bree, the real cooking is done in the other kitchen. This set is just for the show."

"What are you doing?" Libby demanded as Bernie crossed the room.

"Taking a peek, of course."

"They probably have an alarm," Libby told her.

"Don't be ridiculous." Bernie opened the door and stepped inside.

"Looks like our kitchen," Libby heard Bernie say.

"I shouldn't be doing this," Libby told herself. But she followed Bernie inside anyway. What was it her father always said about in for a penny in for a pound?

There was a metal table in the center, clusters of pots hanging from the ceiling, steel racks full of assorted pans, and two large ovens that looked as if they'd seen a lot of use.

One of them was on. Libby resisted the urge to peek: that would be going too far. Instead she went over to the table in the middle and picked up one of the glass pinecones that were in a wicker bowl in the center. "I wonder what these are for?"

Bernie shrugged. "Christmas ornaments?"

"They're pretty." Libby put the pinecone down and looked at the tray of meringue mushrooms on the table. "They're perfect," she said.

"Yours are just as good," Bernie told her.

"Not quite," Libby said as she followed Bernie back out onto the set. Hortense's had more texture to them. Libby was wondering what kind of pastry tube Hortense had used to get that pebbled effect when she realized that Bernie was talking.

"You know," she was saying, "Hortense may be the ultimate bitch but you have to hand it to her in the interior design department. Although I like what you did better."

Libby smiled. "Me, too."

But what Hortense had done wasn't bad at all. She'd just gone in a different direction. And it had taken her a lot less time to execute, something Libby reminded herself she should bear in mind for next year. The mini Christmas tree on the end of the counter was decorated with homemade cookies that Hortense had baked, painted with gold leaf, and shellacked on her last show. The bows that were knotted around the garlands of greenery were made out of a cream-colored organza that had been shot through with gold thread.

In addition, Hortense had taken light green glass bowls and filled them with smooth river stones, into which she'd embedded groups of ivory tapers. She'd put those on the window sills. A huge poinsettia that Hortense had placed in a basket, woven in Africa out of reeds, sat on the kitchen table, while a lavender plant sat off to one side of the sink. The effect was both elegant and homey at the same time.

Libby sighed as she looked around. There was no denying that Hortense was a genius at what she did: she excelled at taking simple household objects and giving them a new look. Although drying cattails, spraying them gold, and making them into Christmas wreaths was going a little too far in her opinion. She was just thinking that the shredded-wheat wreath wasn't a particularly good idea either when she heard a noise.

"What was that?"

Bernie shook her head.

"I didn't hear anything."

"I did. It's coming from behind the door on the left."

"That's Hortense's office." Bernie cocked her head and listened for a moment. "I think you're right. I think someone is in there."

Libby felt a wave of panic. why did she always let Bernie talk her into these things? "What if it's Hortense?"

"It's not, and even if it is, so what? We're not doing anything wrong."

Somehow Libby didn't think Hortense would agree with her sister's assessment of their situation. "How do you know it's not her?"

"Because she's getting her hair done."

"Are you sure?"

"Of course I'm sure. I know the woman who does it."

"I still think we should leave," Libby said.

"You don't mean that."

"Yes, I do."

After all, Libby reasoned, since they weren't supposed to be here in the first place, why not get out while the going was good?

"Don't you want to find out what's going on?" Bernie said.

"Why assume something is going on?"

Bernie pointed to the door. "Then what's that noise?"

"A mouse?"

"A mouse on steroids."

Libby bit her lip. Why had she ever said anything to Bernie? All Bernie eve did was complicate things.

"After all," Bernie said. "What's the worst that can happen?"